BLADE'S
Awakening

Erin Osborne

Blade's Awakening
By: Erin Osborne

Photographer: Reggie Deanching, R+M Photo

Cover Model: Shawn Joseph

Cover Design: Vicky Deviney Chesley

Editor: Darlene Tallman

Dedication

I would like to dedicate this book to all of my fans. You have been loyal and patient with me as I had personal issues come up writing this book. You have sent messages and made comments that have shown the amazing support you are willing to give the authors that you like and stand by. Without all of you this wouldn't be possible.

To Vicky, Darlene, and Jenni my team and ultimate support system. You guys are there for me when you don't have to be and for more than just about book related things. I love ya and I'm glad that we're a team that supports one another through everything!!

Table of Contents

Prologue

Kiera

IT'S BEEN MONTHS since I left the Wild Kings clubhouse. I'm happy that Melody got her family back together and she's happier than I've ever seen her. Since leaving, I've been back there once. The only reason I went was for Melody's wedding. Anthony talked me into going back once more for a family picnic. That is today and I'm not looking forward to it at all. For multiple reasons.

See, when I left, I took a major secret with me. One that would tie Blade to me for a very long time. I knew it wasn't what he wanted, so I left and I haven't looked back since. I've spent every day trying to move on and live my life. Slim helped me find a place to live and a job. He was the only one that knew my secret and wasn't happy about it. But, he's helped me none the less. Now, more people know because I can't hide it anymore.

I'm working at the Phantom Bastards' strip club, Vixen. I'm not stripping, I'm a bartender and the money is good. Good enough that I have a little nest egg started and more than enough for my bills and what the baby will need. Yeah, Blade's going to be a dad.

So, I'm getting ready to go to Clifton Falls when there's a knock on my door. I can just bet I know who it is. There's a guy I've been seeing and I purposely didn't tell him about today. Honestly, I'm ready to break it off with him, but I'm scared. His name is Jason and we met at the strip club. He was there for work, so he says, and he ended up spending most of the night talking to me. Then he came back in a few more times. Jason wouldn't take no for an answer and continued to ask me out. Finally, I relented and let him take me to dinner. Now, I can't get rid of him and things aren't always good. He's got a short temper and there has been a time or two that he's put his hands on me. To him, it doesn't matter that I'm pregnant.

"Coming!" I holler out, making my way to the door from the bathroom.

The knocking turns to pounding and I can already tell it's going to be a shitty day. Maybe I should call Melody and tell her I can't make it. If only Anthony didn't want me to be there so bad, I'd do just that. I don't want Jason around the only people I consider family and to let the bomb drop when he realizes that my baby's dad will be there. Not that Blade and I talk or communicate in any way these days. At the wedding, he ignored me and left with one of the club girls firmly wrapped around him.

Opening the door, I almost get a fist to my face as Jason was going to pound on the door again. He looks me up and down and a sneer covers his face. Here comes the lecture folks! If I'm wearing jeans, tees, shorts, or anything of that nature I get a lecture about my wardrobe and the image I am presenting to everyone. Well, quite frankly, I don't care about what anyone else thinks about me.

"Kiera, is that honestly what you're wearing?" he asks, the judgement clear on his face.

"It is. I'm not changing Jason. We're going to be surrounded by a group of bikers and their women. I don't have to wear a suit or anything like that for this picnic."

Instantly I know this is the wrong thing to say. I can see the fire light in his eyes and I'm praying he doesn't leave a mark on me before heading there. Knowing they're bikers though, I'm sure he won't. I'll just have to wear a long sleeve shirt or something if I'm lucky.

"You will change. I'm not going to be seen in public with you looking like a slut!" Jason yells, grabbing my arm and dragging me to my room.

I can feel his fingers digging into my skin and I know without a doubt there will be bruising left behind. The skin of my arm under his hand is being pinched and I can feel my shoulder starting to ache with the angle he's got my arm in. Long sleeves for sure today, and it's supposed to be hot as hell out. There's no way I can even try to pull my arm out of his grasp right now because I'm afraid of a few different things. The first being that my arm is going to break and I'll end up in the hospital. The second is that his anger will fly off the charts and that he'll do something to jeopardize my baby.

"Now, find something in this pigsty you call a fucking room that will make me want to be seen with you in public. You have two minutes Kiera," Jason growls out.

"You don't have to go you know. I can go by myself," I say, walking to my closet to find my long dress and a sweater to wear over it.

"No, I'm going. I'm going to go see all this trailer trash that you hang out with. That way I can prove to you that you're no better than them. I'm doing you a fucking favor by being in your life."

"Is that what you call it?" I murmur, hoping he doesn't hear me.

"Yeah, that's what I fucking call it, bitch," Jason growls in my ear before spinning me to face him.

Before I can try to protect myself, he lands a punch to my stomach and then backhands me across my face. The pain immediately radiates throughout my entire abdomen and fear for my baby runs rampant through my mind. Getting my feet back under myself, I move away and quickly grab my clothes to make my way into the bathroom. If I don't get away from Jason right now, I don't know that he'll stop. I've seen his anger multiple times but never the rage that I've seen in his eyes in that moment.

Locking the door, I set my clothes on the bathroom counter and make my way to go to the bathroom. Pain is still going through my abdomen and my shoulder is throbbing. No one is going to be able to touch me without knowing that something is definitely wrong with me. Melody won't keep this to herself either. If there's even a hint that someone has hurt me, Glock will know about it in seconds.

Sensing something isn't exactly right, I look in the toilet and see blood. Fear is now the only emotion that I'm feeling. Instead of looking panicked or picking up my phone, I finish changing and make sure that no one will be able to let on that I'm bleeding. It's bad enough that Melody is already going to know something is wrong.

Pulling into the Wild Kings clubhouse, I'm filled with dread and a sense that things are never going to be the same after today. Jason has not kept his hands off me in some sense and I have to hide the repulsion filling my body. I never thought I'd be the girl that let a man put his hands on her. Today, though, that was the last straw. Jason has put my baby in jeopardy and that is not something I will tolerate.

The first person I see is Blade. He's standing outside waiting for someone. I'm not sure what his game plan is, but I plan on avoiding him at all costs today. I will tell him about the baby soon, I'm just not ready to yet. Not while Jason is here and I'm worried about what the hell is going to happen now. The only thing I know about him regarding kids is that he likes kids that aren't his, and he made it clear that he didn't want any of his own. So, we always used condoms and I was on birth control until I found out I was pregnant. I don't know what the hell happened that I ended up pregnant.

"That the guy?" Jason asks, finding a spot to park.

I don't really want to let him know, so I just kind of shrug my shoulders. It's not exactly an answer, but he can't say that I flat out lied to him either. Jason doesn't deserve to know anything about my baby and who their father is.

Almost immediately Jason is out of the car and striding towards Blade. This is not an encounter that I want to be a witness to, but I can imagine what Jason is going to say to him. So, I follow him and wait to see what the fallout is going to be. Someone better give me the strength to get through this day in one piece.

"Who the fuck are you?" Blade asks, noticing Jason striding towards him.

"I'm just the man that wants to know who the fuck knocked up my girl," Jason growls out, while Blade looks at me.

"What's he talkin' about Kiera?" Blade asks, ignoring Jason completely and putting all his focus on me.

"Forget he said anything Blade. He's just being an ass," I respond, letting a little of my control go knowing I'm in the presence of Glock and his brothers.

"No, I think he needs to know that you're knocked up and that he's not having anything to do with the baby," Jason says, grabbing my arm and trying to lead me away from Blade.

Unfortunately, he's grabbed the same arm as earlier and I can't hide the wince that crosses my face. Blade doesn't miss it either. His face contorts and before I know what's happening, he's yelling for Glock and pulling me from Jason's grasp. Jason isn't one to give up easy though. He holds my arms as long as he can, making the pain radiate even further up my arm and down to my hand.

"Let the fuck go, now!" Blade growls out and I can feel him tense up.

"She's not yours. You just used her as a fuck toy because you can't fucking commit and now you're not going to get your hands on her again. Or that bastard she's carrying," Jason yells, getting in Blade's face.

This is a completely different side of Jason. Yeah, I've seen him mad, angry, and with rage filling him. But, to be completely disrespectful and to out me in front of Blade is something so vindictive. I guess today is the day that all his shit comes out. Well, I guess I'm finding a different way home and not speaking to Jason again. I don't need this shit in my life.

"Kiera, get in with Melody. Now!" Glock growls out. I didn't even see him come out here.

"I'm good Glock. Jason was just leaving. Forget my number, where I live, and where I work asshole. Never should have said yes to you," I tell him.

"Fuck you!" Jason yells. "I don't know what I was thinking having anything to do with you. You're nothing but a biker slut!"

Before Jason is back to his car, Blade is telling me we need to talk. I'm not even in the mood to deal with his ass right now. The only thing I want to do is find Melody and Anthony. So, I ignore him and go in search of my best friend. If I'm honest, my only friend. Melody is the only person in the world that knows everything about me.

Going in search of her, I prepare myself to go through everything that has been happening with Jason since I've been gone. She won't let me get away with half-truths and lies. It's nothing but absolute honesty with us. Which is a big reason I have avoided her since finding out I was pregnant. Her wedding day was the only time I could be around her and not have to worry about her questioning me. Let the fun begin!

Chapter One

Blade

IT'S BEEN A MONTH since I've seen Keira. She sends me messages about her upcoming doctor's appointments and how she's doing that day, but that's it. I've been a wreck since that day a month ago when my entire world shifted and I learned I was going to be a dad. Yeah, I said I never wanted kids of my own after my fucked-up childhood. But, I would never turn my back on my child either. Now, I need to convince Keira of that. She thinks that I'm going to pay support and that's it. Well, she's got another thing coming. Keira is mine and she will be coming home to me where she and our child belong.

The day of the picnic, she spent most of the day with Melody, Anthony, and Glock. The other old ladies surrounded her too. Especially once they found out she was pregnant. Everything looked fine with her until she started screaming at the top of her lungs from the bathroom. We all heard her outside and I've never been more scared of anything in my life. Especially when I ran into the bathroom and found her covered in blood. It wasn't just her lower half that was covered in it since she had fallen when she tried to get up from the toilet to get help.

Grim called for an ambulance and I rode to the hospital with her. Keira didn't put up a fight about it, Melody was the one to do that. It's my girl and my baby though, so there was no way in fuck anyone but me was riding in that ambulance. The rest of the club followed close behind and waited patiently until we had news that Keira and the baby were fine but she would need to be on bedrest for a while. That motherfucker that told me about the baby apparently punched her in the stomach knowing she was carrying my baby. When I get my fucking hands on him, he's a dead man.

I'll be heading to Benton Falls today so that I can make it to the doctor's appointment with my girl. I've started formulating a plan in order to win her back, but I'm not sure how it's going to work out. If there's one thing I can say about my girl, she's stubborn as fuck and won't let me back in easily. At least now I know why she truly left. She got scared when she found out she was pregnant and figured that she knew what I was going to say about it. Too bad she's wasted so much time that we could have been setting up a home instead of living apart.

My entire life, I've always said I didn't want an old lady and I didn't want any kids of my own. This has nothing to do with women in general or anything like that. It has to do with the fact that my dad was an abusive alcoholic and my mother was nothing more than a crack whore. I can't count on one hand the number of days in my life that my parents actually said more than one or two words to me. On those rare days it was only to tell me to get the fuck out of their house or to go find them their next score. I never wanted to bring that into someone else's life, so I figured the best way to do that was to only go to club girls and always make sure I wrapped my cock up tight.

All that changed the day I met Keira. One look and I knew she was going to be the one to break me. You could see her fiery spirit and willingness to take on any challenge head on. She has a backbone of steel and even when I could sense her hesitation, Keira always called me on my shit. If I was shying away from her and trying to push her away, she called me on it. When I wasn't giving her all of me in bed, she called me on it. In no time at all, Keira wormed her way under my skin and into my heart. A heart I thought I had locked up tighter than fuck so no one would ever be able to get through my walls. It never had a chance against my girl though.

"When you headed out?" Grim asks me, standing in my doorway.

"As soon as I talk to Rage. Want him to start our house," I tell him, continuing to pack my bag.

"You stayin' up there tonight?"

"If you don't need me, I thought I'd stay a day or two. I want to spend some time with her and make sure that she and the baby are really doin' as good as she lets on."

"I thought you were gettin' updates from Slim and Wood," Grim says, stepping just inside the door and closing it a little.

"I am. No one knows that still and I appreciate you keepin' it quiet. The last thing I want is for her to know that I'm gettin' updates on her and blow it all out of proportion."

"I get it. Just let me know what's goin' on and we'll go from there. Take a few days and be with your girl," Grim tells me, giving me a man hug before leaving the room.

Just as I go to close my door and lock up, one of the club girls comes up and wraps her arms around me. I haven't been with any of the girls since I found out Keira was pregnant. Even then, I was only with one and I was drunk off my ass. Keira's name was still the one I called out and thinking of her is the only thing that got me hard. No one else can get me hard or hold my attention but her.

"When you gonna give me a try Blade?" she asks, trying to get ahold of my neck.

"I'm not. Told you that before and I'm not tellin' you that again," I tell her, pulling her arms from around me.

"I never see you with anyone, Blade. What's wrong with you?" she whines in my ear.

"Someone better get this bitch away from me!" I yell down the hallway.

Glen, a new prospect, comes running down and grabs the girl away from me. I don't even remember hearing her name before so she must be new. She'll learn really quick that when one of us say no, we mean no. This girl doesn't need to know anything else about me and what I do with my time. She's not my old lady and she never will be. Keira is the only one that needs to know anything that's going on in my life.

"Grim, somethin' needs to be done with the club girl Glen just took off me," I say, walking past him. "She was all over me and tryin' to be up in my business."

"It'll be handled before you get back," Grim assures me.

Heading out to my bike, I can feel the nervousness start to build. It's been a long time and I don't know what to expect from Keira. She hasn't been hostile or pissed, but we haven't exactly spent much time alone since she left either. Add in the fact that I'm sure it's going to be brought up about her working at Vixen and I'm sure there will be a fight. One that I don't want to have since I'm trying to win her back. The little bit of time we spent together was definitely not enough for me.

After making sure my bag is secure on my bike, I make my way over to Rage. He's sitting at one of the tables under the canopy out back watching his daughter play on the playground. Sitting down, I take a minute to just watch her and think about what it's going to be like when my own son or daughter gets here. I am beginning to want to have it happen now and get excited about it.

"You okay, Blade?" Rage asks me.

"I'm good. Just thinkin' about what it's goin' to be like when I'm a dad," I tell him honestly.

"Yeah, heard about that. Congrats man!" Rage tells me.

"I'm gettin' ready to head up to see my girl now. Wanted to talk to you first about buildin' a house."

"Where you want it?" Rage asks, chuckling a little bit.

"I guess not too far from Glock and Melody's house. She and Keira are tight and I bet they'll want to be close to one another."

"Anythin' specific?"

"Nope. Just want an open floor plan. I'll see what I can get out of her while I'm up there and let you know as soon as I know."

"Any clue about the number of bedrooms?" he asks, jotting something down in his notepad.

"I'm gonna say probably four, but I'll let you know for sure. I'm out," I tell him, standing and going back to my bike.

I've enjoyed the long ride alone on my bike. It's calmed me a bit and let my mind clear before I see Keira. I'm not worrying about the what-ifs or how it's going to be between us. Well, not until I pass the sign welcoming me to Benton Falls. Now, my nerves are starting to ratchet up again. She texted me earlier with her address and I know it's not far from Slim's clubhouse. He also told me where she was living, but I'm not telling her that.

Pulling up to her house, I see it looks like a cute little house that she's really making her own. I've been by this house before and I know that there were never flowers in front of it before. Instead I see flowers planted on both sides of the porch and winding around the side of the house. There's a swing on the front porch and I can see her spending the evenings out here reading or just people watching.

I pull in behind her car and shut my bike down. Instead of getting off, I just take a minute to sit here and gather myself before I go knock on her door. Or until she comes outside to see what's going on. There's no way in hell she didn't hear my bike pulling in, so I'm surprised she's not out here already. Unless something is wrong with her. Fuck!

Hopping off my bike, I run up the steps and bang on the door. Waiting a fraction of a second, I go to pound again when it opens. Keira is standing there in a flowery sundress with her fiery hair flowing loose down her back. I love it when she wears her hair down and part of me can't help but think that she wore it that way for me. It gives me hope that things might not be as hard as I thought they would be with her.

"You okay Blade?" Keira asks me, standing off to the side so I can move past her.

"I'm okay. I just got a bit worried after I sat on my bike for a few minutes and didn't see you come to the door. Sorry," I tell her, looking around the downstairs of her little house.

"Oh. I was in the bathroom and figured you'd want to stretch a bit before coming in. We got a little bit before we need to leave, do you want something to drink?"

"Sure. Water's fine." I follow her into the kitchen and pull out a chair at the table sitting under a window.

"So, how have you been?" she asks, setting the glass down in front of me.

"I've been okay. How have you been?" I ask awkwardly.

"This is really awkward, isn't it?" she asks, reading my mind.

"It is. I'm sorry, I just don't know what to say here."

"I don't either. But, there is something I want to say to you and I haven't wanted to say it over the phone or through a text message."

"Have at it," I tell her, making myself more comfortable.

"Well, I always meant to tell you about the baby. Please don't ever think that I wasn't going to tell you. I was just trying to figure out a way to do that when you told me that you didn't want kids of your own. The way that Jason did that the day of the picnic was uncalled for and I am so pissed at him for it," Keira tells me. "And I'm sorry that you had to see him put his hands on me and then go to the hospital with me because of him."

"Don't ever apologize for somethin' that involves you, kitten. You need to go to the hospital, I'm there. The baby needs somethin', I'm there. I will always be there for you both. You're right, I didn't want commitment or kids, but things change," I tell her, grabbing her hand in mine and holding it between us.

"What do you mean?"

"I mean, all I've been thinkin' about is you and the baby. Once you left our clubhouse, I realized how empty my life was without you. You are everythin' that an old lady should be and one that I'd be proud to have at my side. As far as the baby is concerned, I didn't ever want kids of my own. Not after growin' up the way I did. But, I'm more than comin' around to the idea of havin' kids of my own."

Keira just looks at me and I can see the moisture in her eyes letting me know that she's not far from tears right now. I guess she's really just expecting me to go through the motions of being there for the baby now and not after he or she is born. That's just not the way it's going to work out. I'm going to be there for every milestone of our child and every day of their life. Keira is just going to have to get used to being with me.

"I don't know what to say to that Blade. I mean, you never once indicated that you wanted anything more than some fun. Now, that I'm pregnant, you've decided that I'll make a good old lady and you want me by your side? It doesn't make sense to me."

"It has nothin' to do with the fact that you're pregnant with my baby. It has to do with the fact that you got under my skin and I can't get you out no matter what I do."

Keira just has to interrupt me at this moment. "Yeah, I'm sure it was such a hardship to fuck all those club girls. Someone has to do it though, right?"

"I don't know what you're talkin' about. I was with one girl, one night, and it was your name that got called out, not hers. Fuck, I can't even remember what the bitch's name is. That was the night that I swore off anyone but you bein' on my cock. You're it for me and I'm not settlin' for anythin' less."

"I saw you leave with the blonde at Melody and Glock's wedding."

"It definitely wasn't what you thought. I was helpin' her to her man out front. She had way too much to drink and there was no way she could get home on her own. She's one of the strippers at the club and I wouldn't touch her if I absolutely had to."

"I don't know what you want from me Blade. I mean, what you truly want from me," Keira tells me, looking down at her lap.

I release her hand and make sure she's looking at me before I continue. "Kitten, I already told you that I want you as my old lady. There isn't goin' to be a day that goes by that I don't want you by my side. I want to go to bed with you every night and wake up to you every mornin'. I'm scared shitless and I don't know how to do anythin' involvin' a relationship. At all," I tell her honestly.

"This is sudden, Blade. All you ever wanted before was a bit of fun and nothing more. Now, I'm pregnant and you're telling me that you want us to be together. I guess I need to think about this before I give you an answer."

"That's fine. Now, before we take off and head to the appointment, you know I'm stayin' here for a few days, right? As in, I'll be in your bed the next few nights," I tell her, knowing that she's going to have something to say about it.

"I figured as much. And you know that I'll be working the next few nights too. Right?" she asks me, trying to goad me into an argument.

"Yep. And you know I'm gonna be there the entire time too."

I stand up and pull her into me, wrapping my arms around her and holding her tight. It's been way too long since I've held her in my arms. Instead of forgetting how she felt, I remember every single time she let me hold her. This time is no different. Keira melts into my hold and I am reminded of the last time I held her in my arms. This time is only different because of the proof of our child resting between us.

"I'm gonna bring my bag in and then we'll head out. I'm drivin' your car so I'll move my bike in front of it," I tell Keira, kissing her forehead and heading out the door.

By the time I head back in the door, Keira's ready to head out. So, I drop my bag just inside the door and follow her back outside. I wait while she locks up and then lead her down to her car. Holding open the door for her, I wait until she has her seatbelt on before I close the door and run around to the driver's side.

Keira gives me directions to her doctor's office. Surprisingly it's only about ten minutes from her house. This reassures me in case anything happens while she's alone. I know that Slim and anyone from the Phantom Bastards will be there in a heartbeat if Keira calls them. Just like I know that she won't call anyone for any reason at all.

"You ready for this?" Keira asks, breaking me out of my thoughts of her being alone.

"I can't wait. Honestly, I've been waitin' to come to an appointment with you. I'm sorry I haven't been able to make it to one before now. I truly wanted to be there for the ultrasound too," I answer, grabbing her hand and walking through the parking lot with her.

"Well, I can give you a copy of the picture. And, I didn't find out what we're having because you weren't there. If we find out, it will be when we're together."

"Thank you for that. It's up to you, kitten. I have no problem waitin' until he or she enters the world to find out."

"Well, I can at least see if I can have another ultrasound done so that you can be there for one. It's amazing to see it on the screen," Keira tells me, her entire face lighting up as she's talking about our child.

"If we can't, it's not a big deal."

"I'll ask when they take us back to the room. If we can, I really want you to see it."

I don't respond because I can tell when she gets like this, there's no arguing with her. My kitten gets an idea in her head and there's no talking her out of it when she gets it. We might not have spent more than a few months together, but I know her more than she thinks I do. I know when she's upset, mad, ready to fight until her last breath, when she's defending someone she loves, and when she's ready to give up. Before she left, I knew she was getting ready to give up, but I didn't want to acknowledge it. So, instead of fighting to keep her with me, I let her go.

Before I knew what was happening though, I realized she had become the center of my world. Keira is the one that can calm me down when I feel like spinning out of control, she makes me laugh when I want to fight everything in sight, and she makes me want to forget my past and try to live a life outside of the demons that haunt me. I need her more than words will be ever to convey it to her, but I know I have to show her how I feel somehow.

"You with me Blade?" Keira asks.

"Yeah, kitten. Just tryin' to figure somethin' out."

"Need any help with that?"

"I do. But, I don't know how to tell you what I've been realizin' since you been gone."

"Well, we'll talk over the next few days and see what we can figure out then," Keira says, heading up to check in.

I stand back and wait for her to decide where she wants to sit and wait. Looking around, I see women in various stages of pregnancy, including ones that have just had babies. The sight used to scare the shit out of me, now it just makes me wonder what my girl is going to look like as she gets further along. At this point, Keira only has a small baby bump. Well, it's what I consider small, but I'm sure she doesn't feel the same way about it.

"Now we wait until they call me back. Then I'll have to have my weight checked and use the restroom before we go into a room," she tells me.

"Okay kitten."

"Why do you call me that?" she asks, turning in her seat to look at me.

"Because I've never met a woman that will go to the lengths you do to protect those you love. You're like a kitten ready to pounce and scratch and claw for what you believe is right."

"Oh."

I'm sure my answer surprised her, but it's the truth. The rest of the old ladies will go to battle over their friends and family being attacked, but Keira is ready to defend people at the drop of a hat. She stepped in more times than I can count without Melody, or anyone else knowing, when club girls would try to go after Glock. She doesn't want recognition and she hates it when Melody sees her defend her. None of this stops her from going after anyone though. Hell, it wouldn't surprise me to see her go after someone like Tank or Dozer without blinking an eye. And those are two big motherfuckers.

"Keira, we're ready for you," a nurse calls from a doorway across the room.

Standing up, I hold out my hand to help her up. She takes it and doesn't let go as we follow the nurse behind the door. I wait until she does her thing and we're led to another room.

"How are you feeling today?" the nurse asks.

"I've been feeling okay. Every now and then I still get sick, but it's been getting a lot better."

"I can see that by the weight that you've gained since your last visit. It's a good thing," the nurse reassures her quickly.

"I know it is. It's not like I'm gaining weight because I'm not eating right. I'm gaining it to provide life for our child," Keira responds with more than a little sass to her voice.

I'm trying not to laugh while I sit next to her, but it's so hard. I can tell by the look on the nurse's face that she wasn't expecting my girl to respond that way. She must not have been around her before. So, I do what I have to and bury my face in Keira's side trying not to laugh in this nurse's face.

"I did want to talk to whoever I need to about getting another ultrasound done. The baby's father wasn't able to make it last month and I want him to experience it."

"I will mention it to Dr. Sanchez after I get your vitals. I'm sure she can arrange it for you."

The nurse does her thing, checking blood pressure and temperature on Keira. I just sit here and wait until she's done. That way I can move the chair closer again and take her hand in mine. Now that I'm seeing Keira, I want to continually touch her to make sure that she's really here with me and in touching distance. Not just something I'm dreaming about. Again.

As soon as the nurse leaves the room, I turn my chair to angle it closer to Keira and sit back down. Keira says nothing as she watches me maneuver to get as close as possible to her. She stays laying in the bed thing they have her settled on and waits for the doctor to make an appearance. Slim has already gotten a complete run down of the doctor so I know that she knows what she's talking about and doing. There was no way in hell Keira was going to have some new, fresh out of school doctor. I want to make sure that the best possible person is taking care of her and my baby.

After just a few minutes, there's a knock on the door before it opens. A woman in her late thirties pokes her head in the door before stepping in the room. Before saying anything to either one of us, she pulls a stool up so that she's sitting where we can both see her clearly.

"I hear that you want another ultrasound done," Dr. Sanchez says, taking a look at Keira's chart. "Your weight looks good today, but your blood pressure seems to be up just a little bit. We'll have to monitor that. Are you sure you're feeling okay? Any dizziness, feeling faint, anything like that."

"No. I've been working and they make sure that I get more than enough breaks and I have a stool to sit on when I need to behind the bar. I've just been feeling a little bit more tired than normal."

"You will as you get farther along. Now, I did place a call to ultrasound and they're going to see you today. They had a cancellation and can get you in as soon as I'm done here. I'm guessing that you're the soon to be daddy?" Dr. Sanchez asks, finally addressing me.

"I am. Sorry I couldn't be here before."

"Keira explained that your job takes you out of town a lot and that you live over an hour away to begin with. I'm happy to see that she has you in her corner though."

"Always."

"I'm going to take some measurements of your stomach and we'll listen to the heartbeat before the tech gets in here."

Doctor Sanchez goes to work taking measurements and feeling around Keira's stomach. Then she pulls something out of her pocket and sets it down next to Keira before pulling out a tube of something she smears on Keira's belly. Before I know it, the sweetest sound I've ever heard is thumping away through the exam room. It sounds like our baby's heart is racing and I look at Keira.

"It's fine Blade. It's always that fast," she explains, holding my hand tighter.

"She's right." Is Dr. Sanchez's only comment.

Taking the machine away from my kitten's stomach, the sound disappears and I want nothing more than to hear it again. I should've recorded that sound for when I'm not with my girl. Next time, I will without fail.

"Okay, sit tight and the tech will be in soon."

I settle back in the chair again, trying to relax and not let my nerves take hold. It's one thing to hear a heartbeat, but I'm guessing my entire world is about to change when I can actually see the baby on a screen.

"You'll be able to see the baby move and everything," Keira tells me.

"Really?"

"Yeah. If they're sucking their thumb, moving an arm or leg, you see it all. It's the most amazing thing I've ever seen in my life."

Yeah, that didn't help my nerves from ratcheting up just that much more. It was real when I found out that I was going to be a dad. Hearing the heartbeat just now, made it just much more real. Now, we're going to be seeing our child and I'm sure that it's going to really hit home the fact that in about three months' time we're going to be parents. That doesn't leave me much time to make sure that Keira is back home where she belongs.

It only takes a few minutes before there's another knock on the door. This time, a woman enters behind this huge machine. I'm not sure exactly what this thing is supposed to do, but it looks weird to me. Keira's already been through this though, so I'll just follow her lead. Not my usual thing, but this is all new for me. I really have no choice right now.

"How are you guys today?" the woman asks, staring at me and ignoring my girl.

"I'm doing fine," Keira answers, the attitude in her voice clear.

"Um…what?" the woman asks.

"I said, I'm doing fine. Now, do your job and quit staring at him. I think you might have some drool hanging there. Fuck!"

I sit there and don't say a word. Without coming right out and saying anything, Keira just claimed me. If she didn't care about me at all, she wouldn't be bothered by someone else looking at me. I mean, she was ignoring the patient, but still. Keira just let me know more than she wanted to and it's going to hit her in just a few seconds.

"Um…I don't know why I just said that," she starts. "Sorry Blade."

"It's all good kitten. You just let me know all I needed to know."

"What do you mean?"

"I mean, you just let me know all I need to know. You'll be home where you belong before too long." Is my only response before the woman starts talking to Keira.

"Since you've had this done before, you know what to expect. I'm going to put the gel on your stomach now."

I watch the woman do her thing and hold Keira's hand in mine. There's not a thing going near her that I'm not going to watch. This is my woman and my baby and I'll do what I have to in order to protect them until the day I die. History will not repeat itself for my child. I will not treat my child the way I was treated and Keira will never know what it's like to feel my hands on her in anything other than pleasure.

"Watch the screen Blade," Keira's soft voice breaks me from my thoughts.

Hearing the heartbeat, I pull my phone from my pocket so that I can record it. Keira doesn't say anything, she just watches me with a soft smile on her face. I guess I'm just proving to her that I will be there for the long road and I'm not going anywhere. Not just for the baby, for her.

If I didn't want to be with her, Rage wouldn't be starting to build a house for us. I wouldn't be making plans to bring her home permanently. And I sure wouldn't be sitting here with her in a place I thought I'd never be in a million years.

"Alright mom and dad, are you ready to see your baby?" the woman asks us before hitting a few buttons on the machine.

Keira looks at me and we both nod our heads. The screen goes from black to a fuzziness that is starting to take some sort of shape. Everything remains black and grey, and I'm not sure what I'm looking at, but I'm guessing I'll find out soon.

"Have you been told that you're having one baby?" the woman asks, looking directly at the screen.

"Yeah. I haven't ever been told anything else," Keira responds, looking at me quickly.

"Let me get Dr. Sanchez really quick," the woman says, pressing a button on the wall.

A few minutes later the Doctor returns to the room and talks quietly with the woman controlling the ultrasound machine. She's pointing something out on the screen and moving the wand around on my girl's stomach.

"Keira, it looks like you are having twins," Dr. Sanchez says, turning around to face us.

"Wh-what do you mean?" Keira asks, almost speechless.

"It looks like the second baby has been hiding behind the baby we've already seen. Until today."

"Is that even possible?" Keira asks.

"It is, and it happens more than you think. Instead of making an appointment for a month from today, I'd like to see you in a few weeks. I'll let them know at reception," Dr. Sanchez says before leaving the room.

I'm sitting in the chair next to Keira and I'm speechless. I was used to the idea of having one baby with my girl, now I have to wrap my head around the fact that we're about to have two babies. But, it's not about me right now, it's about my girl and our children that she's carrying. Instead of worrying about what I'm thinking or feeling right now, I need to be concerned with what's going through her mind.

"Kitten, you okay?" I ask, as the woman at the machine keeps doing her thing.

"I'm okay. I'm shocked, but I'm okay," she says. "Can you tell us the sex of either baby?"

"We can try. Let's see if they'll cooperate."

As she moves the wand around on my girl's stomach, we can see different angles of the babies. Other than being able to tell what the head and arms are, I can't figure out what we're supposed to be looking at.

"Alright guys, baby A looks to be a boy," she says, moving the wand around further to try to get a look at the other baby. "And, baby B looks like a little girl."

One of each, we're having a boy and a girl. I can already guarantee that my daughter will not be happy when she hits her late thirties and wants to start dating. Between her brother, my club brothers, and me she will have to go through a lot. There won't be anyone good enough for my baby girl. No one.

"Blade, are you okay?" Keira asks.

"I'm doin' good, kitten. How are you feelin' about this?" I ask, pulling her hand to my mouth and kissing it.

"I don't know how to feel. I was prepared for one baby, not two. But, we'll adapt and there's still time to prepare for two babies," she tells me.

"Okay mom and dad, let me get you some pictures printed off and you'll be ready to leave," the woman tells us.

Hitting a button, I hear the machine starting to print our pictures. Hopefully she prints enough for me to take back to Clifton Falls with me. At least until I can convince Keira to move back home.

"What do you want to do now?" I ask her.

"I'm hungry, actually. There's still time to go before I have to be to work. Can we go through a drive through or something so I can take a short nap?"

"Sounds good to me kitten," I tell her, accepting the pictures the woman hands us.

After thanking her, we head out so that Keira can make her next appointment. Asking for two appointment cards, she hands me one that I put in my wallet. There's no way I'm missing another appointment. So, I'll have to talk to Grim when I get back.

Chapter Two

Keira

BLADE HAS BEEN HERE for a few days. It's been nice having him around, taking care of me. I'm still not over the shock of learning that we're having twins, but it will be okay.

I could tell the thoughts running through Blade's head as soon as we found out we're having a boy and a girl. My poor daughter is going to be so protected that it's going to drive her up a wall. It's a good thing her mama won't let them get too bad. Hell, I'll even help her get away every now and then. Blade won't like it, but he'll get over it.

He's stuck to his word and been at Vixen every night while I've been at work. There's a corner table that he's chosen to sit at and watch me while I work. Honestly, I haven't seen him really even pay attention to the strippers as they dance. His gaze is always on me.

Slim and a few of the Phantom Bastards have been in more since Blade has been spending time at the club. It's nice to see them on a more regular basis. I know that Maddie is Slim's daughter and that he misses her and the kids like crazy. We've had several talks about it. He's such a good guy and I hope that eventually he finds his happy ever after. He deserves it.

Waking up, I go through my morning routine while Blade is still asleep. This gives me a chance to think about the last few days and decide what I'm going to do. Blade's made it extremely clear that he wants me to come home to Clifton Falls. Technically I don't have a home, this is just a temporary stop along the way I guess. Obviously, I won't go far because of the babies, but I know Benton Falls isn't my home.

Blade hasn't touched me sexually in the days that he's been here. The only thing he's done is hold me at night when we go to bed. I'm so sexually frustrated that it's not funny, but I'm not going to make the first move. If Blade wanted me, he'd make sure I knew it.

My phone ringing breaks me out of my thoughts as I pick it up to see that Melody is calling me. "Hello."

"Hey babe," she responds. "How are things with you and Blade?"

"Okay I guess."

"What do you mean?" she asks, the confusion clear in her voice.

"Well, we found out some news at my appointment. That's not what I'm talking about though. I'm talking about the fact that the man hasn't touched me since he's been here. We go to bed and he wraps his arms around me, then falls asleep. There's no sex. At all," I tell her, getting out the ingredients I need to make breakfast.

"So why don't you start it babe? I'm sure he's just trying to respect you. Not push you into something that he's not sure you want right now."

"I'm not starting anything. If he wanted me, he'd make sure I knew it. He always did before. Blade's the only one I've been with since just before you were kidnapped and he's the only one I want now."

Before Melody gets a chance to respond, my cell phone is taken from me and I can hear the beep of it being hung up. I don't even have to turn around to know that Blade is behind me. His smell and heat meet my back just before he starts kissing my neck.

"Don't ever think I don't want you, kitten," he says. "You want somethin' from me, take it."

Turning around, I wrap my arms around his neck and pull his mouth down to meet mine. He wants me to take what I want, then I'm going to do just that. I move to his neck while running my hands up and under his shirt, bringing it up his body so I can kiss my way down to what I really want.

Blade lifts his arms up so I can remove his shirt easier, tossing it to the floor behind me. Continuing to kiss his neck, I slide my hands in the sweats that he slept in last night. I can hear the groans coming from Blade as I slowly make my way from his neck, down his chest and abs to his cock.

"Kitten, never said you had to do that," Blade says, just before I take him in my mouth.

Without answering, I take as much of Blade in my mouth as I can. Using my tongue, I swirl it around the entire shaft while continuing to bob up and down. The entire time I stare up at him, watching the look of pure pleasure on his face. He's got his head slightly tilted back and his eyes are closed. I can hear his low moans which is just turning me on more.

"Kitten, stop," Blade says, bending slightly to pull me up. "Feels too good and I'm not goin' to last much longer."

Blade picks me up and before I can wrap my legs around his waist, he sets me down on the island behind me. I try to stay in a sitting position, but he uses one hand to gently push me back so I'm laying down. Reaching up under my dress, Blade slides my thong down my legs until he can fling it behind his back. Standing up, he bends over me and grabs my hair so that he can tilt my head where he wants it to go before kissing me in a way that he knows I love. Just as I'm about to break the kiss so I can catch my breath, Blade moves to my neck.

I moan out as he nips and kisses his way down my neck to my chest. Without skipping a beat, I can feel the straps of my dress being lowered down my arms, baring my upper body to Blade. My back arches up off the island as he takes one nipple in his mouth. Ever since I became pregnant, I am so sensitive that he can almost make me cum just from playing with my tits. And it doesn't take long either.

"More Blade!" I moan out, arching up as far as my stomach will let me.

Blade doesn't disappoint. He moves from one side over to the other one. I don't know if it's because I'm already so close, but this side seems more sensitive. Before I can stop, or warn Blade, an orgasm rips through me.

"Blade!" I scream out.

Before I come down all the way, I feel Blade insert a finger in me. Curling his finger in a way that ensures he hits all the right spots, I feel my body responding the way it always does to him. From the very first time we were together, Blade knew my body better than I did. I enjoy sex but no one else has ever gotten the response that he has. Blade makes it more about me and less about himself than anyone I have ever known. Just like I know that he's holding back and not giving me everything that he usually does with other women.

"Kitten, you ready for me?" he asks, stepping in even closer to me.

"Mmhmmm," I murmur.

After pumping his finger in and out a few more times, I feel the head of his cock lining up. Even though Blade won't slam into me the way that he has in the past, he doesn't stop until he's buried inside. My back arches and there's no stopping it if I wanted to. I love feeling Blade inside me, making sure that we both reach our release in ways that are fun and new to me. It's never the same thing with him.

"I need more," I tell him, lifting my hips to meet him.

"I don't want to hurt you or the baby, Kitten."

"You won't. Please, I need more," I moan out.

Blade pauses for just a second before giving into me and giving me what I really want. He moves faster and harder until I can feel my release curling through my body. I know that he's getting closer too since I can feel his legs starting to shake and his movements becoming erratic.

"Give. It. Up. Kitten!" Blade pants out between thrusts.

Leaning down, Blade takes one nipple in his mouth and bites down just hard enough for my release to tear through me. Two more pumps of his hips and I can feel Blade still and know that he's found his release too.

Usually he would lean down on me and hold me while we both came down. I know he won't this time though. He will hold me, but he won't put any weight on me. So, he rubs his hands up and down my sides while our breathing begins to slow. I run my hands up and down his back, pulling him as close as he'll get.

"Kitten, you know that I have to leave today, yeah?" he asks, helping me sit up.

"I know. I don't like it, but I know you have to get back to your life," I tell him honestly, while my heart breaks in pieces.

"Kitten, you know I want you to come home with me. I've already talked to Rage about buildin' our home close to Melody and Glock's. I want us together, you my old lady, and us raisin' our babies together," Blade tells me, kissing my forehead.

"I don't know, Blade. That's a big step up from just wanting to have a little fun. We can't do that just because there's children involved now. That won't be good for anyone. Especially them," I tell him, knowing first-hand what parents fighting all the time does to a child.

"Kitten, we'll work on it. I'll keep comin' down to see you and you can make trips up to see me. I know I want a decision made soon though. I don't want our twins livin' in two different houses," Blade tells me.

I don't want our children raised in two different houses, in two different towns, either. My parents couldn't make their relationship work and I remember the toll it took on my sister and I to go from one home to the other with two different sets of everything from rules to the people we were surrounded by. My kids deserved better than that, but that's not a reason to get back together.

"We'll see what happens, Blade," I tell him, leaning up to give him a kiss good bye.

"Bye kitten. I'll call you as soon as I make it to the clubhouse," he tells me before grabbing his bag and making his way out to his bike.

I stand on the porch watching him leave. After he's long gone and I can barely hear the rumble of his bike, I'm still rooted to the same spot. So much has to be decided and I have to be the one to make those decisions. Can I truly risk my heart and give Blade the chance he says he wants?

Blade

My head was spinning on the drive home. Instead of it being a calm and relaxing ride, I couldn't stop the thoughts of Keira and my kids from flitting through my mind. Was I really ready to be a dad to not only one child but two? How was I going to handle having a daughter? Am I good enough to teach my son what it takes to be a man? Will my girl move back where she belongs with the people that truly love and care about her? If I push too hard, will she pull a runner and disappear with my kids? Will she give me a chance to prove to her that I'm ready to be a one-woman man?

The few days that I just spent with her were amazing. No, I didn't push the sex issue because I want this done at her pace. If she doesn't want me to touch her, then I'm not going to. That theory was good in my mind until I heard her talking on the phone thinking I didn't want her at all. My kitten is the only woman I'm going to want today, tomorrow, and when we're old and gray. Keira knows when to challenge me, when to leave her sass behind, how to give me as good as she gets, and isn't afraid to try anything. She speaks her mind and doesn't let me bullshit her. I also know when it comes down to it, unless I do one of her few deal breakers, she'll have my back no matter what.

With all the thoughts running through my mind, I'm back at the clubhouse before I know it. I back my bike into its normal spot and take a minute to just sit there. It's good to be home, but my girl needs to be here with me. My kids need to be here no matter if they're in her stomach or born. I'm tired of missing out on things.

"Blade!" I hear yelled from across the yard. "You didn't bring my girl home? What the fuck were you doing there?"

"Angel, leave the man alone. He's just gettin' back and wants a minute. He'll come to you when he's ready," Glock tells Melody.

"Let me just give her a call and I'll be right in," I tell her, hoping it will calm her down enough to give me time to call Keira.

Pulling my phone out of my pocket, I pull up her name and listen to it ring. Instead of hearing her sweet voice, I get her voicemail. I know she's not working at the club tonight. Maybe she's taking a nap. I know she usually tries to lay down and relax for a little while during the day. I'll give her an hour and then I'm calling her back.

Knowing I don't have much time before Melody comes barreling at me again, I make my way in the clubhouse and see her and Glock sitting at a table in the corner. Guess we're talking about my trip and why our girl isn't home where she belongs yet.

Making a detour to the bar, Summer hands me a beer before I make my way over to them. I sit opposite of Melody and down half of my beer before I set it down, letting her know I'm ready to talk.

"How is she?" she asks, genuine concern written all over her face.

"She's okay. Tired most days but she's handling everythin' like a champ," I respond, the pride evident in my voice.

"I know she was upset the last time I talked to her. The same way I know I was hung up on, so I'm guessing you took care of that issue?"

"Angel," Glock warns.

"Yeah, I took care of it. We got news, but I know she's gonna want to share with you, so I'm sure she'll be callin' you real soon."

"How are you gonna do that to me?" Melody asks.

"It's not just my news to share. She'll spill the beans when she's ready to and not a minute sooner. You know how stubborn she is."

"I do. I also know how she truly feels about you even if she hasn't admitted it to herself, or you yet. You need to be careful with her and be there when she needs you," Melody tells me. "And you have to let her push you away a little when she needs to. Keira hides her feelings behind a wall thicker than concrete. So, when she loves you and gives you her all, don't break that trust."

"I'm not gonna hurt her," I tell Melody honestly. "I want her here with me. We're goin' to be a family and she needs to know that I'm all in when I say I want to be with her."

"I know you are Blade. I haven't seen you with any bimbos and I know that you're missing her as much as I am. Please, bring her home where she belongs," Melody begs me. "She's never really felt like she's belonged anywhere or that she's had a home. Give that to her Blade."

Learning that my kitten doesn't feel like she belongs anywhere guts me. She does belong somewhere; right by my side. I don't want her following behind me, I want her to be my partner in everything. Keira is someone that I can open up to and share the demons that haunt me. She's the only one that I want to open up to completely about everything. Obviously, there's some club things I can't let her know, but everything else in my life is an open book to her.

Looking down at my phone, I realize that I've been sitting here for almost two hours shooting the shit with Glock and Melody. We've talked about the new house, Melody's babbled on about baby things, and how much she wants Keira here with us all. Making my excuses, I leave the table and head to my room to call my girl. She should be up by now and I want to talk to her. I miss hearing her voice already.

Just before I get to my door, I see a club girl making her way over to me. I don't remember seeing her before and I'm glad that I don't want anyone else but my kitten. This girl is young, she's got make-up caked on so thick I can tell from thirty feet away, her long hair is greasy and unkempt, and she could do with a meal or two to fatten her up. Even if I didn't have Keira, I couldn't bring myself to touch this girl. There's something off about her and I can feel it in my gut.

"Hey handsome," she purrs, trying to sound sexy. "You looking for some company?"

"No. Sorry, my girl would have my cock sittin' in a jar if I so much as looked at another girl."

"What she doesn't know won't hurt her."

"Who the fuck do you think you're talkin' to? My girl means more to me than some used up skank," I say, getting in this girls face. "If you ever come at me like that again, I can guarantee you'll be out of here before you can blink. We don't play that game around here. Our women mean the world to us and we're not gonna fuck it up for someone like you."

"I-I'm s-s-sorry," The girl stammers. "I didn't mean anything."

"You're just lucky it was me you pulled this shit on and not one of the higher members of the club. You would already be gone. Now, run along and find a single guy to fuck with."

I watch the girl scramble off down the hall towards the common room. Shaking my head, I think that it never ceases to amaze me how low some of the club girls will go to try to land a brother. Especially Addison and Chrissy when Skylar first started coming around. Those two were down right vicious and I hope this new girl doesn't turn out to be the same way.

Opening my door, I pull my phone out and try to call Keira again. There's still no answer and I'm honestly starting to get worried. I might have to put a call in to Slim to have him send one of his guys to check on my girl. If anything is wrong and I'm so far away I'm going to flip out.

"'Lo," I hear muttered into the phone.

"Slim, you seen my girl since I left there?" I ask, sitting down on my bed.

"No. We tried callin' her to come in to cover a shift and haven't had a call back," he answers, more alert then when he answered the phone.

"I've been tryin' since I made it back and haven't gotten her to answer the phone. Can you...." I don't even have to finish my question.

"Boy Scout, go 'round to Keira's house and check on her. Tell her that we tried callin' to see if she wanted to cover a shift and were gettin' worried. Call me as soon as you see her," Slim tells the prospect. "Call you back as soon as I hear from him."

Hanging up, I lean back waiting for Slim to call me back. Unfortunately, there are so many possible scenarios running through my head that I can't relax. I won't be able to until I know that she's okay and our babies are okay. Especially if she's not answering for Slim or one of the girls from Vixen. That's what's got my head in a tail spin wondering what's going on with her right now.

Slim: She's good. Just wakin' up

Me: Thanks man

It's a good thing that the clubhouse isn't that far from her house. I know Slim did that on purpose. Now, I can call my girl and find out when I get to see her again. I'm dead serious when I say I'm not missing out on much more of her carrying my babies. She needs to come home. Now.

Chapter Three

Keira

IT'S BEEN A FEW DAYS since Blade left and I've been missing him. Well, I haven't been missing his bossiness. The day he left, I fell asleep and didn't hear my phone or anything. When he could finally get a hold of me, he chewed me a new ass because he was worried about the babies. I mean, he told me that he was worried about me, but we all know that it's the babies he's concerned about. I'm just the one carrying them for him. I know it sounds mean, but I just don't know what he honestly wants from me. I've never been this confused about anyone in my life and then to add all the hormones running rampant from the pregnancy in, to say I'm a hot mess would be an understatement.

I can hear my phone ringing as I sit at my island daydreaming. So, I don't bother looking at the caller i.d. before answering.

"Hello?" I ask.

"It's about time you answer your phone you biker whore," Jason's voice hollers through the line. "Did you have a nice visit with that biker trash?"

"What do you want, Jason?" I ask, the confusion and anger lacing my voice.

"Who the fuck do you think you are talking to like that?"

"I'm the girl that isn't your fucking concern anymore. I'm the one that doesn't care what the fuck you want. And, I'm the one that is hanging up now."

"Don't you dare hang up on me, Keira. If you do, your biker bitch will be the one to pay for it."

"What do you mean?" I ask, getting scared for Blade.

"I got enough on your biker trash and his entire club to put them all behind bars. Not for a little bit of time either. I'm talking for a long, long time. You're going to do exactly what I say or he's going to be the one to pay. Then what are your babies going to do? Who's going to help you take care of twins?"

"And what exactly is it you think I'm going to do for you?" I ask, not wanting to know what this demented man is going to ask me to do.

"It's quite simple. You're going to leave that biker trash and come back to me. You'll do everything I say and you'll make sure that your little biker doesn't contact you ever again. And, when you have his little biker bastards, you will give them up to him and never see them again," Jason tells me like he's talking about the weather and not destroying my life.

"What makes you think I'm going to give my children up for you? And how do you know I'm having twins?"

"I know you will because if you don't, I'll kill the bastards while you watch me do it. And I know everything there is to know about you. You don't need to know anything more than that."

"I have to go to work in a little bit. While I'm there, I'll contact Blade and make sure he knows never to contact me again. When I have our children, I'll make sure that my girl comes to get them and takes them to their daddy," I tell Jason, trying to stall for time to come up with a plan.

"I'll be at Vixen at some point tonight. So, you better make sure you call him early. And if I find out you're trying to double cross me, you won't like the consequences Keira. Don't try me on this."

Hanging up the phone, I slump down on my bed trying to figure out what I'm going to do. If Jason knows things that are going on with me, then obviously there's bugs and taps all over the place here. So, I'm going to have to be careful with what I do and who I contact for the time being. Which means no talking to Melody about anything serious right now. Hell, I'm better off not contacting her at all right now. She's going to hate me, but she'll understand once she finds out what's going on. Now, I'm going to have to alert Slim somehow so that he can get a hold of Blade before I make the call I have to.

Going to the desk that once belonged to my favorite grandmother, I sit down and write down what's going on. I write everything that Jason said to me on the phone and what he wants from me now. That way Slim can tell Blade the whole story and I can make a call that's going to break my heart without truly having to stop contacting Blade. I'll figure something out to still get a hold of him and until then, I will just leave it alone. My only hope is that he doesn't hate me for being so weak.

Before I fold the piece of paper to put in an envelope for Slim, I decide to write Blade a personal little note. That way he knows how much I truly love him and that I would've been moving back with him if it weren't for Jason.

Blade,

Even if we weren't having twins together, I'd still be moving back to be with you. I'm willing to put my heart on the line in order to see where this thing between us goes. But, right now I have to protect the babies, you, and your brothers. So, I'm going to do the only thing I know how to and let Jason have his way. Maybe one day we can find our way back to one another. Until then, take care of our children when they're born and make sure they know how much I truly love you all.

Please make sure that Melody knows I'm sorry for hurting her by doing what I have to do. I don't want to hurt any of you.

Love Always,

Keira

I have about three hours before I have to be at Vixen. Right now, my bed is calling my name. I

can still manage to get an hour and a half of sleep
before getting ready to go. And, I can still be there
early enough to see Slim or have someone call him
to come down. There's no way in hell I'm using my
phone to contact anyone. Not until I can have
someone look at it and get whatever tap he put on it
off. Maybe Slim can get me a burner phone so I can
talk to Blade and Melody when I'm not at home or
in my car. There's got to be a way I can still contact
them without Jason knowing.

    Pulling into the employee parking at the rear
of Vixen, I take a minute to just breathe and see if I
can see Slim's bike here. I see a few bikes parked
by the back door so I know at least a few of the
guys are here. That's going to make it easier for me
to get Slim down here so I can give him the
envelope that's about the crush my entire world.
Well, that's what Jason will think anyway.
Hopefully Slim can get Blade on board with acting
like we're never going to talk again so I can see
what Jason's plan is. Something has obviously
happened to make him act the way he is and making
me do whatever he wants me to do to go back to
him.

    Mustering up all the courage I can, I make
my way into the club. Wood and Killer are the first
two guys I see and I make my way over to them.
Since I don't know if there's anything in the club

that's going to get Jason the information he wants, I need to play this smooth and be careful with what I say and do. Especially once he shows up.

"Hey guys!" I say with fake bravado.

Instantly Killer perks up, knowing that something is wrong. "Hey sweetheart. Everythin' good?"

"Um, I need a minute and I don't know where to go so no one hears what I have to say," I tell them, flipping over a napkin I write 'bug' on it.

"Leave your purse and coat here. We can go in Slim's office and have Boy Scout keep watch," Wood tells me, standing up and grabbing his drink before making his way down the hall.

Killer follows me after I put my things behind the bar. He pulls his phone out of his pocket and hits a few buttons before we get to Slim's office. Instead of putting it to his ear for a call, he makes sweeping motions from about ten feet in front of the doorway to inside the office. Once he's done, he tells me to sit and tell them what's going on.

"I need Slim here guys. I need to make a phone call to Blade but I want Slim to talk to him first. That way this isn't coming out of left field and Blade knows that I have no choice in the matter. This is important guys. You know I never come to you for anything. But I can't handle this myself."

"Alright babe. I'll get Slim here immediately," Wood tells me. "I know he was already plannin' on stoppin' by tonight. He wanted to talk to you about somethin' I think."

"Great!" I mutter. "If I wasn't already a nervous wreck, I am now."

So many things are running through my head hearing that Slim already wanted to talk to me. I'm pretty sure I haven't fucked anything up, so I don't think it's work related. That means that he wants to know what my plans are regarding the babies and Blade. I'm just beginning to wrap my head around the fact that I was going to go back to Clifton Falls. Now all of this shit is happening and I don't know what to do.

The first tear slips out and I know that I have to get to the bathroom before I become a blubbering mess right here in front of Killer and Wood. I've been holding it together since I got the call from Jason. Unfortunately, it seems as though the dam is about to break and I don't want these two men to witness my breakdown. So, I make my excuses and run to the bathroom that the dancers use. It's the only place I know I can get some privacy.

Rushing in, I almost slam into Shy. She's a sweet girl that is only stripping to pay her way through school. Her real name is Cheyanne and she's extremely shy. That's why her stage name is Shy. How she gets up there and dances every night is a mystery to me. But, the men love her and I know that a certain MC president may have a thing for her too. But, he won't ever say anything to anyone about it.

"You okay Keira?" Shy asks, breaking me from my thoughts.

"Yeah, I'm good hun. You dancing tonight or are you helping behind the bar?" I ask, since she does both.

"I'm actually doing both. When I'm not dancing I'll be helping you out. Then I think Lexi is going to be filling in for me. Dante called in again," Shy tells me.

"Doesn't surprise me," I say, feeling the tears getting closer and closer to spilling. "I'll be out soon. Can you let the guys know please?"

"Sure. You take all the time you need and I'll cover for you.

Shy leaves and I make my way over to the little couch against one wall of the bathroom. Instead of sitting down like I usually do, I curl up on my side and let the tears fall freely. Thoughts of not seeing my children grow and learn fill my head. Blade will take good care of them. He's got the support of the club and the old ladies behind him to make sure he doesn't fuck up too bad. This leads to thoughts of Blade and all the time we wasted. Instead of me being here, I could've spent my last few days with him and loved him the way I wanted to. I guess we'll never know what could've been between us.

Before I know it, Slim is crouching in front of me. He's wiping my tears and handing me some Kleenex to clean myself up. He gives me the time I need to compose myself before wanting to know what's going on. Thankfully, before I left the house, I tucked the envelope in my back pocket. So, I pull it out and give it to him. For a minute all he does is look between the envelope and me. Finally, opening the envelope, Slim pulls the paper out and begins to read what I've written. I can see the rage simmering beneath the surface the farther into the writing he gets. This isn't going to be good.

"What the fuck?" Slim explodes. "Is this fucker for real Keira?"

"He is. I should've known when he left Grim's clubhouse after spilling the beans to Blade that I hadn't heard the last from him. Now, he wants me back and this is what I have to do. Please, can you call Blade and explain before I have to make my call to him?"

"Keira, I don't know. There's gotta be a different way to handle this," Slim says, taking a seat at the end of the couch.

"There's not. I need to make this call to Blade before Jason gets here tonight. Please, Slim, I'm begging you so he knows the true story."

"Alright. In the meantime, we'll try to come up with a game plan. You know Blade's not goin' to sit by and let this asshole take you and those babies away from him. I guarantee that he'll be here before the night's over with."

"I know. And I'll have to deal with that once it happens. Just let him know that I do love him and I'm going to figure this shit out."

"*We* will figure this out honey. You are not in this alone. Between all the clubs, we'll take this motherfucker down. I'm goin' to get my guys on diggin' in to him and then we'll come up with a game plan. Don't try to take him down alone Keira. Blade will kill us all if anythin' happens to you."

"I'm not promising anything to anyone," I tell Slim honestly.

"I know babe. Trust me, we all know that when it comes to our old ladies. And don't even say you're not because it's only a matter of time before you're Blade's old lady. I'll let you know when I'm off the phone with him."

Instead of saying anything to him, I turn and make my way out to the bar so I can get to work. I know that it's now only a matter of time before Jason gets here and I'm not looking forward to it. Especially when I look around the main room and see members of the Phantom Bastards sitting spread throughout the room. That can only mean that Killer and Wood let Slim know a little bit of what was going on before he got here. So, he brought re-enforcements. Great!

Shy is behind the bar and it's starting to get busy so I move as fast as my pregnant ass will let me to start helping her out. She smiles at me and continues working without missing a beat. There's a few older men that are regulars at the club sitting at my end of the bar. They know I'm pregnant and they always sit in my section so that they can help me out with the tips they don't have to leave.

Before I know it, Slim is heading towards the bar. The rage on his face is worse than when he was reading what I wrote earlier. That can only mean that Blade is throwing a fit and it's not going to end well. Guess it's my turn to find out exactly how bad it is.

"Shy, I need to make a quick call. I'll be right back," I say, wiping my hands down on the bar towel.

"Take your time sweets. I got this, and if I don't, I'll pull Boy Scout back here to help me. It's not like it would be the first time he's had to help out," Shy tells me, laughing.

I make my way out the back door to calm myself down a little bit before making a call that I don't want to make at all. I'm already crushed and I know that Blade's going to be just as crushed. Even if he knows what's going on in advance. Just knowing that I'm never going to see him again is breaking my heart. Add in the fact that Jason is telling me that I have give my kids up and my heart is breaking into a million pieces.

Knowing I can't waste any more time, I open my phone and pull up Blade's name. For a minute I forget that I'm calling him as I stare at the picture of the two of us. I took it one afternoon when we were just lounging around in his bed. We're wrapped around one another and he's staring down at me. I love the picture and look at it more than I should. That's my secret though.

"Hello? Kitten? Kitten, are you there?" I hear Blade's voice coming through the phone.

"Oh, sorry Blade. I got lost in my own head for a minute," I say, putting the phone to my ear.

"It's all good babe. What's up?"

"I need to tell you something and you're not going to like it. But, it has to be said," I start, willing the tears to stop before they begin.

"Okay. Are you tellin' me that you're finally comin' home?"

"No. As a matter of fact, I'm calling to tell you the opposite. Not only am I staying in Benton Falls, I don't want to talk to, or see, you again. We were kidding ourselves thinking anything could ever work between us. And, I'm just not ready to be a mom to twins. So, when they're born, I'm going to have Melody come get them and bring them to you. I'll get through the rest of this pregnancy without you and then you can raise them with the help of your club," I say, my heart breaking into a million pieces.

For a full minute, Blade doesn't say a word. He knew this was coming, but he's still shocked as fuck and I know I'm hurting him. "What are you talkin' about kitten? What's happened since I last talked to you?"

"Nothing happened. I've just decided that I can't be what you want and I'm too young to be a mom. It will be hard enough trying to be a single mom to one baby. Make it twins and it's going to be even harder. So, I just can't do this. I'm going to move on with my life and I suggest you do the same. If you try to contact me, I will change my number. There's nothing more you can say that will change my mind about this. And tell Melody that I won't be contacting her anymore either. Bye Blade," I say, hanging up before I start crying and he knows it.

Slumping down against the wall, I let the tears flow without worrying about what anyone else is going think. I'm sure most of the guys from the club sitting in there right now know what's going on. So, if they see me they'll know I'm crying for a reason. Most of them will know to leave me alone while I get this out of my system. Not that they want to be dealing with a crying girl.

Slim is the one that finds me slumped against the wall, tears streaming down my face, staring at my phone and the picture of Blade and I. He takes my phone from me and pulls me into his embrace, rubbing my back in a soothing manner. Out of all the men, I would expect him to be the one to comfort me. He might be new to the whole dad thing, but he's not one to back down from showing his softer side.

"I-I-I'm f-f-fine," I stammer out, trying to control my tears and breathing.

"You're not fine sweetheart. No one would expect you to be after the call you just made. We'll figure it out though. I've got Boy Scout goin' over to your place to look for taps and bugs. Anythin' that's givin' this asshole the information he has on you. By the way, he just walked in the door and is lookin' for you."

Straightening my spine, I wipe my tears away, and make sure that I am steady on my feet as I stand up. Not like Slim would let anything happen to me, but I'm still independent. I nod my understanding that Jason is here and Boy Scout will be going over to my place. It's not like they need a key considering the club owns the house and they already have one.

"I'm ready to just get this over with," I tell Slim, starting to head back in.

"The guys will be here the rest of the night sweetheart. Wood is goin' to be stationed on your end of the bar and Killer will be in the middle. If they even get the hint that this motherfucker is steppin' out of line, they're goin' to step in."

"I don't think that's a good idea," I begin. "He already hates you all. Especially knowing that Blade is friends with you guys. He's going to be extra mean in your presence."

"No, he won't. Not if he knows what's good for him," Slim says, his voice taking on the menacing tone showing that he means business.

Heading back into the bar, I look in one of the mirrors on the wall before making my way behind the bar. I can see Jason sitting at my end, his foot tapping on the floor impatiently. Unfortunately, I know that means bad things for me. He's not going to care if I'm pregnant or not now. In fact, I won't be surprised if he were to purposely make me lose the babies or go into premature labor. It would be just like him to do that. Even if he already told me I'm not allowed to keep the babies.

"It's about fucking time you come back from break, Keira," Jason growls out at me. "Get me a fucking beer and keep them coming until you're ready to leave."

I pull one of the bottles from the top of the cooler, knowing that they're going to be warmer than the ones farther down. If he wants to be an asshole, then I'm going to treat him like one. I'm not going to cater to him anymore and I'm not going to go into this "arrangement" willingly.

As soon as he takes a sip, Jason knows what I've done and he's not happy. I can tell by the look on his face that he's about to go off on me. So, I try to lean in closer so he's not yelling, drawing Wood and Killer's attention to him any more than it already is.

"Listen bitch, you better start acting like you want to be with me. It's only going to make things easier on you in the long run. I don't want to have to pass you around to the men that I associate with. They won't be gentle with you. And they will take what they want with no regards to the bastards your carrying."

"Fine, Jason. Whatever you want, Jason," I mutter sarcastically. "It really doesn't matter considering you've already ruined my life and are taking the only things that I love and care about away from me."

"Oh, you will care. Every day you show me disobedience, it's just going to get worse and worse on you. You'll be lucky to be able to leave the house without having bruises showing, Keira. I'm not playing games."

Knowing that Jason is serious as he's talking to me, I decide to reel in my inner bitch and pretend that I want to be with him. It's going to take all of my acting skills to be able to pull this shit off. But, for the sake of my children and my body, I'll do what I have to. The only concern I have is if he thinks I'm going to fuck him. That will be something I'm not willing to cave for. Jason will *not* be touching me no matter what he thinks.

My shift is finally coming to an end and I'm not looking forward to leaving with Jason. It's the last thing I want to do, but I know he'll either be coming to my house or I'll be going with him. Hopefully he makes me go to his house because I don't want him in my space. I don't want him tainting the memories from the few short days that Blade spent there.

"Keira, you're following me back to my place. Tomorrow you can get some of your clothes and bring them over to my house. Nothing else of yours will be coming there. It's nothing but garbage and I don't want it in my home," Jason tells, me standing up and heading for the door.

"Okay Jason. Just let me cash out and take my drawer back to the office," I tell him, turning my back to him.

"You have about five minutes. I'm not waiting all night for you. Do you understand me?"

"Yes," I mutter, knowing that I better move as fast as I can.

Quickly printing off my reports, I count my drawer down and take everything in to Slim. He usually has one of the guys from the club take care of everything else. They let us know if our drawers are okay when we come back in for our next shift. Usually if you don't get talked to, your drawer was fine.

Without saying a word to Slim, or anyone else standing in the office, I make my way behind the bar to gather up my belongings. Shy tries to talk to me, but I can't afford to make Jason wait. So, as politely as I can, I let her know I'm in a rush and that we'll talk when we both work together again. She says she understands and gives me a quick hug.

I exit the club through the back door and I can see a few of the guys from the club standing around. Usually one or two are out here to make sure no one bothers us as we head to our cars. Tonight, there's at least ten guys standing around. Some are talking quietly while others are smoking. I can see Jason parked next to my car and I quicken my pace. He's on the phone as I unlock my door and get in.

"We have a pit stop to make," he tells me, after rolling up next to my door and telling me to open my window. "You are to stay in the car and wait until I come back out. I don't know how long I'm going to be and it really doesn't matter. You are to sit there and wait."

"What if I have to go to the bathroom or something? You know it doesn't take much with the babies sitting on my bladder."

"I don't give a fuck. You will not move from the place until I'm ready to leave."

Jason pulls out and waits for me to pull in behind him. then he leads me out of town towards Dander Falls. I don't know where the fuck he's taking me, but I know that we're getting closer to the other Wild Kings club. This isn't going to be good. Not with the mood Blade's in. I'm sure that they know what's going on now too.

We drive about forty-five minutes before Jason pulls down a dirt road. After a mile or two, he pulls up to what looks like a hunting cabin. I roll down my window as I see him walking over to the car again. I'm sure that he's simply going to remind me not to move. And, I'm right. He growls out what he wants to say and then leaves me.

As he enters the cabin, I can see a bunch of people hanging out and hear the music blaring. Apparently, he wants me to sit in the car while he's at a party. What the fuck is that shit about? Why do I need to even be here when I could've just gone home? That doesn't sound like a bad idea honestly. I'll give him a half hour and if he's not out, I'm leaving. I don't care what he does to me.

While I'm waiting, I decide to clean my car up a little bit. There's an empty bag sitting on the floor in my passenger side so I grab it before sliding my seat all the way back. I reach under my seat to grab out any garbage that may have fallen under there and my hand wraps around something that feels like a phone. So, I pull it out and see a flip phone. It looks like one of the ones that I've heard the guys say are their burner phones.

I flip open the phone and see that there are three text messages. So, I hit the button to pull them up and see that one is from Slim, one is from Blade, and one is from Melody. Must be the only numbers programmed into the phone. I pull up Slim's first so I know what's going on.

Slim: So you can contact us in case of emergency. Someone will be followin' you at all times. Always use this phone.

I figured it was from him and that one of the guys put it in my car while Jason was still sitting at the bar. He won't know I have it and I can still contact those that I need to. I can still talk to Blade without him knowing. My heart beats a little faster knowing that I can still have him in my life without Jason knowing.

Blade: Kitten, I know you didn't want to make that phone call. Please text me when you find this to let me know you're okay. I love you.

Me: I'm sitting outside while he's at a party. He told me not to go anywhere until he comes back out but I want to go home. I love you more.

I pull up Melody's message while I wait for Blade's response. Her message just says that Blade told her what's going on and she won't contact me on my regular phone. She also tells me that she's worried about me and that she's not going to rest until I'm home where I belong.

Blade: You should do what he says kitten. I don't want anythin' happenin' to you or our babies. Please, just stay there until he tells you that you can leave.

I know Blade's right but I'm so tired. The only thing I want to do is crawl into my bed and forget that today ever happened. If I weren't pregnant, I would just leave, but I need to think about the lives I'm carrying and not just myself.

Me: I'll stay put. Only to protect our children. I miss you so much.

Blade: I miss you too. We're goin' to figure this out as soon as we can. Then you're comin' home, where you belong.

There's no point in responding to him considering I know he's right. I will be moving back to Clifton Falls when this is all said and done. Blade will be getting the chance that he's been telling me he wants and I'm going to give him my all.

After an hour goes by, my other phone starts ringing and I look to see that Jason is calling me. I answer it and hear a girl moaning from right by the phone. Apparently, the motherfucker is in there getting fucked while I've been out here waiting. He tells me that it's taking longer than he thought so I can leave and go directly home. I am to text him as soon as I pull in the driveway.

Once I make it down the road so I can't see the lights from the cabin, I pick up the phone they left in my car and pull up Blade's name. Pushing the call button, I expect to have to wait for him to answer, but he does so immediately.

"How are you callin' me right now kitten?" he asks, worry lacing his voice.

"He told me he was going to be longer than expected so I could go home. I'm to text him as soon as I pull in my driveway," I answer honestly.

"Okay. Well, we can only talk while you're in your car. Boy Scout isn't sure he got everythin' out of your house. We don't want to take any unnecessary risks right now."

"Alright. At least we can talk for a little bit. If you're not busy that is."

"I've got all night Keira. Nothin' is more important than you."

"Then what do you want to talk about? For some reason, I have no clue what to say to you," I tell him honestly.

"To start, let's talk a little about the babies. Do you have any idea about names yet?" Blade says.

"I have a first name picked out for our son. But, I don't know if you're going to like it," I say suddenly nervous.

"Hit me with it," Blade says, I can hear a door opening and closing before complete quietness overcomes the call.

"I was thinking Kenyon. I don't have a middle name or anything like that, but I really like the name. It's unusual," I say without taking a breath.

"Slow down kitten. I like the name a lot." Blade says. "What about Kenyon Alexander? Do you like that?"

After thinking for a minute, I answer. "I actually really like it. Do you have any ideas for our daughter?"

"I had a baby sister. Her name was Cory Jaqueline. Is there any way you would consider namin' her somethin' for my sister?"

"Absolutely," I answer. "Do you want to use her full name or do you want to do something else with it?"

"I'd like to keep her name intact. Then, she can shorten it to CJ when she gets older or somethin'."

"It's perfect. Can I ask you what happened to your sister?" I ask hesitantly.

"You can ask me anythin' you want to kitten. My sister was my entire world when we were little. From the second my parents brought her home, I was by her side. Watchin' over her because I knew my parents weren't goin' to. You see, they had an issue or two with drugs and the only thing they cared about was gettin' their next fix," Blade starts. "One night, Cory was just under a year old, a guy they owed money to came stormin' in the house. He raped my mother while my dad watched. Then, when he was done, he opened fire. Cory was hit in the chest and there was nothin' I could do to save her. My dad was hit in the arm and I was grazed by a bullet in the leg. My mom was also killed. Anyway, when the cops got there, they didn't even try to find out what was goin' on and simply arrested my dad. I was in so much pain over losin' Cory that I didn't do anythin' to help my dad."

I sit in stunned silence for a few minutes, soaking in Blade's tragic story. "I'm so sorry you had to go through that."

"It was a long time ago," Blade responds. "I deal with it every day. But, you're the first person I've ever told that story to."

"I'm honored that you chose me to tell."

Blade and I talk for the rest of the ride back to my house. Before we hang up, I tell him that he might as well tell Melody our news since I have no clue when I'm going to be able to talk to her again. Once I park, I tell him that I better get off of the phone in case Boy Scout didn't get everything out. He tells me to call him as soon as I can and he'll drop whatever he's doing to talk to me. Hanging up, I sit there for a few minutes and think about the situation I'm currently in. How did my life get to this point? What am I going to do now? Will I survive whatever is going to happen with Jason?

Chapter Four

Blade

I'M SITTING IN THE CLUBHOUSE, wondering if today is a day that I'll be able to hear from Keira. It's been a few days since she called that first time when she was driving home and I can't stop the thoughts running through my mind about what he's making her do, if she's okay, if our babies are okay, and everything else. None of it's good and I need to be there but I know it's just going to cause problems for her.

"Blade, you okay?" Melody asks, pulling me out of my head.

"No, I'm really not. But, my girl will get through this and we'll figure out how to help her. I do need to talk to you though."

"Okay. What's up?" Melody asks, sitting on the stool next to me.

"Since Keira doesn't know when she'll be able to talk to you, she wanted me to tell you our news. You're gonna flip out, so I need you to promise me that you won't try to call her or contact her any way."

"You're scaring me right now, but I promise, I won't contact her. I'll wait until she can talk to me."

"Well, we're not havin' just one baby. We're havin' twins. A boy and a girl," I tell her, bracing myself for the screaming and shrieking that I know is about to happen.

"Oh my!" Melody screams, pulling the attention of everyone in the main room of the clubhouse. "Are you fucking serious right now?"

"I'm dead serious," I tell her, pulling out the ultrasound picture I have in my wallet. You can see the wear and tear on it from me handling it so much.

"I can't believe this. But, I guess you can tell her our news when you talk to her again. Glock and I are having another baby," Melody gushes, staring down at the picture I handed her.

"Congrats! I know she'd want to be here for you like she was before. The same way I know it's killin' you not to be there for her right now."

"You can say that again. But, we need to let this thing with Jason play out. So, do you have any names or anything picked out?"

"We do. Kenyon Alexander for our son and Cory Jaqueline for our daughter," I tell her, not going into detail about Cory's name. That's personal and just between the two of us until Cory is old enough to know where her name comes from.

"Those are so cute! I can't believe you guys are having twins! I have to go tell Glock," she rushes out.

"Just don't tell anyone else. She said you could know and I know that she was includin' Glock in that. Only because you can't keep your mouth shut," I tell her, smiling to let her know I'm teasing her.

"Oh shut it! I can keep my mouth shut. But, I'm going to tell my man."

I tell Melody bye and motion for Summer to hand me a beer. There's nothing I have to do and I don't plan on going anywhere, so I might as well have a drink or two. Then I might take a nap to forget things for a little bit and see if Tank wants to work out later this afternoon. He told me when they all found out what was going on that he spent a ton of time in the gym when Maddie was taken. Yesterday I spent most of the day there, I'm sore as hell but it took my mind off shit for a little bit.

Drinking down my beer, I motion for another one. I slam that one and get up to make my way to my room. Just as I'm about to unlock my door, my phone starts ringing and I rush to pull it out of my pocket. I never know when my girl's going to call so I need to keep my phone close at all times. I'm not missing a single call from Keira if I can help it. The only thing that would make me miss one is if I'm in church and don't have my phone on me. Glen knows to keep an ear out for it when I'm there, but he also knows not to interrupt or answer it. Unless she calls back-to-back. Then I know it's an emergency and he better answer the fucker. So, I put mine on the table, instead of in the box with the rest of the guys' phones.

I look down and see Tank's name flashing across my screen. Not wanting to talk to anyone right now, I just silence the call and figure I'll call him back when I wake up.

For the last few hours, I've tried so hard to take a nap and just forget that this dumb motherfucker is taking my girl away from me. Nothing will make me forget that though. This asshole truly doesn't know who he's fucking with right now. I'm not going to wait around for long, with my thumb up my ass to come up with a plan to get my kitten back.

Knowing that I'm obviously not going to go to sleep, I sit up and call Tank back. I'm not sure what he wants, but I'm hoping he's going to be heading to the gym so that I can exhaust myself.

"'Lo," He answers.

"What's up, brother?"

"Was gonna see if you were headin' to the gym today? I know I spent a shit ton of time there when Maddie was taken. I'm guessin' you're goin' to be the same way."

"Yeah. I was gonna try and crash for a bit. That's why I didn't answer earlier. It didn't work out that way though," I tell Tank honestly.

"It never does. The only thing that's gonna happen is you have the what if's runnin' through your mind and they don't stop until your girl comes home. So, let's go blow off some steam and try to get you exhausted so you can manage to get a little bit of sleep."

Before hanging up, Tank tells me he'll be over in about ten minutes. We always use the gym at the clubhouse so we don't have to deal with any bullshit. And we don't have to leave to get a good workout in.

I get up and make my way in my bathroom. There's no point in taking a shower right now, but I need to get changed into my shorts and a tee shirt until I get in the gym. I'm not walking around here unless I'm fully dressed. Not with all the club girls walking around, thinking they're going to get their claws in the single men. I'm not single. My girl just isn't here right now.

The only thing that would've made this situation with Keira worse would be if she had left here. Hell, she didn't even have to give me a heads up about what was going on. But, she wanted Slim to make sure I knew it wasn't her saying the words she spewed to me. That was one of the hardest phone calls I've ever had in my life. Another man telling me that my girl was in trouble and we had to come up with a plan before we just went in and took her back. He was right though. My girl and unborn babies are the most important things in my world and we need to protect them. I just fucking hate waiting and leaving her to deal with the bullshit that dead man walking is putting her through.

Walking out into the main room, I see most of my brothers sitting around. Some are already drinking, some are sitting around talking, there's a few playing pool, and one or two are with club girls. Typical for a slow afternoon at our businesses. The scene just doesn't interest me anymore. I want my kitten back and with me.

"Blade, come sit for a minute," Glock calls out to me.

"Goin' to workout with Tank. We'll catch up later," I tell him, continuing on to the gym.

"Melody told me your news, brother," Glock tells me, catching up to me quickly. "I can't begin to guess what you're goin' through right now. You need anythin', call me."

"Thanks. I'm good. Just want my family safe and whole. I want my girl here and we need to come up with somethin' like yesterday. If not, I might decide to go on my own. I can't stand this shit."

"Grim's been talkin' to Slim constantly. You don't know all the details and we're keepin' it that way for a reason. All you need to know right now is that Keira's still at Vixen and she's okay. Phantom Bastards are posted all over the club the days she works. Slim's been workin' on his end since that's where she is."

"It's not me though!" I yell, getting closer to Glock. "I should be the one there, keepin' an eye on her, protectin' her anyway I can, and makin' sure our babies are doin' okay."

"You are protectin' her by bein' here and not doin' somethin' stupid, Blade," Glock tells me. "You don't think we've all been where you're at right now? Try goin' through it for years and years."

"I know. I just feel so helpless while she's out there havin' whatever he's doin' to her. You didn't hear her on the phone the last time we talked, Glock. She's gettin' scared which means he's spiralin' out of control sooner than we thought he would. He's gettin' desperate," I tell him, thinking back to the last time we talked.

Keira was trying to sound normal and act like she wasn't scared. I could hear the fear in her voice though. Even talking about the babies wasn't helping take the fear out of her voice. That's one topic that's guaranteed to get her excited and rambling on and on. Instead, she was hesitant to even talk about the babies. It was like she wanted to avoid talking about them at all costs. Maybe it was because he's telling her she has to give them up. I don't know, but I know I never want to hear her sound so small and weak again in my life.

"Blade, you here man?" Tank asks, standing next to Glock.

"Yeah. Sorry."

"Nothin' to be sorry about. We've been there. Let's hit the gym and get some of that pent up rage out," Tank says, leading the way inside.

Tank always puts the music on. It's usually something hard to get our blood pumping. Today is no different. I hear the beginning cords of *Failure* by *Breaking Benjamin* blare out of the speakers. This is exactly what I feel these days. I haven't protected what's mine. Again. First with Cory and now with Keira. I would say that it's telling me that I shouldn't have anyone else in my life, but I'm a selfish bastard and I'm not letting her go. I'm not letting my kids go.

I spot Tank while he starts lifting and he can see the rage that is threatening to explode. It's getting worse and worse with every passing day. Yeah, Glock said that Slim's working on it and keeping an eye on her. But, it's not me doing it. I need to be there. Grim won't let me anywhere near there though and I can't say that I blame him.

"Blade, we're not liftin' today. Today, we're gettin' in the ring. Come on," Tank tells me, leading the way and starting to wrap tape around his hands.

I follow suit and wrap my hands up before stepping in the ring. Tank is known for his underground fighting in the past and I know I stand no chance against the man. But, we're just going to spar. I hope.

"Don't look so relieved princess," Tank says. "We're not sparrin'. You need to get some of that rage out and I'm gonna help you do that. I won't go full out, but I'm not takin' it easy on you either."

"Fuck!" I say. "Alright, let's get this show on the road before a bunch of brothers get word and come watch me get my ass handed to me," I tell Tank, taking my fighting stance.

It seems like I no sooner get set and I have to duck a right hook. Tank doesn't let up and I'm soon finding my rhythm. We dance around the ring and I try to land as many hits as I can, but Tank is a fast fucker and he lands almost every hit he throws.

Within minutes, I see a few guys come in the gym and I know it's only a matter of time before everyone else is in here watching. They never pass up the opportunity to watch a few brothers throwing down. Too bad my focus is on that and not Tank. He lands a hit and I can feel my eyebrow split open. This just makes my rage flow and I start throwing punches for all I'm worth.

Hollers and bets are being placed as Tank and I go punch for punch in the ring. It's the same any time there's someone in there. Although it's been a while since any of us had to get any pent-up aggression and rage out. I never thought I would be in here doing this, but Keira changed my life and I want my kitten back. There will be no rest for me until she's in my arms again.

Keira

It's been days since I've been out of Jason's house. Well, other than going to Vixen to work.

Jason won't let me go to the store, he won't let me go sit on the porch, or anything else. The only thing I can do is clean and make sure there's dinner on the table for him. He lets me eat, but I have to serve him first and whatever is left over is what I get. Honestly, I'm surprised that he lets me go to work at all. But then again, he takes any money that I earn.

"Bitch, what time do you have to be to work?" Jason asks, his latest blonde bimbo draped all over him.

"I'm going to get ready now. I have to be there in an hour," I tell him, continuing to scrub the counters in the kitchen.

"I won't be in tonight. Any tips you get you can leave on the counter for when I get home. Not sure when that will be and it really doesn't matter. You better be here, cleaning this pigsty," he tells me, before slamming the back door.

I make my way into the bathroom and start the shower. Jason told me I was going to be sharing his bed, but I guess plans changed. Now, he parades a string of women in front of me. I'm not sure what he's hoping to accomplish by doing that. I don't care about anyone he's with. The only thing it means is that he's not coming to me for sex and that's fine by me.

Stepping under the relaxing spray of the shower, I let myself think of Blade. I miss him, and everyone else, so much. He's missing so much of the pregnancy because I shut him out and now he's going to miss out on the rest of it. Looking down, I see my stomach that has expanded so much since the last time I saw him. I'm huge now and don't have much longer to go.

My doctor told me yesterday that everything looked good and that I would more than likely go into labor early. As it is now, I only have about a month and a half left. I put my hand where our children are resting and feel a kick that makes me laugh.

The first time Blade felt one of the babies move, he lost his ability to do anything. He sat there and stared at my stomach, resting his hand there for what felt like hours. Hell, he didn't even want to let me up to go to the bathroom until I told him my bladder was going to explode if he didn't move. Remembering this puts a smile on my face as I get out of the shower and finish getting ready to go to work. Tonight, I need to talk to Slim and let him know that Jason's taking all my money when I get it.

Pulling into work, I can see Slim, Killer, and Wood's bikes parked in the back parking lot. They've been here almost every night I work since everything happened with Jason. I think the main reason is to make sure what's really going on so they can report back to Blade. He's got to be going crazy, but I can't think of that right now. I need to focus on getting out of this alive and protecting our children.

"Slim," I say, knocking on his office door. "Can I talk to you for a minute?"

"Come on in sweetheart," comes Slim's booming voice from behind closed doors. "How are things goin' today?"

"They're okay. He paraded another skank in front of me this morning. But, at least that means he's not touching me."

"He better not touch you! Now, I know you didn't just come in here to shoot the shit."

"Well, I was wondering if you could start holding my pay. At least a portion of it," I ask, hesitantly.

"What's goin' on sweetheart?"

"He's taking all my money. I have to hand over my tips and everything to him."

"He's what?" Slim yells, scaring the shit out of me.

"I have to hand all of my money over to him. When I get home, it either goes in his hand or I have to leave it on the counter for whenever he decides to grace me with his presence."

"And how does he expect you to live? To buy what you need for the babies?"

"He doesn't care about the babies because he says they aren't staying with me. Blade has to take them as soon as they can leave the hospital or he's going to kill them," I tell him, finally letting go of the strength I've been trying to display and breaking down.

Slim comes around his desk and wraps his arms around me. He lets me get everything out and get myself back under control before he starts talking again.

"Sweetheart, I'll keep a portion of your money in the safe. It'll be put in an envelope with your name on it. How are you gonna get it though so that he doesn't know?"

"I'm just going to leave it there so that Blade can use it for the babies. I know he's got his own money, but I want my money to be used for them too. Is there any way that one of the guys can meet me at my doctor's appointment in a few days? Make it look like they're there with someone?"

"Yeah, why?"

"There's a nursery set that I want the babies to have. I've taken pictures of it and I want someone to give them to Blade. It's the only thing I want for our children."

"I'll have Killer meet you there with Shy."

"Thank you, for everything," I say, before heading out the door to start my shift.

Shy is behind the bar with me again and I can't wait to get busy working. It might not be as easy to move around now, but I still make decent money in tips. And with Shy working with me, we make even more. Wood is stationed in my section of the bar again so I know tonight is gonna be a fun night. He's always making me laugh.

"Hey honey!" he says in greeting.

"Hey Wood. How's everything tonight?"

"Goin' good. I got a surprise for you," he says, a Cheshire cat grin taking up residence on his face.

"What's that?" I ask, intrigued.

"I'm gonna video chat Blade and leave my phone on the counter so he can see you. And you can talk to him."

"Are you sure? I mean, I don't think Jason's coming in, but I don't want anything to happen to any of you."

"I got this," Wood says, before hitting some buttons on his phone.

Within a matter of seconds I can hear Blade's voice ringing through the speaker of the phone. He sounds in pain and I can't wait to see him. But, I'm scared as fuck too. I don't want Jason to learn of my betrayal any more than when I called Blade from the burner phone.

"Got someone here you might want to see," Wood says, before setting his phone up on the bar facing me.

"Kitten, is that you?" Blade asks, and I can hear some emotion in his voice.

"Yeah. Hey babe!" I say, my fear of talking to him forgotten. "What happened to you?" I gasp.

"I got in the ring with Tank, kitten. I'm okay. It looks worse than what it is," he tells me. "I want to see you, see our babies."

I back up and pull my shirt tighter around my stomach so Blade can see. A grin breaks out on his face and I know he wants to make a smartass comment about how big I've gotten in what seems like overnight. He knows better than to say a word though.

"They're gettin' big in there, kitten. How much longer now?" Blade asks.

"About a month and a half. I probably won't last that long though."

"What do you mean kitten?" he asks, the concern evident in his voice.

"If women carry multiples, they usually tend to go in to labor early babe. There won't be anything wrong with them. I promise. I wish you could be here with me. With us," I tell him honestly.

"I know kitten. I wish I were there too. This is such bullshit that I have to miss out on the pregnancy and delivery of our children," Blade says, barely holding onto his rage.

"And then I have to miss out on their lives until I can get away from him."

"We'll get you away from him, I promise. Now, what's this that I hear Slim is puttin' money up in the safe for you? Tell me it's not what I think it is kitten."

"He's taking my money. All of it. I don't get anything I make, including my tips."

"What the fuck!" Blade yells out.

"It's okay. I've got a way around it for now. Now, I'm going to have pictures delivered to you of the nursery set I want."

"Okay kitten. I'll make sure I get it and get it all set up."

"Where are you gonna set it up? In your room in the clubhouse?" I ask, confused.

"No. I'm rentin' a small place for now. It's big enough for the babies and us. At least until Rage gets our house done. Then we'll move it in there."

"You got Rage building us a house?" I ask, the tears filling my eyes.

"I do. Not how I wanted you to find out, but we really don't have a choice at this point. It's close to Glock and Melody so you can be close to your girl. I knew that's what you'd want, so I made sure that Rage knew."

"You were pretty confident that I'd come back to you, weren't you?" I ask, bringing a little bit of sass back into my voice.

"Yep. Now, we have a plan in place for when you go into labor kitten. Shy is goin' to be there for you. We know that none of the guys are goin' to be able to be there for you. Not that I would let them in the room. So, Shy is takin' on the role of bein' in there. She'll keep her phone on her and have me on speed dial so I can get constant updates and pictures. If she can, she's goin' to video chat so I can feel like I'm there."

Looking to the opposite end of the bar, I see Shy looking at me. It's not too loud in here yet, so I'm sure she heard Blade telling me that she's going in with me. Shy sends me a smile and nods her head. Out of all the girls at Vixen, she is the one that I've gotten the closest to. So, if Blade can't be with me, then I'm glad she can be.

"So, I want to know something about you Blade. I think I should since we're having children together," I say, a smile on my face.

"What's that kitten?"

"I want to know what your real name is. I need it for the paperwork after all."

"My real name is Michael Branch," Blade says.

"Well, my name is Keira Case," I tell him, knowing it's only fair to share.

"I know we're doin' this all ass backwards. Aren't we kitten? Blade asks.

"Yeah, I guess we are."

"I don't care though. I know we never intended this to be more than somethin' casual and a bit of fun, but I'm dead serious when I say I want you by my side as my old lady," Blade tells me. "I want you to come home, kitten."

"I would be there already if I could. But, I need to sort this situation out with Jason before I can even think about coming there Blade. You know this," I tell him, tears filling my eyes once again.

"I know. We'll get everythin' figured out. The sooner the better because I don't want to miss anythin' else," Blade says. "But, I'm gonna let you get back to work. Call me when you feel safe enough to do so. And don't ever call me when you're in his house. We don't know what he has there as far as surveillance or bugs."

"Okay babe. I'll call you as soon as I can."

After hanging up, I make myself busy with making sure I have enough of everything before we get hit with the evening rush. Wood stays in my section, sipping his beer and watching the people coming and going. I know without a doubt he's looking for Jason. The guys are just waiting for him to make an appearance and give them a reason to beat his ass. They haven't said that, but I'm not stupid. I know what they're doing.

Within the hour, the club is starting to pick up and it's getting busier than normal. In some ways I'm glad because it doesn't give me a chance to think about my current situation. On the other hand, if Jason walks in he'll expect me to bring in a shit ton of tips. That's just not going to happen.

So, hopefully he stays gone and occupied with whatever skank he's with. Knowing my luck though, he'll be in at some point. When he does make a pit stop in, he always looks at the tip jar to see how much is in there. That's my concern right now. I don't need him to see a ton of tips, the jar is almost overflowing already, and then see me bring hardly any home to him.

"Keira, I'm gonna empty the tip jar," Shy tells me. "I'm taking it in to Slim to count and separate. I'll be right back."

I don't know if she was reading my mind or what. Shy is going to be my savior through this whole thing, I can already tell this. Seeing a customer trying to get my attention, I just nod at her and go about my work. Wood and Killer are sitting in their bar stools, watching and waiting. I can already tell that they're going to be ready to jump into action at any given second. Which is probably a good thing as I see Jason making his way towards the bar.

"Bitch, get the fuck over here!" he yells over the pounding music and other customers.

Looking at the two men standing guard, I gently shake my head so they don't make a move. I acknowledge the waiting customers and make my way to Jason at the end of the bar closest to Slim's office.

"What do you want Jason?" I ask, the contempt clear in my voice.

"You better watch yourself, you won't be surrounded by biker trash forever," he starts off. "Give me money. I know you've been making money already and you need to hand it over."

"I honestly haven't made any money yet. We're just starting to get busy," I say, looking at the crowd surrounding the bar.

"Don't fucking lie to me. I need your fucking money and you're going to give it to me. Now!" he yells, getting in my face and grabbing my arm.

"I think you heard the lady tell you she didn't have any money. Now, I suggest you get out of my club and don't make another appearance. Ever!" Slim says, coming to stand behind me. "And if you ever think about layin' a hand on her again, I'll find out and you will pay."

"Fuck off biker trash! This is between her and me. No one asked for your fucking opinion."

Wood and Killer suddenly appear behind Jason and I can feel him tense up. Unfortunately, my arm is still in his grasp and it makes him tighten his hold on me. I wince as the pain gets worse and the three bikers close further in on him. This is the last thing I need to be in the middle of right now.

"Shy!" Slim yells, "Get Keira back behind the bar and trade ends with her. I don't want this pussy to be able to get close to her again. Not that he'll be steppin' foot back in here."

Shy comes over and waits until Jason releases my arm. Then she leads me over to her section of the bar and pours me a soda. She knows that I've been mainly just drinking water while I'm here, but tells me to drink the soda. Playboy, who I didn't even know was here, sets me down a bag of food from a restaurant and takes up residence in front of me.

"Take a minute to eat sweetheart. These guys will wait so you can calm down and feed my brother's babies," Playboy says. "Shy, let her eat and watch the bar. If you need help, let me know and I'll jump back there to help."

"Okay Playboy," Shy answers before turning to me. "Take all the time you need hun. I'm not going anywhere and the guys will wait for their drinks."

I see Slim, Wood, and Killer still dealing with Jason. He's trying to fight and argue his way out of having to leave the club. Jason is definitely used to getting his way and he's not going to like this. I know for a fact that I'll be paying for this whenever I leave the club. There won't be any waiting for me to get back to his house. He'll make sure that I pay before I we make it back there.

"Bitch, I'll see you in a few hours. You know you're gonna pay already, so be prepared."

"You're not gonna touch a hair on her fuckin' head cocksucker!" Killer yells out, his voice raising above everyone in the club's.

"You won't be there to protect her forever biker trash," Jason yells out. "She'll be in my house before the night is over."

"I don't have to send her to your house. If you want, I can get the cops involved in this shi,." Slim says.

"She'll be back in my house before sunrise tomorrow," Jason threatens "One way or another, she'll be back with me. Or, your entire club will be fucked."

"You think you scare us?" Wood asks, dragging Jason towards the back door. "You want to threaten one of ours and tell her that she can't even keep her babies because you have plans for her. What, are you gonna sell her to the highest bidder?"

"How the fuck do you know that?" Jason asks, his face becoming fire engine red.

I stop eating, the fork half way to my mouth. Everything that I've eaten is threatening to come back up. Rushing past Shy and around the bar, I move as fast as possible to the back so I can use the employee bathroom.

As soon as I get in the stall, I barely make the toilet as the entire contents of my stomach comes up. Soon, someone is holding a wet cloth to the back of my neck and is rubbing circles on my back. Meanwhile, the only thought running through my head is that Jason is going to sell me to the highest bidder. That's why he won't touch me and is taking all of my money. I'm not going to need it when I'm a slave of some sort.

"It's going to be okay honey," I hear Shy's sweet voice say.

"No, it's not. The only reason I'm still here is because I'm pregnant. Now that I know the truth, there's nothing stopping him from making me go into labor early and then moving me from here until whenever this sale is," I say, crying uncontrollably.

Before Shy can say anything else, there's a knock on the door. It's one of the guys if the pounding is anything to go by. I don't want to see anyone right now and I tell Shy that. She tells me not to worry and that she'll get rid of whoever it is.

Unfortunately, no one is going to tell Slim what he can and can't do. I hear Shy telling him that I'm okay and I want to be left alone for right now. They're arguing back and forth but I can't hear what the conversation is, until I hear Blade's name mentioned. Then I perk right up to hear what's being said.

"Slim, where's Blade?" I ask, wanting him by my side more than ever.

"He's on the phone sweetheart. He needs to hear your voice and know that you're okay. Can I please come in with my phone?" he asks.

"Just you," I tell him, using the washcloth to wipe up my face.

Within seconds, Slim is entering the bathroom followed by Shy. She's pissed as hell that he's in here right now if the glare she's sending his way is anything to go by. I try to tell her it's okay without using any words, but I'm not sure she gets my meaning.

"Kitten! Kitten!" I hear Blade's voice say through the phone Slim's holding. "Someone tell me what's goin' on."

"I'm right here babe," I tell him, taking Slim's phone from his outstretched hands.

"Kitten, nothin' is goin' to happen to you. I promise you that. I'm not lettin' any motherfucker get their hands on you," he tells me, the promise evident in his voice.

"Blade, you can't come here and get me. We need to play this smart for Kenyon and Cory. They're the most important ones in this situation," I tell Blade, trying to get him to listen to reason.

"And the only way I'm goin' to make sure that they're okay is to have you by my side. You need to be away from that dumb fucker. He's right,

Slim and the guys aren't goin' to be with you every second of every day," Blade tells me, ratcheting my nervousness and fright up a few more notches.

"I'll do what I have to do in order to protect the babies," I tell Blade, meaning every word. I'll die to protect our children.

"I know you will, kitten. But we need to know you're safe too. They can't survive without you right now and we already know Jason doesn't give two fucks about them."

"I know he doesn't. But, now that he knows that I know, I'm worried about him taking off with me or something like that so no one can find me."

"It won't come to that. We're gonna be on the phone and comin' up with a plan. If I have to be there tonight to make sure you don't go anywhere I'll be there," Blade tells me, trying to get me to calm down.

"Son, I know you want to be here with your woman, but we need to play this carefully. He knows we know too much now and we need to tread lightly. We'll keep an eye on Keira and I'll move her into the clubhouse if I have to," Slim tells Blade and me.

"Can you move her in there tonight?" Blade asks. "I don't want her goin' anywhere near that house so he gets a chance to snatch her. Get her whatever she needs and I'll get the money back to you."

"Blade, I got my own money. Well, a little bit," I tell him, the attitude starting to come back again.

"I know you do, kitten. But, I want to do this for you. Please, let me do this."

"We'll see. Now, I'm gonna get back to work so Shy can get a break. I'll talk to you later babe," I tell Blade.

"Kitten, be careful and stay aware of your surroundings," Blade tells me as I walk out of the bathroom.

Slim is still on the phone with him, and I'm sure they're coming up with a game plan for when I get out of work. For now, I'm going to act like nothing is wrong and go back to doing my job. There's really nothing I can do about anything right now anyway.

Chapter Five

Blade

HANGING UP WITH KEIRA is one of the hardest things I've ever done. I want to keep her on the phone so I know for a fact that she's okay. When Slim called and told me what they found out, I lost my shit. The main room of the clubhouse is destroyed now. While I feel bad I made a mess, the only thing I can think about is my kitten, Kenyon, and Cory.

"Blade, if you want in on the meetin' to figure out what we're gonna do about your girl, I suggest you calm the fuck down," Grim tells me, coming in my room.

"I'm sorry, brother. You've been there and know what I'm goin' through. It's not an excuse and I'm not gonna be anywhere other than in that meetin'," I tell Grim, knowing I have to get my shit together

"Then let's go. We need to get Slim on the phone and come up with a game plan."

"The quicker the better. I need my family back with me. Nothin' can happen to them Grim. I mean it. I won't know what to do if somethin' happens."

"I know Blade. We'll get them back, no matter what we have to do. Now, let's get to church so we can figure this shit out."

We've been in church for close to two hours now, with Slim's club on the phone the entire time. Guys in both clubs are on computers finding anything out about Jason they can, anyone he associates with, and members of any club his belongs to. They're leaving no stone unturned to find out who could possibly be behind wanting to sell my girl. Jason certainly isn't fucking smart enough to come up with this plan himself.

Slim's guy, Fox, seems to think Jason has ties to a cartel but we're not sure. We can't find anything concrete to support that idea. About the only thing that can be said for Jason is that he's careful. Other than when it comes to his drug and gambling habits. He's never been arrested for either, but he's not careful about where he shops around for his shit either.

"Blade, I'm gonna get a room ready for Keira at the clubhouse. I want her here from now on. At least until we can get her back to you."

"I want her home. Now. But I know we have to play this carefully. So, if that's the best we can do for right now, then I'll take it," I tell everyone in the room and on the phone. "My only concern is him gettin' to her between the clubhouse and Vixen. And, her not havin' anyone there to talk to other than club girls."

"I'm bringin' Shy in to stay with her. We got a room big enough that they can share. Shy already knows and is packin' her stuff now. She also knows that she's not to be with anyone in the club while Keira is here. At least not in the room they share," Slim tells me.

"Okay. How about her gettin' to and from work? Doctor's appointments?" I ask.

"We're gonna have at least three to four guys on her at all times."

"She trusts Wood and Killer," I tell Slim. "Those are two of the ones I want on her the most. The third guy is up to you, but I definitely want them on her. And, I think if she's gonna be at the clubhouse, she needs a girl's day or somethin'. This shit is wearin' on her and she's not gonna say anythin."

"Can do that too. I know she likes Shy from Vixen. I don't know who else to have though. Not without introducin' a lot of people here and runnin' the risk that Jason has his hooks in one of them."

Since some of the guys from Gage's club are on the call with us, Trojan pipes up. "Crash and I can get Darcy to go there. We'll tell her that you want to pamper Keira for the day and we only trust her with our women."

"Is she gonna listen to you though?" Cage asks. "We all know she's a fuckin' hell cat when it comes to you two and gives you a run for your money."

"She'll listen. She's all about helpin' out a girl in need of some pamperin'. Besides, there's reasons she's startin' to come around to the idea of us," Crash tells us all. "When do you want to do this?"

"Can we plan on tomorrow? I want her to get her mind off shit for a while."

"I can put it in motion. Trojan and Crash, let me know when you leave and I'll make sure the girls are here and ready. Not like we're lettin' them out of our sights anyway."

"We'll leave as soon as we can get Darcy's ass movin'," Crash says.

"Give us an hour and we'll be out the door. Just gotta find firecracker first. She's been hidin' for a few different reasons and we're tryin' to get to the bottom of the shit. Probably a good idea to get her out of town for a few hours or so," Trojan tells us.

"You need help, let us know," Grim says before saying his goodbyes and turning to us. "I know you want to be there Blade. Especially with her bein' in the Phantom Bastards clubhouse. But, we need you here. We need to make everythin' look as normal as possible. That way Jason might think Slim is doin' this shit on his own and not plannin' anythin' with us."

"I hear ya. I don't like it, but I know I have to put her, Kenyon, and Cory first."

The room goes absolutely silent. There's no movement or anything from any of the guys sitting around me. I just look from one face to the next until Cage speaks up finally.

"Twins? For real man?" he asks.

"Yeah. We found out when I was up there last. Keira wanted to make an announcement together, but I don't think that's gonna happen anytime soon."

"Well, congrats man!" Joker says, standing up and pulling me in for a hug. "We'll get your girl back. No matter what we'll have her home to you soon."

"Thanks." There's nothing more for me to say but that.

The rest of the guys all follow suit and offer their congratulations while I think that Keira should be here with me. She should be getting told congratulations and being asked how she's doing so far. Everything that a pregnant woman is supposed to hear. Not my girl though. Instead, she's suffering in the hands of some twatwaffle that wants to sell her to the highest bidder.

Tank, seeing my mood deteriorating faster and faster, pulls me from church after looking at Grim. I know we're heading to the gym because that's where he always takes me these days. He's about to hand my ass to me and I need to put all this shit I'm feeling into fighting him. It's either that, or just let him beat the shit out of me.

After changing real quick, I crank the stereo and hear *Broken* by *Seether* blaring through the speakers. This song definitely fits my mood right now. Without Keira, I am a broken man. I thought I was broken before, losing my sister, having drug addicts as parents, being left alone more than having anyone be there for me, and having daily ass beatings. Now that I know what it's like to have a woman have my back no matter what, I can't imagine going back to being out for loose pussy and having a different club girl every day. Hell, every few hours sometimes.

"You ready?" Tank asks, taping his hands up.

"I guess. My head's not in it. Not gonna be much good in the ring today."

"You'll get your head in the game. Or you'll find yourself with some broken ribs, a battered face, and whatever else I choose to do to you," Tank tells me, meaning every word of it.

Tank isn't trying to be an asshole. He's trying to help me get my head away from thinking about all of the what ifs about Keira and our children. He knows after going through it when his girl, Maddie, was taken. Yeah, he had his daughter there to help keep his mind occupied. But, the girls had her more than he did. That way he could concentrate on looking for Maddie and bringing her home safe.

The only thing I need to concentrate on right now is not getting my ass handed to me. Again.

There's nothing more I can do about getting my girl out of Benton Falls. I can't get her away from that scumsucking, dead-man walking, Jason. For now, I have to trust in Slim and his club to keep my girl safe and away from Jason. There's more to him than we know and I don't think we're going to like what we find out.

The only thing that eases any of my tension is knowing that the guys are going to be watching her even more now that she's going to the clubhouse. And, they're making sure she gets a girl's day out, well, *in*, to feel pampered. She'll be having a little bit of fun because I know Darcy is going to make sure of it. At least if the things I've seen in the past are anything to go by. The only thing that matters to me is my kitten's happiness. It means more to me than anything else in this world. Until our son and daughter are born anyway.

Keira

I've been at Slim's clubhouse for a day and a half with Shy and his club. For the most part, I've stuck to the room they put us in and I haven't ventured out too far from there. The main time I leave is when I have to go to Vixen. And I now have an escort to go to and from work. Wood or Killer usually drive me in my car while two or three other guys follow us. I don't necessarily feel all that safe, but it's better than being in Jason's house. Even if it's just temporary until he can find a way to get me back.

Shy comes walking in the door and sits down on the end of my bed. I've been laying here daydreaming about Blade and the life we could've had. Because I know that I'm not getting out of this alive. Hell, I'll be lucky to get out of this with minimal scarring if they do end up selling me. And I know Jason's not working alone. There's more people involved, I just don't know who.

"Honey, apparently we're gonna have visitors today," Shy tells me. "Slim said they should be here in about an hour or so."

"Who?" I ask, my hopes raising thinking that Blade is coming.

"I'm sorry babe, but it's not your man. I guess a few guys from the other Wild Kings charter are coming here with someone named Darcy. I'm not sure if there's gonna be any other women or not though."

"Oh," I say, a sinking feeling in my gut. "Well, I guess I better get in the shower so I can get dressed."

"Alright. I'm gonna go see if the few old ladies that are here need help. Have you met any of them yet?"

"No. I know that only a few guys here have an old lady. But, I've been trying to stay to myself until this mess gets sorted."

"I'll be right down the hall if you need me," Shy tells me, heading for the door.

"Shy? Thanks for everything," I tell her, walking into the bathroom.

Before getting undressed, I adjust the water until it's the hottest I can stand. I'm not sure exactly why members from the other charter are coming here, but I'm sure that Blade knows and had a hand in setting it up. I know I've heard the name Darcy before, I just can't remember where right now where. I'm sure it was when I was staying with Blade though.

I don't really want to have this girl's day, but if they've already arranged it then I'll go through with it. There's just so much that I could be doing and I've been so tired because of the pregnancy. My stomach makes it so I can't see my feet, I'm tired, my back is killing me, and sleep is almost impossible these days. But, I wouldn't trade it for the world knowing that soon Kenyon and Cory will be here. I might get to hold them for a minute or two before they go to Blade and that's going to have to be enough for now. Even though my heart is breaking.

So, I get ready as quickly as I can considering the fact that I've also been having some dizzy spells that no one knows about. I haven't even had a chance to tell the doctor about these spells yet. Hopefully no one figures it out and tells Blade about it.

Chapter Six

Darcy

IT'S BEEN A LONG few weeks and I'm ready to crash into oblivion. So, I turn on the water to run a hot bath before climbing into bed. I've already stripped and I'm just getting ready to step in the tub when there's a pounding at my door. With everything that's been going on, my heart is in my throat and I don't want to leave the sanctuary of my bathroom. Unfortunately, whoever is knocking at my door doesn't care. So, I grab the pistol I just purchased out of my bag and cautiously make my way to the front door.

"Who is it?" I call out, aiming the gun at the door.

"Crash and Trojan," Comes the muffled reply.

Lowering the gun, I keep it at my side and walk to unlock the three locks I now have on my door. Crash and Trojan are standing there looking hot as fuck as usual. Trojan takes in the fact that I'm only wearing a tiny silk robe and nothing more before taking in the fact that I'm holding a gun at my side.

"What's with the gun firecracker?" Trojan asks, stepping through the door followed by Crash.

"You need to tell us somethin'?" Crash asks.

"Um, a girl can never be too careful," I answer hesitantly.

"There's more to it than that and we're gonna get to the bottom of it. Now, that's not why we're here." Trojan says, stepping in my kitchen and helping himself to the contents of my fridge. "Blade wants Keira to have a girl's day and get pampered. We thought you could help us out with that."

"When are we doing this?" I ask, more than happy to get out of here for a while. "I need time to get some things ready."

"First thing in the mornin'. She's been goin' through some shit, she's about ready to pop with Blade's twins, and everyone thought she could use this."

"Okay. Now, if you two don't mind, I'm taking my bath and then going to bed. I'll be up early to get everything ready and text you when I'm ready to leave."

"We don't mind at all firecracker. You do your thing and we'll be out on the couch. Not goin' anywhere tonight knowin' somethin' ain't right with you."

I don't even have the energy to argue. So, I leave them to do their thing and make my way into the bathroom, making sure to lock the door. Just because I'm letting them stay in my house doesn't mean I want them coming in my bathroom while I'm in the tub. That's the last thing I need right now. Especially considering the fact that they both seem to star in my nightly fantasies and have gotten me off more, and better, in the last few months than anyone ever has in real life. Tonight is going to prove difficult with them sleeping under the same roof as me, invading my space.

Last night was one of the longest nights of my life. Today doesn't seem to be going any better as I'm sitting in between my two leading men on our way to Benton Falls. I'm excited to know that I'm going to finally meet the woman that stole Blade's heart since I've already heard all about her from the rest of the girls. And I get to do my thing and make her feel better for at least a little bit. I'll make sure she forgets about everything while I'm at the clubhouse.

"How much longer until we're there?" I ask, squirming in my seat.

"About fifteen minutes or so. Somethin' wrong firecracker?" Crash asks, leaning in closer.

"Nope. Just want to get out and stretch my legs after sitting between two cavemen the size of elephants. Not a lot of room in here."

"You can always sit on my lap and have more room to stretch out," Trojan says, acting like he's going to place me in his lap.

"Back the fuck off caveman. I'm good where I'm at. No need to see what little you're working with," I say, trying to mask the fact that I'd love to be sitting in his lap right now.

"Firecracker, I'll take it out right now and show you what I'm workin' with. It ain't little and I don't want you passin' out with want when you see it."

"Same goes for me firecracker," Crash says, putting his two cents into the conversation.

"You guys keep telling yourselves that. I get what I need and I don't need the likes of you two thinking anything is *ever* going to happen between us."

"That's a lie and we all know it. You go to your shop and go back home. Every. Single. Day. The only other places you go are the store and when you go to one of the clubhouses for the girls. You haven't been fucked since we met you and even then I'm sure it was lackin'," Crash tells me.

"Are you guys following me or something?"

"Nope. We just know your routine. Whenever there's a lockdown or any trouble we make sure that a prospect is on you. You just don't ever see him."

I'd like to say something in response to that but I can't. It's really not a surprise that they've been having me followed when there's trouble around. I look and we're pulling into the clubhouse. So, I can finally get a break from the Neanderthals for a while.

As soon as Trojan is out of the door, I hop out of the truck and grab my bag. I don't wait for them to follow me in the clubhouse, I know where to go and I don't need these two overbearing men on my ass any more than they already have been.

The first person I see after my eyes adjust is Slim. He's a good looking older man and he scares the shit out of me if I'm being honest. Slim is sitting next to two women and I can already tell who Keira is. She's got long, gorgeous red hair and there's a sadness to her that I haven't seen in someone in a very long time. Not since I left my ex and could finally breathe again.

"Let me go to the bathroom quick and I'll be with you two ladies," I tell them, making my way down the hallway where the men's rooms are.

About halfway down the hallway, I hear moaning coming from one of the rooms and just shake my head. This is nothing new and it really doesn't surprise me. However, the open door does shock me. Quietly taking a few steps closer, the sight before me has me intrigued and wanting to get closer. In the middle of the bed is a girl between a guy I don't know and my good friend, Wood.

The guy I don't know is laying on the bed while the club girl is riding him. Wood is behind her and I can just imagine where his cock is stuffed. From what I can see Wood and the other man don't touch at all, it's all about the girl in between them. Is this what it would be like if I gave Crash and Trojan one night?

Before I can continue watching them, I feel heat at my back and instantly know that it's the men in question. After a few seconds, Trojan is yelling at Wood to close his fucking door the next time he wants to get his dick wet, especially with me being in the clubhouse and the trouble we always seem to get into.

"You see somethin' you like?" Crash asks, pulling the door closed.

"Um…." I can't even answer him.

Trojan takes up his spot at my back while Crash closes in on the front side of me. It's easy to handle one of them at a time, but the two of them together is almost impossible to ignore. There's no denying that I want them both. I'm just not sure if I can act on my feelings and accept only one night with the two of them. So, instead of answering them, I squeeze my way out from in between them and run to the bathroom.

Keira

Darcy came rushing through with two men following her closely even though she didn't realize it. A few minutes after she disappeared down the hallway, there was some yelling and then a door slammed. Slim started laughing his ass off while Shy and I looked at him like he was crazy.

"You just met the entertainment while Darcy, Crash, and Trojan are here," he informs us between fits of laughter. "Wait until Wood is done doin' his thing and you'll really be laughin'."

Shy and I look at one another and I can't wait to see what's about to happen. Wood is a good guy and I hope he doesn't get into too much trouble. I just wonder what the hell is going on to make all the commotion we just heard. I guess we'll find out when the time is right though.

"What are you having done today?" Shy asks me.

"I think I just want a trim. Nothing too outrageous. What about you?"

"I think I'm going to get a trim and some purple highlights added."

"Why purple?" Slim asks, very interested in what Shy's doing.

"Just something different. Why?"

"I liked it when you had the blue in your hair," he says, shrugging his shoulders.

"Well, we'll see what happens when Darcy gets out here then."

Things between Slim and Shy get more and more interesting the more I watch them together. You can tell they're interested in one another, but neither one wants to make the first move. I'm sure they both have their reasons, and I'm not about to try to play matchmaker. Not this time. They'll figure it out or they won't.

Finally, Darcy makes an appearance and she's lugging a bag that I didn't notice before behind her. I guess she brought everything she thought she'd need so no one would have to go anywhere else to get her something.

"Alright ladies, what are we doing today?" she asks, plopping down and ignoring Slim.

"I just want a trim and Shy wants a little more done," I answer.

"Okay. Well, let me get a drink and we'll get started on things."

As Darcy has her drink, the three of us sit and talk about things that don't really matter. I can tell that she has questions for me that I don't want to answer right now. Thankfully she doesn't ask, just lets us be and steers the conversation in other directions. That is until Wood and Boy Scout make their way out from the hallway. Looks like things are about to get interesting.

"Darcy, why you turnin' red on us?" Wood asks, plopping down in the chair next to her.

"Um....no reason really," She says, looking back and forth between him and Boy Scout.

"Did you like what you saw of the show?" Boy Scout asks, sitting between Shy and me.

"Well, um, it was different," she answers as Crash and Trojan come up behind her.

"You ever let her see that shit again, Wood and we'll be havin' problems. More than what we've already had," Crash says, closing in on Darcy and staking his territory. I'm surprised he just doesn't piss on her to mark her.

"Why does it always have to involve me though?" Wood asks.

"You tell us why you seem to always be around firecracker and we'll tell you the answer. Every time somethin' happens with her, it always seems to involve you," Trojan speaks up, placing his hand on Darcy's shoulder. "And if I ever see her face by your fuckin' cock again, you won't have to worry about it anymore."

"That wasn't my fault!" Wood exclaims.

"You didn't move her though, did you?" Crash questions him.

"No. You tellin' me if you had a girl's face near your cock that looks like Darcy, you'd be movin' her?"

From the looks of Crash and Trojan, Wood just said the wrong thing. Especially when I see Crash lunge for him and land a hit to his face before anyone around the table can even blink. Darcy screams and goes to rush over to him before Trojan picks her up and places her on his lap, circling his arm around her waist. He's holding her in place and she's fighting like hell to get away from him. Shy goes over to him and grabs a rag to hold over his nose. I'm just sitting in my chair, watching the show unfold so I don't get in anyone's way.

"You two are un-fucking-believable!" Darcy screams. "I'm not yours and the sooner you realize that, the better off everyone around you will be. Leave me the fuck alone!"

Finally, Darcy can get up and she takes off down the hallway. I'm guessing she's running into the bathroom to hide. Sensing that they're going to go after her, I hold my hand up and waddle after her. That's about the only thing I can do these days it seems. And I want to make sure she's okay and doesn't need any help. I know something is going on between them, you can sense it whenever they're in the room together.

"Darcy, it's Keira," I call out, knocking on the bathroom door.

"Give me a minute," she says, as I hear the water turn on.

After a few minutes, I hear the door unlock and it opens just barely enough for me to get through. Darcy's face is red and her eyes are puffy. She's definitely been crying. The water she splashed on her face isn't doing a thing to conceal that fact.

"Are you okay hun?" I ask.

"I just don't get them. I'm such a clutz and every time something embarrassing happens, it just so happens that Wood is the one there. It's not like I do these things on purpose or anything," she cries.

"I know. But, they seem to have claimed you, so you're going to have to accept the way they act. Or stay away from them. What do you want to do?"

"I know they only want a bit of fun. And, I'm not sure that I'm cut out for that. At the end of the day, it's all about getting their dicks wet and nothing more. I want, no I need, more than that."

"Why do you think they only want a bit of fun and nothing more?" I ask, confused.

"Look at them and then look at me. They're men that love the chase once in a while and once they get me, they'll get bored. I'm not dumb and I know how these things work. They've got all the easy pussy they can handle at the clubhouse."

"You didn't see the look on their faces though, hun. I did. They aren't looking for a bit of fun and nothing more. Are you willing to give them a chance to find out though?"

"What look?" Darcy asks.

"The look of men that wanted to murder someone they thought was trying to move in on their woman. Hell, all they need to do to finish claiming you and marking their territory is piss on your leg."

"That's so disgusting!" Darcy says, finally laughing. "But, I don't know if I can risk it with everything going on right now. There's things that I can't tell anyone and I'm not putting them on the spot to get hurt when it's my mess to handle."

"If they're anything like the guys I see in the other charter, then they're going to stick their noses in it whether you want them to or not. I'm guessing they already know something is going on and it's just a matter of time before they find out what it is. Why don't you just give them a chance if that's what you want to do?"

"Like I said, I don't know if I can risk it."

"I think you already know what you want to do. You're just afraid to take the leap and a chance. What's the worst that's gonna happen?" I ask, realizing that I'm living the same way when it comes to Blade right now.

"I get my heart trampled into a million pieces because they want some fun while I fall for them. Hell, if I'm honest, I'm probably already there."

"Why do you say that?"

"They've been coming around more and more since I first saw them. I don't get a chance to guard myself from the sweet they show me when they're not being cavemen. And now, it'd just be so easy to let them take care of things going on with me, but I'm not gonna drag them through that," Darcy says, thinking about what else she wants to tell me from the look on her face. "Maybe if I make it through this shit in one piece I'll give them the chance they've been pushing for."

"What do you mean by that last part?" I ask, wanting to help this woman any way I can if she's in trouble.

"It's nothing. I'll be fine," she quickly says, letting me know she's definitely hiding something. I don't want to be a rat, but I think in this case, someone definitely needs to know something is wrong.

"Well, let's get back out there and get this pampering started. I'm ready to get off my feet already and I've hardly been on them today."

"Alright mama to be, let's get you taken care of," Darcy says, wiping her face down one more time and fluffing her hair up a little.

We walk back into the main room and the guys have disappeared. Shy is sitting there nursing a beer and waiting patiently for us to return. I don't know what I'd be doing without her keeping me company these days. When I do go live with Blade and our children, she's going to be the one I miss from here. Hopefully I can convince her to come visit me every now and then. If Slim will let her out of his sight, that is.

"Okay ladies, mini break down over. Let's get this day started," Darcy says, downing a shot and trying not to make it noticeable that she's looking for her men.

We've been sitting in the main room being pampered and talking to the guys when they venture in to check on us. I'm honestly ready to call it a day, but Darcy just finished my nails so I need to give them time to dry. She was adamant that I have my nails done because I won't have time to do it once the twins are born. And she didn't want me to look like a hot mess when I went into labor. Her words, not mine.

Shy has been making sure that I have plenty of fluids and things to eat when she hasn't been getting work done on herself. The guys have also been making sure that we've got whatever we need. Especially Slim, Crash, and Trojan. They seem to be the three that come in the most. Slim even put his phone on speaker a little while ago so I could talk to Blade. He was happy I was being treated good by Darcy, but concerned because he could hear how exhausted I am. I can't lie to him, but I left out the dizzy spells when we were talking. There's nothing he can do for me and he's already going crazy. This will just push him over the edge and make him drive here now instead of letting this play out. I'll talk to my doctor when I go in a few days. And there's only a little over a month left to go before I'm due anyway. Basically, I can go into labor any day now and the babies would be delivered.

"Okay Keira, let's get you back to the room," Shy says, just as the guys all walk back in.

"Sounds good to me. Can one of you please help me up? I'm ready to fall asleep where I am and

I know I'm gonna have a hard time after sitting for so long."

Darcy and Shy each get on a side of me and help me stand. Just my luck that a dizzy spell chooses this moment to hit and I sway on my feet before landing back in the chair I was sitting in. Thankfully the girls were right there because with the impact of my fall and not landing right on the chair, I almost tipped over backwards. Before I can even blink, I'm surrounded by the guys and the women are pushed back so they can get to me. This just makes my head swim even more with all of the sudden movement around me. Knowing I have to find something to focus on, I choose Slim since he's the closest one to my head.

"Are you okay sweetheart?" he asks.

"D-don't t-tell Blade," I manage to get out around the nausea.

"I have to. He's gonna wanna know. Or he'll have all our heads. Wood, I want you to call for an ambulance while I call her man," Slim orders before crouching down in front of me.

Killer is bringing me a cold bottle of water while the rest of the guys are moving furniture and getting everyone out of the main room that doesn't have to be here. They want it as easy as possible for the EMTs to get to me when they get here. I know they must be worried if they're calling people in considering that more than likely cops are going to be accompanying the ambulance here.

"Sweetheart, Blade wants to talk to you. Can you talk now?" Slim asks, holding the phone against him to muffle our conversation.

"Yeah, I think so," I say, the tears building up in my eyes.

"Kitten, what's goin' on?" Blade asks, panic lacing his voice.

"I don't know. I've been having a few dizzy spells but thought I'd be fine until my next appointment in a few days. I didn't want to worry you when I know you're already going crazy," I manage to get out.

"I don't care what's goin' on, you need to tell me this shit. What if somethin' is really wrong? You should've immediately called the doctor."

"I know. I just didn't want to bother anyone."

"You wouldn't be botherin' anyone sweetheart," Slim breaks in.

"Exactly! I don't give a fuck what's goin' on with Jason or anyone else right now. I'm headin' out and I'm gonna be there in a little while. We'll make it so no one knows I'm in town, kitten. I love you and I'll see you soon."

Slim takes his phone back and I'm glad because I don't know what to say right now. This is the first time that Blade has told me he loves me and I don't even know what to do about it. I know that I love him, but I never thought I'd hear the words from him. Not yet. I just hope it's not because something might be wrong with Kenyon and Cory.

Slim is guiding someone closer to me, but I can't even concentrate on anything but trying not to puke all over the place. It's never been this bad before and I don't know what is going on. There's two people surrounding me that I'm guessing are EMTs. They're trying to get my vitals since my arm is being squeezed by something. And a light is being shined in my eyes.

"Ma'am how far along are you?" one asks.

"I'm almost eight months."

"Can you tell me what's going on?" the same one asks me.

"I've been having dizzy spells the last few days. I don't know why. I haven't had a chance to tell the doctor about it yet. I was waiting until my appointment."

"You're blood pressure is up a little bit right now. I'm not sure if it's because of what's going on or something else. Let's get you loaded up and to the hospital. One person can ride with you."

Slim points to Killer and he follows us out. I'm happy that he chose one of the guys and not Shy honestly. I don't want her to flip out if something happens to me. She seems like she would be screaming and hollering if something happened and she didn't think the EMTs or doctors were doing their job correctly. Not that Killer won't be doing the same thing. I know he will just because of Blade.

I've been at the hospital for a few hours now. Every time I go to close my eyes and try to relax, another nurse or doctor is in here seeing what other tests they can run. Don't get me wrong, I'm glad that they're being so diligent trying to figure out what's wrong, I just want to rest though. Right now, they've got me hooked up to the monitors so I am constantly hearing the babies heartbeats too. They're nice and strong so there's something that seems to be going right.

"Kitten?" I hear asked.

Opening my eyes, I see Blade walking in the room. His face is full of panic and worry. I'm sure he's not the only one here from his club, seeing the look on his face right now. He pulls up a chair and sits down next to me, taking my hand without the IV in his. I lean up and kiss his lips, needing more of a connection to him. Now that he's here, I can't hide my worry over what's going on with our children. Jason isn't even a blip on my radar at this point.

"You came," is the only thing I can say.

"I told you I was comin' kitten. You mean more to me than anythin' that's goin' on right now.

Grim didn't even try to stop me when I was gettin' ready to leave, he just made sure a few guys were with me so I didn't have to drive."

"I'm so scared."

"I know you are. I am too. But, we'll find out what's goin' on and then we'll know what we have to do so that all three of you come out strong and healthy."

Just then another nurse comes in to take some more blood. I feel like a damn pin-cushion right now. She tells us that they're running more tests to make sure that I don't have some sort of infection running through my body that's not a cold or the flu. Something they would be able to tell based on my symptoms. Blade just sits back and stays out of the way so she can do her job. Before leaving, she tells us that two more people can come in for a few minutes. I say I want Shy to come in and Blade tells them he wants Joker to come in with her.

Blade

We've been in the hospital for hours and hours now. I wouldn't want to be anywhere else other than by my girl's side right now. She's hooked up to monitors and I know all she wants to do is sleep. But she's too worried to let herself relax enough to close her eyes. Even though she says that it's everyone coming in and out of the room.

Finally, I see the doctor making his way into the room to talk to us. Hopefully it's good news and nothing that is going to put anyone in jeopardy. Grabbing her hand again, I brace to hear what the verdict is.

"I think that we figured out what's going on with you Keira," he starts out. "I am keeping you in the hospital overnight for observation, but at this point it looks like your blood pressure is high and that's what's causing you to get these dizzy spells. When you get released tomorrow, as long as nothing happens tonight, you are to be on complete bedrest until I see you in the office in a few days. Is that understood?"

"Do I really have to stay here tonight? I want to go home and sleep in my own bed. I won't do anything that I'm not supposed to," Keira asks, practically begging the doctor to let her go home.

"I'd rather keep you here tonight."

"Why don't you stay, kitten. I'll stay with you and then we'll go back to the clubhouse tomorrow and I'll stay with you until we hear more," I tell her, wanting her to do what the doctor wants.

"I don't want to stay here where there's a better chance that he can get to me. At the clubhouse, there's more protection and I'll feel better. I won't be as stressed out."

"What do you need protection from?" the doctor asks.

"She's just havin' an issue with someone and we've got it under control," I begin, not wanting cops or anyone else involved. "I do see where she's comin' from though. What if we promise to make sure she's on bedrest and we bring her in to see you first thing in the mornin'? That way you can check her for yourself."

"I don't really like the idea, but if it will help keep the stress levels down, then we'll do it," the doctor says. "I don't want you getting out of bed other than going to the bathroom. No activity of any kind for you. Do you understand?"

"Yes. I won't do anything at all. I promise. I just want to go to sleep. We'll be in the office first thing in the morning and go from there."

The doctor nods her head before leaving to fill out the discharge paperwork. I know he's not happy, hell I'm not happy about taking her out of the hospital. But, I'm sure that Jason knows we're here with her by the way he knew other things and is just waiting for the right time to make his move. He's not going to put Keira, Kenyon, or Cory in jeopardy. There's enough going on with them right now and it doesn't need to be added to.

"I'll be right back, kitten. I'm gonna let the guys know what's goin' on and they can make arrangements before we get back to the clubhouse."

"What arrangements?" my girl asks, her eyelids already beginning to droop again.

"We're not stayin' in a room with Shy. I want you all to myself. And I want to make sure that there's goin' to be guys watchin' out around the clock. Jason seems to know more than we're givin' him credit for and until we know how, we have to stay ahead of him."

There's no response from Keira as she's already fallen asleep. I hate that I'm gonna have to wake her up when we leave, but she's the one that wanted to go back to the clubhouse tonight. Walking into the waiting room, I see that most of the guys and Shy are still sitting here waiting to see what's going on. So, I motion for Slim to follow me so we can talk about what I want done at his clubhouse.

"Everythin' good man?" Slim immediately asks.

"I don't know. Her blood pressure is high I guess. They wanted to keep her overnight but she wanted to go back to the clubhouse. She's on complete bedrest for now and can't do anythin' other than go to the bathroom. And I kind of see her point with not knowin' what that Jason fuck is goin' to do next. You got an extra room available?"

"Yeah, we can make sure one is ready. Anythin' else?"

"Yeah. Any way we can get round the clock surveillance or somethin' to make sure that fuckwad doesn't show his face?"

"Already done. Had that in place when we knew she was comin' back there."

"Okay. I'm just waitin' for her to be discharged and then we're headin' back there. I'll probably make her somethin' to eat and then she'll crash for however long she can sleep. I know she ain't sleepin' for shit these days."

"Shy already planned on makin' her somethin' to eat when we got back. She didn't have dinner or anythin'."

"If she could still do that, I'd appreciate it."

"Anythin' man. We're gonna head out then and I'll see you when we get there. I'll find out who's stayin' from your club and make sure there's room for them too. I think Crash and Trojan planned on stayin' with Darcy. She wanted to be here but they wouldn't let her after the way she got upset seein' your girl almost pass out."

"I'll talk to her when we get back there. How's that workin' out with Wood bein' there?" I ask, trying to lighten the mood even a fraction.

"It's been entertainin' so far. Let's just say that as soon as they got there, Darcy got an eyeful of more than the guys wanted her to see with Wood and Boy Scout."

"Fuck! I bet they loved that one."

I can just imagine what Crash and Trojan did. Pretty soon Wood is gonna get a beat down and he's innocent in this. Darcy keeps saying that she's a clutz and I can believe it. If there's something bad that can happen to someone, it happens to her without fail. Wood just happens to be the poor victim that's around whenever catastrophe strikes.

"Anyway, we're gonna get out of your way. We'll see you when you bring your girl back," Slim says, turning to round everyone in the waiting room up to head out.

"Alright," I respond, heading back to Keira. It doesn't matter if she's still sleeping or not. I need to be with my girl.

Finally, we can leave the hospital. Keira is tired as hell and wants to go get in bed. She doesn't even want to eat, but she's going to. Feeding the babies is more important and won't take that long. Especially if Shy already made dinner for her. It's going to be a fight but I'll make sure she eats.

"You ready to go back to the clubhouse kitten?" I ask, helping her off the stretcher.

"Yeah. I want to climb in bed and pass out. I'm so tired I feel like I could sleep for two weeks and it still wouldn't be enough."

"I know you want to sleep kitten, but we need to get you fed before you can pass out. Shy was goin' back and makin' you dinner," I tell her, gearing up for a fight.

"Okay. I know I gotta eat for the babies even though it's the last thing I want to do."

"Good girl," I tell her, taking her hand in mine. "Let's get out of here and back to the clubhouse."

The short drive back to Slim's allows Keira to get a cat nap in. I'm hoping it's enough so that she can keep her eyes open for a few minutes. Everyone is going to want to check on her and make sure she's truly okay before they let her disappear into the room that we'll be staying in for now. Pulling out my phone, I send a quick text to Slim asking him to have Shy get her a plate ready so she can sit right down and eat. There was no way she was going to eat the hospital food the nurses were trying to get her to eat and I had to promise them I would make her as soon as we walked through the door.

I look over and take in my entire world sitting by my side. Keira is leaning against the door and her eyes are closed. Based on the even breathing, I know she's sleeping right now. That just gives me a minute to take in all the beauty my girl has. It's not about her looks, it's about who she is as a person and I'm a lucky son-of-a-bitch to get to be the one that calls her mine.

Pulling in to the clubhouse lot, I see Grim, Glock, and Slim waiting outside for us. Glock was going to stay back in Clifton Falls, but Melody wanted to know her girl was okay and a phone call from me wasn't going to be good enough. She wanted to hear it from her man and so he had no choice in coming down here. Not like he wouldn't have any way. I just think he wanted to stay close to his girl and son. Especially considering that I think Mel is going to have another baby but hasn't said anything to anyone yet.

"You need help?" Glock asks, as I get out of the truck.

"Nope. I've got her."

Glock walks over to us anyway and I know he's going to stick close by until he leaves. I've already told Grim that there's no way in hell I'm leaving without my girl. So, if she has to stay here for the time being, then I'm here. He's not happy with my decision, but he does understand it and isn't going to stand in my way.

"Shy got her plate all ready and it's in the microwave still to keep warm. I'll run in ahead of you and let her know to get it out and find her somethin' to drink. She got any meds she has to take?"

"Not right now. That may all change tomorrow though. I'm not sure what's goin' to happen yet. Other than we have to be at the doctor's office first thing in the mornin'."

"Okay. One of the prospects has a room ready for you two and Shy already moved her stuff into it. There's a bathroom in the room with a tub so she can relax if she wants to."

"I'm pretty sure that all she's goin' to want to do is eat and then go to bed. I know all I want to do is lock her away and hold her in my arms. It feels like it's been forever since I've gotten to hold her."

"I hear ya. I'm stayin' for a few days to make sure she's okay. Not likin' bein' away from my girl and son, but she's adamant that I keep an eye on her girl for a little bit. It's either I stay or she comes here. Not puttin' her in danger of whatever is goin' on."

"I'm sorry man. I wish I could take the threat away and bring Keira home. It's gotta be on her terms though. I'm not forcin' her to come back with me or be with me."

"You won't have to. Anyone can see the love she has for you. She's just independent and doesn't know how to stay that way and be with you. Plus, I think she's got shit in her past, like we all do, that is holdin' her back. She'll be home before you know it," Glock says, running inside while I go to get my girl out.

Knocking on the window of the passenger door, I get Keira awake enough to lean away from the door so I can open it without her falling out. I help her down and she doesn't fight me putting my arm around her to help her inside. Hell, if anything she leans in closer to me and I can't fight the smile forming on my face.

"Shy already got your plate ready. So, we're gonna sit in the main room while you eat so everyone can make sure you're okay. Then we'll go to whatever room they put us in, kitten. Glock said they made sure it was one with a tub if you wanted to relax in a hot bath before layin' down."

"No. I just want to eat and go to bed. You can visit and hang out."

"Not happenin'. I'll be in bed with you, holdin' you in my arms. Been too long, kitten."

Keira gives a slight nod of her head while Slim holds the door open for us. I know she wants to say something to him, but she just thanks him and continues on her way. My girl is never quiet so I'm hoping she's just tired as fuck and nothing more is running through that head of hers.

I lead her in and see that Glock put her at a table that isn't right in the center of things, but it isn't in the corner either. That way people that want to see my girl can and not feel like she's closing off from everyone. Hell, he's already sitting there waiting for us to make our way over to him. Unfortunately, Darcy gets away from Crash and Trojan and stops us before we can get too far.

"Are you feeling okay?" she asks Keira.

"I'm feeling better hun. Thank you."

"I was so scared for you and those babies. The guys wouldn't let me come to the hospital though because I was flipping out a little bit," she tells my girl, trying to get a smile to appear on her face.

"I'm better. My blood pressure is just elevated a little bit so I have to go on bedrest and go back to the doctor tomorrow morning. We'll go from there."

"Well, you eat and I'll be here if you need anything at all," Darcy tells her, being pulled back by Trojan.

Everyone else waits until Keira is sitting down and has finished most of her food. For someone that wasn't hungry she sure did demolish the food Shy made for her. I think maybe her exhaustion is just overruling everything else right now and she honestly didn't think she would eat the way she just did.

"Babe?" Keira asks, looking at me.

"Yeah kitten?"

"Can we go to the room now please? I can't eat anymore and I just want to collapse. Besides, I'm supposed to be on bedrest and not sitting at the table right now."

"We can do that," I tell her, helping her up from the table and letting Wood lead us to the room they chose for us.

He tells me that we're right between him and Killer. Slim is across the hall and Grim and Glock are going to be staying just a few doors down. It reassures me to know that everyone Keira likes and everyone I trust are so close to us in case something happens. I'm not just talking about with this fuckwad Jason either. If something happens to Keira or the babies, then they're all right there. They'll hear us yelling and come running in.

Wood leaves us and I get Keira settled in the bed after giving her one of my shirts to change in to. She tried fighting me on it, but I want her in something of mine. I need to be as close to her as I possibly can right now. Before I climb in to bed with her, I make sure I have crackers, a bottle of water, and the remote for the tv right on the stand by the bed. That way, I can just grab whatever she needs and not leave her side. Am I going a bit overboard on not wanting to leave her? Probably. But, I've been kept away from her for too long and I'm not letting her out of my sight any time soon. Not with the asshole running around and none of us knowing what he has planned.

Chapter Seven

Keira

IT'S BEEN ALMOST TWO weeks since I was in the hospital. I'm going crazy because I'm being kept on bedrest until it's time to have the babies. Blade is driving me crazy, in a purely good and loving way. He won't let anyone visit with me for too long, only certain people are allowed in, and he's got me eating every time my eyes pop open. Today, I've about had it though. I'm ready to get out of this room and I'm going to no matter what Blade says.

"I need to talk to Dr. Sanchez please," I say when a receptionist answers the phone.

"Give me just a minute and I'll see if she's available."

When I'm on hold still, Blade comes walking into the room. I don't even care. I need to get out of this bed and room. A person can only stare at the same four walls for so long before they end up going insane.

"Keira, what can I do for you?" Dr. Sanchez asks, coming on the line.

"Can I please go out in the main room and sit? I won't do anything other than walk from the room to there. I'll stay sitting and if anything happens to stress me out, I'll come back to the room."

"I don't see why not. Your blood pressure was still elevated when we last saw you, but it wasn't quite as bad as it has been. Now, are you feeling any contractions or anything like that?" she asks.

"No. Well, I don't think so. I mean my back has been bothering me a lot so I'm not sure."

"Okay. Tomorrow when you come in, I might send you over to the maternity ward and have them hook you up to the monitor. If we can catch your labor early, I'll admit you right then so we can make you comfortable and monitor everything closely."

"Sounds good. Thank you Dr. Sanchez," I tell her, hanging up.

Blade is standing there staring at me and I know he wants to know what the doctor just told me. So, I quickly relay what was said and Blade stares at me for a full minute. He doesn't say a word, he just stares at me. At least until I can't take it anymore.

"What's the matter babe?" I ask, standing up.

"Why didn't you tell me your back was botherin' you? I would've rubbed it or somethin' to see if it helped."

"You've already done so much and I didn't want to bother you anymore than I already have."

"You carryin' my babies? You my girl?"
Blade asks me, coming into my personal space to
help me up.

"I am your girl and I am carrying your
babies. But, that doesn't mean I want you to do
everything for me."

"It's my job though. I'm your man and I
need to take care of you and our kids. It's what I
want to do. You just need to let me do it," Blade
tells me, pulling me in for a kiss.

"Now, let's get in the main room so I can sit
down and relax," I tell him, grabbing a blanket to
put on my legs.

Blade and I walk out to the main room and
he leads me over to one of the couches. Glock is
sitting nearby and I see him walk over to where I'm
going to be sitting. Slim, Wood, and Killer also
make their way over to us. Wood and Killer bring
over chairs to sit across from us and we all just
shoot the shit. Shy also sits with us for a while until
the club girls start tossing dirty looks her way.

"Well, Keira, I'll catch up with you in a
little while. Maybe when you're back in your room.
I'm gonna go find something to clean."

While Shy walks away, I watch Slim
watching her. He wants to say something to her
about not sitting with us, but he doesn't. I don't
know why he's holding back and not saying
anything to her about staying with us. Slim wants
Shy as much as she wants him but neither one of

them will admit it. One day they will and I can't wait to see the fireworks that explode when they come together.

"How you doin' kitten?" Blade asks, leaning in to me.

"I'm doing okay. I'm having fun sitting here and talking with everyone."

"You let me know if you get too tired, yeah?"

"I will," I answer.

Before anything else can be said, there's a horrible shaking coming from outside and the sound of an explosion. Blade covers me as much as he can while the rest of the guys surround us. Slim is on the phone and I can hear him telling more guys to run outside and help cover the fence. From what little I can hear, I'm guessing that someone used explosives to breach the fence surrounding the clubhouse and yard.

Just as Blade goes to tell me something, I feel extreme pain in my stomach and back before a gush of something runs down my legs. Blade looks at my face and I know he sees the panic overtaking my features. He's yelling something and I can't hear him because I'm so focused on the pain and worry that I'm going into labor before it's time. This is not how it's supposed to happen.

"Kitten, are you okay? What's goin' on?" Blade is asking me, getting right in my face.

"My water just broke. I'm going into labor and we should probably head to the hospital now," I say as calm as I possibly can.

"What are you talkin' about?" Blade asks. "How are we supposed to go anywhere right now?"

"What's goin' on?" Slim asks, coming closer to us.

"I'm in labor. My water broke right after the explosion," I explain, becoming a little more panicked.

"We'll figure out how to get you guys out of here." Slim responds, calling Grim and the rest of the guys over.

I can vaguely hear him telling them what's going on and how we're gonna get out of here. I'm just trying to concentrate on my breathing and everything else right now and let the men do what they do. I feel as safe as I can be right now and I know they're not going to let anything happen to me or these babies.

Just as Blade goes to tell me what's going on, a contraction hits and I lose my breath. I double over in pain and grab onto Blade's arm so I don't hit the ground. Blade bends down with me and makes me look in his eyes. He holds my gaze and doesn't let me look away from him during the entire contraction. Grim, Wood, Killer, and Joker surround me and don't let anyone else see what's going on. The less people that know what's going on, the better off it's going to be.

"Kitten, we're goin' to get you out of here. Slim has a back way that only a few people know about and we're takin' that out of here. You ready?"

The only thing I can do is nod. So, Slim gets in front of us, pulling Shy with him. Joker gets on the other side of me, and Wood and Killer get behind us. We all make our way behind Slim while he leads us to our way out. The only thing that registers in my brain is whether or not there's going to be a car waiting for us and how it's getting there. My reasoning for this is because I'm not moving from panic to fear that something is going to happen to us before we can make it to the hospital, even though it's not far from the clubhouse.

"We're almost to the entrance," Slim tells us, moving us as fast as he thinks I can move.

Blade and Joker don't try to make me move any faster than I am while Killer is watching our backs to make sure that no one sneaks up behind us. I know that Blade is scared as hell right now and he's trying not to let anyone see. But, I feel the death grip he has on my hand and he's constantly asking me if I'm okay.

"Kitten are you ready to meet our son and daughter?" he asks, just as Slim opens a secret doorway.

"Uh huh. I want the pain to stop and I know it's only going to get worse before it gets better," I grit out as another contraction hits.

Blade tries to stop moving while I'm having the contraction, but I want to keep going. I slow down to a turtle's pace even though I just want to curl up into a ball on the floor. Every time he tries to get us to stop moving, I tug on his arm and don't let my feet stop moving. Honestly, I think the only reason I'm not stopping right now is because of the threat that's happening outside the clubhouse. I know it's Jason that's behind it and it just makes me realize even more that he's not going to stop until he gets what he wants. Me.

"I think we need to talk after I have the babies," I grit out to Blade.

"About what?"

"I'm letting him take me when the babies are born. Our son and daughter are not going to know what's going on and be put in the line of fire because this asshole wants me."

"The fuck you are!" Blade yells out. "We're gonna handle it and you're goin' nowhere but home to Clifton Falls when you all can leave the hospital."

Instead of saying anything in response, I just feel tears start to stream down my face. I know what I have to do to protect everyone. The guys will do what they can to get me back and I know in my heart that they will get me back. I just hope that it's before I'm too broken to be a mother to Kenyon and Cory.

I know the other guys have heard what I've said and I can feel the tension ratchet up so much more. I'm not going to argue my point or let anyone talk me out of doing what I gotta do though. It's not just Blade or myself that I have to look out for anymore. We're gonna have two little ones that need to be protected and guided to grow into strong, loving, loyal people. Blade and the rest of the club will make sure that happens.

"About fifty more feet and we'll be at the car. Playboy is waitin' for us already. I called him since he was the only one that was out of the clubhouse when this started," Slim tells us all.

By this point, I don't know how I'm going to make it another ten feet, let alone fifty feet. I think Blade and Joker can sense this as I feel myself being picked up on each side. The two men carry me the rest of the way and all I can do is hold on.

Blade

We've been at the hospital for an hour or so now and Keira is definitely going to be giving birth to our children today. Dr. Sanchez has been here and they're keeping a close eye on the babies. She's already had to move around once so that one of their heart rates would pick back up. That was scary as hell, hearing the monitors going off and not knowing what was going on.

One of the nurses taught me how to read the paper printing out of the monitor so I can help let my girl know where in the contraction she is. I know when one is going to hit now and I can tell her when she's at the peak of her contraction. Now we're just waiting for the doctor to come back in to let us know what the next step is. I know my girl didn't want to have a cesarean section, but she might not have a choice in the matter. At this point, it's a matter of getting the babies out before anything happens to them.

"Almost done, kitten," I tell her, as her latest contraction reaches the peak and starts to go away.

Before it's fully over with, Dr. Sanchez comes back in and looks over the monitor. I can tell just from her face that Keira isn't going to be happy. So, I brace myself to find out what's going on.

"Keira as soon as this contraction is over with, I'm going to check you. If you haven't progressed at all, then we're going to take you in for a cesarean. I know it's the last thing you want, but we need to think of the babies right now," she tells her, reassuringly.

"I know. Honestly, I don't know how much longer I can do this. It feels like it's been days instead of a few hours. And I know that you guys are watching the babies closely. So, whatever you think has to be done, let's do."

The doctor does her thing and tells us that we are going to surgery instead of delivery. I knew it was a matter of time before we heard that news. Don't ask me how I knew, but I knew Keira wasn't going to deliver the way she wanted to.

"Go out and let everyone know. Take a breather and come back to me babe," Keira tells me, taking a break to relax a little before the next contraction hits.

"Not leavin' you alone," I tell her.

"Send Shy in and go take a break. Shy won't let anything happen and she'll come get you as soon as we're ready to head back."

"I want her in here before I leave this room," I say, pulling my phone out to let Slim know to send her here.

Within minutes, Shy is knocking on the door and poking her head in. She takes my spot by Keira's head so she can watch the monitor and help her through her contractions. It's honestly almost like she knows what she has to do to help her already without me saying a single word to her. Has she been through this before and no one knows?

"I'll be back in a minute or two," I say, kissing my girl before I leave the room.

Walking down the hallway, I make my way into the waiting room Shy told me everyone was moved to. The guys are all sitting there watching tv, reading, or playing on their phones. Grim is the first to look up and notice me standing there.

"You okay brother?" he asks, coming over to me.

"Yeah. She's got have a cesarean done. Not what she wanted, but it's in the best interest of the kids," I tell them all.

"Most women carryin' multiples end up havin' that done any way," Joker says, joining us.

"I know. I've read and done research," I answer honestly. "She wanted me to take a break before we go back."

"Cage is havin' a hard fuckin' time tryin' to keep the girls in Clifton Falls. Especially Melody. Glock is debatin' headin' home right now to make sure she stays there," Grim tells me.

This is the first time that I'm truly realizing that the men and women that are in the club are going to be by our sides no matter what. I look around and see the few men that are here right now, knowing for a fact that more would be here if things at the clubhouse weren't going to shit right now.

"Any news of what's goin' down at the clubhouse?" I ask.

"Not talkin' about that now. You take your break and when the little ones are here, we'll talk business," Slim tells me.

His tone alone tells me that I'm not going to get an answer from anyone in the waiting room. So, I sit down in one of the chairs and close my eyes for a second. I'm not going to sleep, instead I'm praying. I'm praying that my girl, my son, and my daughter are going to make it through this okay. I don't want anything to happen to anyone in my little family. This includes my brothers and their women in the clubs we surround ourselves with.

"Why don't you get back in there so we can meet our niece and nephew," Glock says, walking into the waiting room.

"Where's Melody?" I ask.

"Finally sittin' at home where she belongs right now. More goin' on than you know, Brother."

"I got a pretty good idea. But, I'll wait until you're ready to tell everyone," I say, a smirk on my face at his shocked expression.

I don't let anyone else say anything to me as I make my way back in to my girl. Shy is there, holding her hand and holding a wet rag against her forehead. Seeing this makes me scared that something is wrong and no one got me while I stepped out for a second.

"Nothing is wrong daddy," Shy says, reading my expression. "She was getting hot and they don't want her to have ice chips or anything. So, this is about all we could do for now. It's just about time for you to get ready to go in though."

"Thank you," I tell her, taking my spot back at Keira's side.

Kenyon and Cory made their entrance into this world in less time than I expected. Right now, the nurses have them and are cleaning them up and doing whatever else they have to do, my girl is in recovery, and I'm making my way to the waiting room to let the guys know. Keira did an amazing job and I couldn't be more proud of her than I am right now. Dr. Sanchez told me that I'd have enough time to go talk to my brothers and Shy before the kids were brought back in to us. So I'm going to gather myself so I can be there for my new family.

"Are they here?" Shy asks excitedly.

"They are. Right now, the nurses have them and Keira is in recovery. You guys should be able to see them soon but I'm pretty sure they're goin' to limit the number of people goin' in and out for now," I tell them.

"I bet they're cute as fuck," Shy says.

The men are paying attention to me, but they don't want to seem too excited over seeing my babies. They have to act like the badass bikers they are. But, I've seen them when the kids are around and I know they all melt and become wrapped around the little fingers belonging to every child of every club we're friends with.

I sit down and talk to my brothers to find out what happened at the clubhouse since we've been gone. Apparently, it was Jason that was trying to breach the gate and fence around the clubhouse. I'm not sure where the men with him came from, but he had a lot of guys with him. His ultimate goal was to have them distract us all enough so that he could get to Keira. This was all told to the remaining men by a few of the guys they captured. Jason managed to get away and some of Slim's guys are out looking for him now.

"You know he's mine when they find him, right? I don't give a fuck what you all do to him before I can get there as long as I get the kill shot and my time with him. It's my girl the fucker is after and I want him!" I say, making sure everyone is paying attention to me.

"You'll get him son," Slim assures me. "I'll make sure that there's more than enough left for you. I will also be gettin' my hands on him. Keira has become like a second daughter to me and I want him almost as bad as you do."

Wood and Killer are nodding their heads right along with Slim. I know they've been the main two to watch my girl and they treat her like their little sister. She looks at them as her friends, brothers, and guys that she can depend on no matter what. The four of us want him more than anyone else here. We better get him soon before something worse happens. My children are here now and I get what Keira meant about protecting them at all costs.

"Alright, I'm headin' back in. It should be about time for my son and daughter to be brought back to us."

"You go enjoy some time with your family and tell the nurse to let us know when we can come in," Grim tells me, offering his congratulations.

"Okay. You guys don't have to sit here though. We're good," I tell them all.

"Not leavin'. The guys at the clubhouse got it under control and we want to meet little Kenyon and Cory," Grim tells me.

"Besides, if we don't get pictures to take home with us, our women are goin' to kill us. Or at the very least, make us sleep on the couch," Joker tells me.

The only thing I can do is laugh because I know that Joker's right. Skylar has made them sleep on the couch more than once. Cage and him both vowed never to do anything to make that happen again. And I know that Melody will be worse than her because Keira is like her sister. I bet she's just bitching about not being able to be here right now. More than likely, she'll talk Glock into letting her and Anthony come here so she can be with her girl.

"Glock, I think you need to make arrangements to bring Mel and Anthony here," I say, pausing at the doorway. "You know she's already formin' a plan to get here anyway."

"I've been thinkin' the same thing. I wouldn't be surprised if she talked the new prospect, Glen, into bringin' her here. Hell, she's probably already on her way."

We all laugh because we all know that Glock is right. Melody gets something in her mind these days and she does it. It doesn't matter what it is, Melody is like a lioness when she wants to do something. Especially when it concerns her family. Keira is the closest thing to family she has besides Glock.

Turning around, I continue to make my way down to recovery. About halfway there, a nurse stops me to tell me that Keira is back in a room and they're getting ready to bring the kids in. I quicken my pace to get in the room before the bassinets are wheeled in. Nothing is going to stop me from being in there when my son and daughter are brought back in to us.

Quietly opening the door, I don't want to disturb Keira if she's sleeping. However, she's sitting up in bed looking as relaxed as she can be right now. I know she's in pain but my girl is going to tough it out like she always does. No one will know the amount of pain she's in unless she wants you to see it.

"I'm not sleeping," Keira tells me. "I'm waiting for them to come back in with us. What's taking so long?"

"They'll be here in just a few minutes. One of the nurses told me they were just finishin' up."

"I can't believe we're parents."

"I know. You did amazin' kitten. I'm so proud of you."

"Didn't do anything other than lay on a table and get cut open babe."

"You didn't throw a fit because you had to do it that way. You accepted what the doctor said and let them do their thing so nothin' happen to Kenyon or Cory."

"Told you they are more important to me than anyone else in this world. It's why I made the decision I made and why I'm seeing it through."

"Not talkin' about that today. Maybe when we get back to Clifton Falls. Now, some of the guys are waitin' to get in here. You tell me how many and who."

"I don't care babe. I'm fine and if they all want to come in at once, have at it. As long as the nurses don't care."

Within a few minutes, there's a knock on the door and I'm expecting to see my brothers since I sent a message to Grim. Instead, two nurses are on the other side of the door and the greatest sight in the world, my son and daughter. I hold the door open so they can be wheeled in and I don't let them out of my sight. It's only going to get worse from here I think.

One of the nurses checks on my girl while I move to stand between the two bassinets. Our son and daughter are so tiny and I don't know how any clothes are going to fit them. I'm not worried about hurting them by holding them or dropping them though. I will do everything in my power to protect them.

Cory is smaller than her brother and seeing her little face makes my heart melt. She's going to be the spitting image of her mama and I know we're gonna be beating the boys away. No one is going to ever be good enough for my little girl. Switching my gaze from Cory, I look down at Kenyon. He looks more like me and I know that I'm going to teach him everything I know. He'll grow up to be a man that is loyal, caring, strong, and determined. Someone that he can be proud of and someone that doesn't back down from a fight.

"You okay over there, daddy?" Keira asks me, sitting up a little higher in the bed.

"I'm just looking at our kids and thinking about how opposite they are."

"How do you figure?"

"Already I know that Cory is gonna grow up lookin' just like you. She already takes after your looks. Kenyon is going to look more like me. Cory is so much smaller than he is and I know she's already wrapping me around her little finger."

"She's only a few hours old, how can she be wrapping you around her little finger already?"

"Because she's gonna be a daddy's girl."

"Well, hand me Kenyon then so I can make him a mama's boy," Keira tells me.

Before I can respond, there's another knock on the door and I open it to see the guys waiting to come in and meet our son and daughter. For right now, it's just the few guys from my club. Joker, Glock, and Grim come in and give Keira a hug and offer their congratulations before they walk over to meet Kenyon and Cory. Joker looks at me, silently asking permission to pick Kenyon up. I nod and go to pick Cory up at the same time. It's definitely going to be harder to let someone else hold my little princess.

"Come on Blade, let her go. It's your brothers and not some random person. They all have kids of their own," Keira tells me, knowing what's going through my head right now.

"I won't hurt her, I promise," Grim tells me, stepping in my space to take my daughter from my arms.

I hesitantly hand my daughter over to Grim and stand between the two men holding my world in their hands. Keira is the only other part of my world and Glock is standing with her, getting ready to hand her his phone. Must be he called Melody and she wants to talk to her girl. Hopefully Glock warned her that we want to surprise her so we're not letting her know that Melody and Anthony are coming here.

Instead of paying attention to my girl on the phone though, I watch the guys holding my children like a hawk. Glock has made his way over and is shaking his head at me. Joker goes to hand off

Kenyon to him and I'm just glad it isn't my daughter. Not that I don't trust these men with my life, and the lives of my children, I just need to keep them close where I can watch over them. Call me overprotective or whatever else you want to, I really don't care. I see this being a matter of conflict between Keira and myself though.

"Has it hit you yet?" Joker asks me.

"It has. As soon as Kenyon was born it hit me. My life is changing for the better and I couldn't be happier than I am right now. Well, I will be when we get this threat taken care of."

Another knock on the door has us stopping our conversation. Joker walks over to the door and lets in the rest of the guys. Slim is leading them all and he makes a beeline for Grim and Glock. Keira laughs at him, knowing he's about to turn to mush. Shy is close on his heels, but she at least says hi to my girl. Wood and Killer surround Keira on the bed and talk to her while everyone else surrounds the guys holding the babies.

Stepping back, I take in the scene before me. Once again it hits me how much family Keira and I truly are blessed with. The guys are laughing and joking, including my girl, and talking about my kids like they're the greatest thing on Earth. In my eyes, they are the greatest and I can't wait to watch them grow and learn. These men and women will be by our sides the entire time and they'll help us guide them to become the adults they are meant to be.

It's been a long day and the last of the guys have finally left the hospital. Well, Wood and Killer are still here standing guard, but everyone else went back to the clubhouse. Glock wanted to stand watch too, but Melody and Anthony should be here in a few hours. He's going to have all he can do to keep them at Slim's instead of coming here.

"Are you okay kitten?" I ask, sitting on the edge of the bed while she nurses Kenyon.

"I'm more than okay. How are you daddy? Gonna have a heart attack yet?" she asks, a smile lighting up her face.

"You saw that huh?"

"I did. It's gonna be okay ya know. They won't ever hurt our children and you don't have to be so overprotective. Especially of Cory. We got this and they're going to help us along the way."

"I know. I just don't want to let them out of my sight. Especially with that fuck out there still. He's gettin' more dangerous and becomin' a loose cannon."

"We'll all be fine. He won't be able to get the kids when you take them out of Benton Falls and back to Clifton Falls with you."

"Not up for discussion kitten. We got this."

We sit in silence, each lost in our own thoughts. The main thought I have is that I will give up my life to protect the three people surrounding me right now. Looking down into my daughter's sleeping face, my heart expands and I know I'm where I'm supposed to be right now. Life is perfect and I can't wait to start living with my girl, son, and daughter.

Chapter Eight

Keira

IT'S BEEN TWO WEEKS and I'm just getting released from the hospital. I ended up getting an infection in the incision and Cory ended up getting jaundice. To say Blade flipped the fuck out is an understatement. He was right by her side the entire time she was baking as I call it. Now, we're more than ready to leave this place and go back to something that resembles normal. Personally, I think Blade arranged for us to be in the hospital this long to give us a chance to be a small family without the threat of Jason.

"Slim will be here soon kitten. You ready to go?" Blade asks me, coming back in the room from checking on our girl.

"I am. I just want to get the kids dressed and then we'll be all ready to leave."

"They'll be bringing Cory in here in a little bit. I got somethin' for them though," he tells me, bringing out a box.

I've heard that Ma usually gives outfits to any new babies born to members of the Wild Kings. I just didn't think that it would happen with us because I haven't been around. Apparently, it doesn't matter to her though because Blade is a member. I can't wait to see what the outfits look like.

Opening the box, I peel back the tissue paper and find the two most adorable outfits. For

Kenyon there's a pair of tiny jeans, with a onesie saying 'Property of Blade' under the Wild Kings patch. A blue hat is also included in his outfit and a small pair of little shoes looking like boots. For Cory, there's a little jean skirt with a pink onesie. Her onesie says the same thing as Kenyon's and the hat is pink instead of blue. Her little shoes are little dress shoes. The outfits are so cute and I instantly tear up at seeing them.

"I can't believe she sent us these. It's just because of you since I made the decision to come here instead," I tell him, trying to stop the tears.

"It doesn't matter if you were there or not kitten. Kenyon and Cory are Wild Kings regardless. Please don't cry anymore."

"These are happy tears," I answer, slowly getting up to pick Kenyon up to get him dressed.

Blade helps me as much as he can but I'm still feeling independent and it's hard for me to take the help. Kenyon stays asleep while I get him dressed before Blade puts him in his car seat. Now, we're just waiting on Cory to be brought in to us so we can get her ready to go home. Well, back to the clubhouse at least because we don't have a home to go to.

I must get a weird look on my face because Blade wraps his arms around me and pulls me into his body. I've definitely missed being wrapped in his arms since I left and it seems like he puts me as close to him as often as he can. Before long, he releases me and I know that we're going to be having a conversation that I don't want to have right now.

"Kitten, what's with the sad look on your face?" he asks, kneeling in front of me.

"I just realized that Kenyon, Cory, and I don't have a home to go to. We get to go to Slim's clubhouse. And you're going to be leaving soon to go back to Clifton Falls."

"The kids and you are comin' home with me kitten. When I go back to Clifton Falls, you'll all be comin' with me. I'm not leavin' my entire world behind so you can try to do this with the help of Shy and the Phantom Bastards."

"I know you mean that, but it's just not a reality right now. You have to get back to your life and I have to move on here. Not that I'm going to be with anyone. You're it for me."

"That's why we're leavin' together kitten. If I could make you my wife today, I would. I'm that serious about not lettin' you out of my sight and out of my life," Blade says, making me look at him to realize how serious he is.

"Then why don't we do it?" I ask honestly.

"What? Get married?" he asks, shocked.

"Yeah. We don't need anything fancy or big. We can just grab a few witnesses and get married in front of a judge. I don't need to go all out babe. Later on, we can have a party for everyone, but I don't even care about that."

"You serious right now?"

"Dead serious," is my only response.

I can see the wheels turning and I know that before the end of the day I will be married to Blade. I will be Mrs. Michael Branch. On one hand, I can't wait for that to happen. But, on the other I'm scared shitless that he'll get tired of me and realize that I'm not worth all the trouble. Or that he's only keeping me close because of Kenyon and Cory. I guess when that day comes I'll figure out how to deal with it and what to do from there.

"Slim just sent me a text and said he's just pullin' in. I told him to come on up while we're waitin' on our girl," Blade tells me.

"As soon as they bring our girl in to us, we'll be ready to leave. Can you go see what the hold-up is please?"

"Yeah, I'll be right back kitten," Blade responds before giving me a kiss and walking out the door.

I watch Blade walk out the door and stare down at Kenyon in his seat. He's so tiny and fragile right now. I'm scared that I'm going to accidentally do something to hurt him and Cory because they are so small. This is just one of the fears that have gone through my head since I first found out I was pregnant.

Now, I need to focus on what we're gonna need to do in order to get a marriage license so we can get married today. I wasn't lying when I said I didn't need anything fancy. The only thing I need is for Blade to be with me and want to stay with me for the long haul. It's not like I have any family that I want there. And I know he doesn't either. I'm pulled from my thoughts by a knock on the door.

"Come in," I call out, thinking that it's going to be Slim walking through the door.

"Hey girl!" I hear Melody call out.

I'm speechless that my only friend in the world is here. I never dreamed that she'd be here with all the threats running rampant right now. Glock is crazy for letting her anywhere near me. Especially when I see Anthony poke his head in the door from behind his mom.

"What are you doing here? You need to be as far away from me as you can," I ask, confused.

"There was no way I was staying away when my sister just had my niece and nephew. Glock knew this and allowed a few guys to bring me down."

"But why? You know it's dangerous," I say.

"Like I said, you need me here. So, I'm here. Now where are these babies?"

"Kenyon is the only one in the room with us right now. Cory should be here shortly. Blade just went to see what the hold-up with her is."

"Let me see the little guy," Melody says, walking over to the seat Kenyon is sitting in.

Melody squats down in front of Kenyon and pulls his blanket back a little bit to see more of his face. She 'oohs' and 'ahhs' over him while Anthony makes his way over to me. He hugs me and tells me that he's been so excited waiting for me to get out of the hospital. Apparently, they've been here a few days and Glock made them stay in the clubhouse until today so Jason didn't know they were here. I guess they got put on lockdown since they decided to come here.

"I'm not going to wake him up just so I can hold him. But when we get to the clubhouse, he's so mine," Melody tells me.

"Okay," I respond, smiling. "Now, do you want the big news?"

"What can be bigger than my niece and nephew being here?" she asks, coming to sit next to me on the edge of the bed.

"Blade and I are getting married today. Glock and you can be our witnesses since we're just going in front of a judge," I tell her. Not giving her a chance to squeal just yet I add, "don't tell anyone. It's just going to be us and our witnesses. I don't want a fuss and it's not going to be anything extravagant. Hell, I don't even want a party."

"What? Oh my! You think I'm going to keep this to myself?" she practically screams.

"If you don't keep it to yourself, I won't let you be there Mel. I'm dead serious."

"You're serious huh? But why?"

"Because of everything going on. I don't want to call attention to me, to us, any more than is already there. Jason is not playing around this time. So, please, keep this quiet."

"Okay. I'll keep it quiet hun. I'm not happy about it, but I'll do it for you."

"Thank you babe."

Before we can say any more, Blade comes back in the room carrying Cory. She's cradled in his arms and I know that he's not going to be giving her up any time soon. Cory is going to be his little princess and he's not going to let anyone get near her. Hell, other than feedings I'll be lucky to get near her. That's how overprotective he is already. It's going to be real interesting when she gets older and discovers boys as being something other than gross.

Blade lays our daughter down on the hospital bed and unwraps her blanket. I have the outfit that Ma sent to her laid out already so he can just put it on her. If anything, he has been more hands on than I anticipated. I figured that I would be doing all the diaper changes, feedings, and getting the babies dressed all alone. Nope. Blade has been right by my side from the time they wake up until the time they fall back asleep. Even when they're asleep he's watching over them. I honestly don't know how much sleep he's gotten since they were born.

"Melody knows our news," I tell him. "She's keeping it a secret so Jason doesn't get wind of it. Glock and she are going to be our witnesses. I figured that way she could be there for us, have a little piece of home there."

Blade doesn't say anything for a minute. A huge smile breaks out on his face though. "Love hearin' that come out of your mouth kitten."

"What?" I ask, confused.

"You callin' Clifton Falls home. Means you're ready to really go back with me and make a life together."

"I told you I have been ready babe."

"Until now, you weren't truly ready though. Words are different than actions. I could tell by the look on your face that you weren't quite ready. Now, you are. I'll have to make some calls before we leave to make sure the house is ready for us."

"The house Rage is building?"

"No. The little one I told you I was rentin' until that one's done and ready for us to move in."

"Babe, we don't have anything for the twins when we get out of here," I say, finally realizing that we may not be as ready as I thought we were.

"Don't worry about it. We got this covered," Blade says, a smirk spreading across his face.

Obviously, he knows something I don't know. There's no way I'm going to get it out of him, so I leave it be for now. It's only a matter of time before I find out what he's hiding any way. Glancing over at Melody, I can see a similar look on her face. This only tells me that whatever is going on is big. It's something I'm not necessarily going to like, but it's already been done.

"Alright. I'll let you two have your secret for now. If I don't like it, I will let you both know."

Their response is to laugh at me. Little do they know that I've gotten better at holding a grudge since being around Jason. I can go days and days without uttering a single word. Blade will be affected more than he realizes. Not only will I not talk to him, but I will move the babies and I to a different room and not let him in. He'll be ready to go back to Clifton Falls in no time. Even if we are married.

"How are we going to get married today Blade?" I ask, switching gears while he finishes up with Cory.

"Got it taken care of. Made a call to Slim and he's doin' what he can to get us a license immediately. He knows a judge and has already called him too. We're gettin' married today no matter what kitten," he says, making sure I know he's serious about it.

"Okay babe."

Blade

Keira has no clue that Melody brought all the gifts here that were supposed to be given at the baby shower. She put one together once she found out we were having a baby and just changed it up once I told her we were having twins. I'm sure that most of the gifts came from her and Glock, but he won't care. Glock and I both know how close our girls are. We're both willing to do whatever we have to in order to make sure these two girls stay as close as they are.

I finally have Cory buckled up in her car seat and I'm doublechecking to make sure we haven't forgotten anything. Keira is moving to the wheelchair she has to be wheeled out in with the help of Anthony. He loves his aunt Keira so much and I'm glad that he made the trip with his mom. Not that she would leave him at the clubhouse with them being here.

"Let's roll kitten. I'm more than ready to get out of here," I tell her.

"Can I wheel you out?" Anthony asks her.

"You sure can buddy."

"Yay! I promise not to run you into anything," he responds, not hiding his excitement.

"I know you won't."

We all make our way out to the elevators and wait while it makes it way up to us. Anthony is talking a mile a minute and I'm surprised he's not spilling the beans about the presents waiting for them. I may have gotten her a thing or two. And one definitely isn't for Kenyon and Cory.

Glock is waiting for us in the SUV outside. Anthony and Melody climb in first so they can sit in the very back while we strap the car seats in the middle seat. Keira climbs in between them while I take the passenger seat. I imagine Keira's pretty cramped so I'm glad it won't take us more than ten minutes to get back to Slim's. Glock tells me everything is set up and I know he means with the presents and little baby shower Melody decided to throw along with what we need for the wedding.

"How you doin' back there, kitten?" I ask, turning to look at me girl.

"I'm good. I can't wait to get back so I can take a small nap before later on."

"We'll see what happens," I tell her, not giving her any information.

Melody and Glock make small talk the entire ride so that Keira won't be able to ask any questions. Anthony chimes in every now and then but Keira and I stay quiet. I keep looking back to check on her and see that she's only paying attention to Kenyon and Cory. It's going to be different now that we aren't in the hospital. At least there the nurses would give my girl a break when she needed one. Now, it's just the two of us. Yeah, we have the members of the three clubs to help, but I know we won't take them up on it very often. We're gonna want to keep them close to us.

Finally, we pull into the clubhouse and I can see the influx of cars and trucks in the parking lot. There's definitely more bikes here too and I know that Keira is going to notice as soon as she takes her eyes off our children. Glock and I step out and open the passenger doors. We each take a car seat so that the other three can get out.

Keira still hasn't looked up to see the full parking lot. At this point, I don't know that she'll notice anything until she walks through the door and sees everyone waiting for us. Anthony takes her hand as soon as he gets out and pulls her towards the door. He knows what's going on and I'm honestly surprised he hasn't spilled the beans to her yet.

"Aunt K, you ready?" he asks, just before opening the door for her.

"Ready for what honey?" she asks, looking at him.

"You'll see. Let's go," he says, the excitement radiating from every part of his little body.

He finally manages to get the door open and I can hear all the talking inside stop. Keira looks up and takes in every member of the three clubs standing there waiting for us. Skylar, Bailey, Maddie, Darcy, Shy, Ma, and now Melody are in front of everyone. They want to be the first ones to embrace Keira and see the babies.

"Welcome back!" everyone shouts.

"What is this?" Keira asks.

"Since things happened and you couldn't wait to have a baby shower, we brought the baby shower to you." Bailey says, hugging my girl.

"You guys shouldn't be here. There's too much danger right now," Keira tells everyone.

"There is danger," Grim starts. "However, we have two new members of the club and it's time we celebrate that. With all of us here, we're gonna make sure everyone is protected and prospects are surrounding the entire clubhouse. It's good Keira."

I see my girl relax a little and take in the main room of the clubhouse. There are pink and blue streamers and balloons, a table with nothing but gifts that make their way onto the floor, two more tables with nothing but food, and in the center two new glider rockers. The girls lead us over to the rockers and tell us to sit while they look at the babies still sleeping.

"Thank you for putting them in the outfits we sent down," Ma tells Keira, pulling her in for a hug.

"Of course. Thank you so much for sending them to us."

"Any time at all honey. Now, you tell us what you want to do first. We're not doing any of the games or anything because I'm sure that you're going to want to rest soon. So, it's either open gifts up or eat."

"I think I'd like to start with the gifts."

"If she gets hungry, I'll get her a plate Ma," I tell her, looking at my girl.

"You better Blade. I wouldn't want to have to beat your ass in front of everyone here," Ma says, to the laughter of everyone surrounding us.

"My girl will want for nothin'. Both my girls and my son won't ever want for anythin'."

The girls start bringing the gifts over and put them down between the two of us. I guess I'll be helping her open everything. That's completely fine by me because it means that we get to the wedding portion of the day even quicker. I can't wait to have Keira as my wife and I wish that we decided to tell everyone, but she wants to keep it quiet so we will. At least for now.

As we begin opening all the gifts, everyone surrounds us and I'm hit with an overwhelming sense of family and belonging. Melody and Bailey are each holding one of the twins after they woke up, Keira fed them, and they got changed. Keira is getting teary-eyed over all the gifts and how much it means to her that everyone from all three clubs got the babies something.

"I'm goin' to say now that I did get Kenyon and Cory things, but they didn't make it here. They couldn't kitten. I got the nursery set you wanted and it's already set up in the house. I also get them some clothes, blankets, bottles, and a few other things."

"You didn't have to do that babe. I have money that Slim's putting up and I was just going to send that to you."

"It's not just your responsibility. They are our children and it's up to both of us to support them financially, emotionally, and to help them grow and learn the right way," I tell my girl.

"I know, but like you said, it's my part of the financial responsibility. I hope it doesn't come to that, but I know if it's Kenyon and Cory or me, I choose them every time. You won't stop me Blade. I will give myself over to Jason before any harm comes to them or you."

"Not havin' this discussion now."

I didn't realize that Grim and Glock were right behind us. I can feel the glares at the back of my head while I sit and continue opening gifts. It's not a good feeling to have and I know that I don't want to ever be on the receiving end again.

"We will be discussin' this later. Before anythin' else happens after this baby shower, we'll all be talkin' about that statement," Grim tells us. "And I mean all three clubs. We will be on the same page and you will know what's goin' to happen."

I look over at Keira and see that her face is now a sick shade of white. She's gone as pale as a ghost and I know she's scared of the upcoming conversation we're about to have with all three clubs. I rub her arm and try to give her comfort, even though I know it's not working.

We've opened all the gifts and now have a mountain of things for the babies. I don't see how we're going to run out of anything for a very long time. Keira says it will be gone before I know it though. We got everything from clothes, onesies, blankets, bottles, toys, diapers and wipes, pacifiers, and so much more.

Everyone has eaten and now we're just relaxing and having a good time. Well, everyone but Keira. She's putting on a good show but I can see the tension and nervousness pouring off her. Keira is only concentrating on the upcoming conversation. Which is about to happen right now if Grim, Gage, and Slim walking towards us means anything.

"Let's go," Grim says, not waiting for us to follow them.

I grab Keira's hand and help her up. She's looking all over the place trying to find a way out. There isn't a way out and she's not going to find any help from any of the girls. I'm sure they heard what's going on from their men and want this conversation to happen as much as I do.

Instead of going in to the room Slim uses for church, we head out the back of the clubhouse. It's still warm out even if it is getting pretty dark outside. I know that Slim has lights and everything else out here right by the back door. He's got a pretty sweet setup on the patio before the fire pits start and the picnic tables are set up.

"Alright, we overheard a conversation that I'm sure we weren't meant to hear," Grim begins, making sure Keira and I are front and center. "We all know what's goin' on with Keira and the fuckwad that thinks he's gonna sell her to the highest bidder. What you don't know is that she thinks she's goin' to give herself up to him in order to protect her old man and children."

Grim pauses and lets that information sink in with everyone. I can hear some men growling and others are muttering curses. Keira is standing next to me with her face downward so that she doesn't have to look at anyone. I know she does this when she doesn't want to face something hard and it's probably a mechanism that's left over from her childhood. Even though I don't know all the details, I do know that it wasn't good. You can tell by watching her when she's in certain situations.

"Now, Gage, Slim, and myself have been in constant contact since this all began. We haven't told Keira or Blade what we've been talkin' about. This is mainly to protect Keira and ensure that Blade doesn't flip the fuck out," Grim continues before turning it over to Slim.

"We've had someone on our girl from the second she left with the fuckin' twatwaffle. Someone has been studyin' his every move and seein' where he goes when he's not with Keira.

He's in bed with some pretty heavy hitters. And we're pretty sure that he's involved with the cartel. I'm not sure in what capacity just yet, but we're workin' on findin' that out now. Fox, Tech, and Irish have been doin' everythin' they can to find any and all information on this man. Unfortunately, it's not easy. There's nothin' on him. That's why we've been havin' them followed. Closely," Slim states. "Keira, you will not be turnin' yourself back over to the scum-bag. When everyone heads back to Clifton Falls in a few days, you will be headin' back with them."

Keira stands there stunned. She never expected to be coming home with us so soon. I knew she thought eventually we'd be heading back together, but not right now. Honestly, it's probably safer for her to be there away from Jason than still here where he knows she is.

"Keira, I can see the panic on your face darlin'," Gage says. "I'm sendin' a few of my guys over with you for about a month or so, and I believe Slim is too. We'll let you get into your own routine and see if Jason figures out where you went. I'm sure it's not goin' to be hard since he's already been there once. But, this gives Grim and the guys enough time to get everythin' in place as far as your protection goes. Until then, Wood, Killer, Crash, and Trojan will be your security team. They'll be crashin' at your house, followin' you everywhere you go, and posted outside when you're home."

I nod, liking the sound of what they've come up with so far. It's not ideal, but it's better than spreading our guys thin until everything is settled. I'm guessing Grim is going to have Rage working around the clock to get our house done so that we can be inside the fence and not somewhere else.

"Rage isn't here because he's got three crews workin' on your house. When we left a few days ago, it was honestly only goin' to be a matter of days before it was ready to go," Grim tells us, almost reading my mind.

I simply nod and let him know with a look that we have somewhere we need to be. I'm pretty sure that we've gone over everything that they're willing to share in front of my girl. Now, it's time that Glock, Melody, Keira, and I get ready to meet with the judge. Even though we're not leaving the clubhouse, there's still things that need to be done.

The first thing I need to do is talk to Ma and Pops and see if they'll keep an eye on the twins. Then I need to get the rings from the room without Keira seeing what I'm doing. Melody went out earlier and got a new dress for her that she doesn't know about. And, we're going to be staying in one of the cabins out back. Grim and Bailey will be keeping the babies overnight. Although, I don't know that Keira will be on board with that so it might end up being just for a few hours so we can be alone. I know we can't do anything yet, but I just want some one-on-one time with my girl.

"I think that a few of you have somewhere to be right now," Slim says, a smirk gracing his face. "So, you guys get out of here and we'll see you when we see you."

I grab Keira's hand and lead her away from my brothers. Glock follows behind us and I know we're going to his room to get ready, so I drop her off with Melody as soon as we get in the door. Glock doesn't say anything until we get in their room and the door closes behind us.

"Are you sure you know what you're doin'?" he asks me.

"Never been more sure of anythin' in my life. She's the one I wanna grow old with, I want to wake up with her in my arms every day, and I can't imagine anyone else havin' my babies. She's already given me two gorgeous babies and I know it's just a matter of time before we have more."

"Knew you were. Just wanted to make sure it was for the right reasons. I might not be close to your girl, but Mel is. I'm not gonna see her hurt because you think you have to marry her because of the twins. Not enough of one and you'll both end of regrettin' it."

I don't say anything in response. Instead I get my things together and head into the shower. I'm ready for us to be married now and I know it's going to be at least a little while still. Melody is going to make sure my girl looks good and that's going to take time. Darcy is here so they might as well put her talents to good use.

Glock rushes in after me so that he can get ready. I know he's ready to get this done with so he's going to be just as quick as I am. Before I can think about anything else, there's a knock on his door. Opening it up, I see Pops standing there.

"Hey son. I hear congratulations are in order. More than for just Kenyon and Cory."

"Yes sir. I'm officially makin' her mine today."

"You got a rag already?" he asks.

"No. I'll take care of that once we get home. I don't want to push too much shit on her at once."

"I can see your point. I just wouldn't wait on it too long. I know how these women think sometimes when they see the other old ladies wearin' theirs and they don't have one. Don't want that girl thinkin' those thoughts."

"No, I don't. Did have a question for you though. Can you and Ma watch the kids for a little bit? Just while we do the ceremony. Keira didn't want anythin' fancy and she doesn't want a party afterwards."

"Of course we will. But, you know these women won't let you guys get away without havin' a party of some sort. Today should be proof of that with the baby shower."

"I know. I'm just not gonna say anythin' to her until it's time to go. That way she can't bitch about havin' it done."

Pops starts laughing his ass off. Probably because he knows as well as I do that it's more than likely not going to work out the way that I want it to. Keira will find out about the party and try to put a stop to it if she finds out about it. Melody and the rest of the girls won't let that fly though. If there's one thing they love to do, it's plan a party celebrating something. What's bigger to celebrate than a baby being born or a brother getting married?

"I'm gonna go let Ma know we're gonna have those adorable babies with us for a while. You go marry your girl. Did you get rings or anythin' son?"

"Yeah. She doesn't know it yet, but I bought her weddin' set a while ago. I knew deep down it was always gonna be Keira. It just took her leavin' for me to realize what I truly have with her."

"Sometimes it just works out like that son. It's a hard lesson to learn and one you won't ever repeat again. Trust me, I know," Pops says, making his way out of the room.

I'm not sure what he's talking about, but I'm glad that I woke up before it was too late and I really didn't lose her. I don't know what I'd do if I actually did lose her. It's something I won't ever have to worry about happening now.

As I've been sitting here thinking about losing my girl, more time has passed then what I realize. Next thing I know, Melody is in her room telling me that it's time to head down and wait for my girl to walk out. She also gives me the gift that

Keira somehow managed to get me. Yeah, I got her something too, but I've had it with me for a little while.

Opening up the gift, I see that she got me a silver bracelet with a matching necklace. It almost looks like a tire tread from a tire burning rubber. I've never seen anything like it before. My girl definitely knows me and knows that I would fall in love with it as soon as I saw it. I'll have to see where she got it from so I can see if they have anything else like it. Maybe for a female.

Melody takes one look at my face and before I know it I have her and Glock peering over my shoulder to see what I got. I pull it out and Melody has tears in her eyes. She obviously had no clue that my girl was getting me anything. Melody helps me put both on before Glock and I head downstairs.

I figured by now the nerves would start to kick in. I'm doing something I never thought I'd be doing and I don't know what to expect. However, I'm as calm as ever and I don't even care what to expect after we get married. Keira is my world and has already given me two beautiful children. I can't wait until we add more to the mix.

Before too long, I hear the girls making their way into the room that Slim told us to use so no one else would know. What I see has my breath leaving me and I can't help the smile I know lights up my face. Not only does my girl look absolutely amazing in the simple, white dress that Melody got her. But,

Pops is walking her in to me. No wonder he came in and talked to me while we were getting ready. Somebody either told him what was going on, or he just knew like he usually does. Either way, he didn't let my girl walk in by herself. He's choosing to give her away to me. This moment means more to me than he could possibly understand.

Keira

Today is the day that I marry the love of my life. After I sent Melody in with the present I got for Blade, Pops made an appearance in the room we're staying in. I know that no one opened their mouths about what's going on today, but he just seemed to know. I've never had any real interaction with him, but from listening to everyone, I know he is respected and loved by everyone associated with the club.

"Hey sweetheart. How are you doin'?" he asks, closing the door behind him.

"I'm doing okay. How are you doing?"

"I'm good. Now, I know you and my brother are gettin' married today. No one opened their mouth, I just got a feelin' that this was gonna happen. I'm not sure what your family situation is, but I would like the honor of walkin' you down to Blade."

There's nothing I can say for a few minutes. Tears are forming in my eyes and I can't stop them from starting to spill over. This man is offering to take the place of my dad when I haven't talked to him in over ten years. Hell, I don't even know where my dad lives anymore. My mother isn't in my life either. Quite frankly, I've been better off without them around. And my children will never know the chaos that surrounded me until I left home when I was fifteen. Here this man is, barely knowing me, offering to be there for us on one of the most important days in our life.

"I'd be honored to have you walk me down to Blade," I tell him, opening my arms for a hug.

Pops pulls me in for a huge hug. This is the kind of man that I wish I had for a father. Not the one that I did have that cared more about his latest piece of ass then he did my mom or me. Thankfully I was an only child so no one else had to go through what I did. Knowing my dad was cheating with a different woman almost daily drove my mother crazy. No matter what she did, he wouldn't stop. Most nights I would either hear my mom crying herself to sleep, if she slept at all, or I'd hear them arguing nonstop. It got to the point that when I was about ten years old, I was taking care of myself. Any meals I ate, I made myself. My laundry was done by me. All of the housework was done by me. Hell, I was even grocery shopping and getting everything else we needed for the house. The only thing either one of my parents did was give me the money I needed for it.

Instead of leaving me alone in the room, Pops stays with me. I'm sure Melody told him that we didn't have long until we had to meet my man downstairs. She shouldn't be long giving Blade the gift I got him, and then they'll be heading down. Now, it's just a matter of time until the rest of my life starts. The best part of my life.

"You ready hun?" Melody asks, coming back through the door.

"I am."

"By the way, love the set you got him. It's awesome! Where did you find it?"

"I'll never tell!" I say, making Melody pout because I won't let her in on my secret.

Glen is actually the one that got the necklace and bracelet for me. I just gave him a little bit of information as to what I wanted. At this point, I'm not even sure where he got it, but I fell in love with it as soon as I saw it. Hopefully Blade likes it.

"Alright girls, let's get you down to your man and get this show on the road," Pops tells us. "I'm goin' to leave as soon as I hand you over. Don't want anyone else to know what you're doin'."

"Thank you. We'll tell everyone as soon as things calm down. We just didn't want to wait to get married."

"You don't have to explain anythin' to me sweetheart. Everyone does it in their own way. This is how you guys want to do it, then it's all you."

I'm glad that he understands and isn't upset with the choice that we've made. We're not doing it this way to leave anyone out. I just didn't want a big fuss made when everything with Jason is up in the air. Knowing him, he would do everything in his power to make sure this didn't happen. He'd figure out some way to get into Slim's clubhouse. Or, he'd make friends with one of the club girls to get the information he needed.

"Fuck!" I say, a thought coming to me.

"What's the matter sweetheart?" Pops asks me.

"I need to talk to Slim. He needs to know that Jason will use the club girls if he thinks they'll give him an in for information."

"I'll let him know. You concentrate on gettin' married," Pops tells me, continuing to make our way down to Blade.

"Thank you Pops," I tell him, taking his arm and letting him lead me to my man.

By the time we round the corner, there's butterflies in my stomach and I wonder if Blade really wants to go through with this. All of my doubts creep back in and I feel like I'm trapping him into marrying me just because of the twins. In the back of my mind, a voice is telling me to turn around and run as fast as I can. Set Blade free to live his life without the twins and I trapping him. But, then I wouldn't be with the love of my life and I'd constantly be running from Jason, looking over my shoulder wondering when he's going to find me.

"Don't do it," Pops says. "You are his world and he wouldn't be doin' this if he didn't want to."

I chuckle a little bit at the fact that Pops seems to know everything that's going on, and through people's heads, before anyone else does. It's kind of creepy, but it's also comforting to know that my doubts are just that, doubts. I nod my head to acknowledge that I heard him and we continue on our way to my future.

The smile I see light up Blade's face tells me that we're doing the right thing. I can see love shining from his eyes and it proves that he's not just telling me words that he thinks I want to hear. When he tells me that he wants to marry me, he sincerely means it.

Pops stops just before we get to Blade and we wait until the judge asks who is giving me away. "I am, along with the entire Wild Kings MC and the Phantom Bastards MC."

For a minute, no one moves and no one says a word. I've never heard anyone be given away at a wedding by an individual and two entire MCs. Blade and Glock suddenly get huge smiles on their faces because I'm guessing that you never know what you're going to get when it comes to Pops. He genuinely cares about everyone tied to the club. That's why he walked me to Blade and gave me away. And gave credit to both clubs. Pops doesn't need any recognition for the things that he does and gives to others.

"Okay. Let's continue with the ceremony then," the judge says.

The entire time the judge is talking, I'm not focused on what he's saying or doing. I'm focused on the man standing before me and our little family. Blade and I stare at one another and I don't even know if he's hearing a word that the judge is saying. Before too long, I see Glock nudge Blade.

"You can say your vows," the judge tells him.

"Keira, in the beginning, I didn't want anythin' serious. I didn't want to live the life I grew up watchin' with my parents. But, you broke down my defenses without even tryin'. When you left, my world got dark and the only thing I could think of was gettin' you back. You have already given me the greatest gift of all by makin' me a dad. Now, I want to spend the rest of our lives treatin' you like the queen you deserve to be treated. I will do my very best to make you happy, no matter what it takes. I love you more than my life. Kenyon, Cory, and you are the three most important people to me."

"Keira, you may say your vows," the judge repeats.

"Every day since I met you, I've become a stronger person. I still have my doubts, including on the walk down to you. But, I overcome them and move on. You are the love of my life and I can't wait to see what the rest of our lives bring. I will do my very best to love you and make you as happy as you can possibly be. Kenyon, Cory, and you are my entire life and I would do absolutely anything to protect you all. I love you more than you'll ever know."

The judge tells us that we can exchange rings after repeating him. Not only did I get Blade the matching bracelet and necklace, but there's a ring that almost matches the set. I turn to Melody and she hands it to me. Repeating after the judge, I slip the ring on Blade's finger. When it's Blade's turn to repeat the same words, I'm shocked to see him have not only a wedding band, but a matching engagement ring. The set is silver and it has a red stone surrounded by diamonds. Going down the side of the ring are alternating red stones and diamonds. It's the most beautiful ring I've ever seen and I can't stop the tears. Blade reaches up and wipes them away with his thumbs ever so gently.

"I now pronounce you husband and wife, you may kiss your bride," the judge says.

Blade barely waits for the judge to finish the sentence before he's holding my face between his hands and gently kissing me. It's a kiss that I've never felt before. He's so gentle and almost hesitant to kiss me. Blade is known for taking what he wants, without force, but not being gentle in doing so.

"May I announce for the very first time, Mr. and Mrs. Michael Branch," the judge says before moving over to have Melody and Glock sign in the witness spots to make our marriage legal.

The entire time, Blade continues to kiss me. That is until Glock taps him on the shoulder so that we can add our signatures to the license. Before leaving, the judge tells us that he'll file it with the necessary people and we should have our copy soon. We thank him and he leaves the room. Blade, Melody, Glock, and myself take a few minutes for ourselves to celebrate before we head back in the main room of the clubhouse.

"I'm so happy for you two," Melody tells us, wrapping me in a hug.

"Thank you," I tell her, hugging her back. "I'm happy that you're here and were able to be here for it. It wouldn't have been the same without you."

"I wouldn't miss it for the world. Blade, you're lucky that my man stopped bein' pigheaded and I made it here. Otherwise, you might be missing an appendage or two right now."

"You know why I didn't want you comin' here," Glock says.

"I do. And I also know that I'm being careful. Nothing is going to happen, so quit worrying about every little thing."

"Guys, you do know that at least the two of us now know that you're having another baby. Right?" I ask.

"What?" Glock asks, feigning shock at that statement. "We just wanted to make sure that she made it to the safe point in her pregnancy before we announced it to anyone."

"We won't tell anyone. I basically told you at the hospital I knew what was goin' on," Blade says. "It's not gonna be long before everyone else figures it out either."

"I know. Glock is the one that wants to wait. He's worried something is going to happen since he wasn't around when I was pregnant for Anthony."

We all take another few minutes to just talk and relax before making our way back out to my babies. Ma and Pops are surrounded by the rest of the old ladies and a few of the other kids. Jameson is right in the middle being his normal protective self. I can see him trying to make sure no one gets too close to the twins and that they're both okay.

A smile overtakes my face as Blade wraps his arm around me and we watch our family. Both clubs are our family and I don't know where we'd be without them. I know that I can't thank them enough for everything that they've done for us, and me personally. Slim took me in when he didn't have to and now my life is fuller than I ever dreamed possible.

Chapter Nine

Blade

IT'S BEEN ABOUT A MONTH and a half since Keira and I brought our children home and got married. Within a week of us getting married, Rage had our home finished and it turned out amazing. Keira had tears in her eyes as she walked through it, going from room to room and inspecting everything. Somehow, I managed to have Rage build her perfect home.

For right now, the twins are going to be sharing a nursery. When they're old enough they will have their own bedrooms that are already painted a blue for Kenyon and yellow for Cory. We're not set on the colors because who knows what they're going to want their rooms to look like, but it's a start for now.

Since I no longer needed the house that we were renting, Grim and I decided to buy it. We're going to keep it and hold it until we find a worthy individual to rent it to. Basically, the girls are all getting behind those that have suffered at the hands of domestic violence. So, what better way to help them out than to have a place that we can shelter a woman, or small family, that is trying to get away from their abuser. The girls fell in love with the idea and I'm glad that I talked to Grim about buying it.

Keira has been a champion. I've had to go away on club business a few times. The first time was just after we moved into our new home. So, she not only had to put our home together, but she had the twins to look after as well. When I talked to Melody, she didn't ask a single person for help with the house or Kenyon and Cory. The girls all chipped in, but she did most of it herself. Not once did she bitch, whine, or complain about me not being there to help. Instead, she made our home as cozy as it can be and someplace I don't ever see myself leaving, and took care of the kids.

We've talked about her going back to work, but I don't think she honestly wants to. It's fine by me if she wants to stay home and raise our children. There are things that she can do from home to make money if she truly feels the need to do so. Which brings me to today. I happened to find something that I think needs to be addressed. So, I go in search of my wife to have a talk.

"Kitten, where are you?" I call out, leaving our bedroom.

"In the nursery."

Making my way there, I pause at the doorway to admire the view before me. Keira is holding Cory and rocking her back to sleep. Kenyon is already sound asleep in his crib and it's just a matter of minutes before Cory joins him. I can see her little eyes fluttering closed before she pops them back open. Cory is so curious about everything that she hates taking a nap. Our little princess is already afraid that she's going to miss out on something happening, that she'd rather be crabby than to get some sleep during the day.

Seeing Keira get ready to put Cory in her crib, I stay put. There are days that I walk in and Cory wants nothing to do with Keira putting her to sleep. I end up having to do it. I don't mind those days at all, I cherish the fact that my daughter can be a daddy's girl. Today, I need to talk to my girl though, so I stay rooted to my spot in the doorway until I know Keira is on her way towards me.

"Did you need something babe?" she asks, joining me in the hallway.

"Yeah. I was goin' through the last of the boxes in the closet and I came across somethin'. Mind tellin' me what this is?" I ask, holding out a stack of handwritten papers.

"Oh, um…." Keira starts, a blush creeping up her pale face. "Well, in my spare time, I've been doing a little writing. It's nothing major and I was honestly going to just burn it."

"Don't you dare!" I tell her. "I've read a little bit of it and I think you have some real talent. I think you need to keep going and see what happens."

"What do you mean?"

"What are your plans for this? Were you plannin' on turnin' it into a book?" I ask her, honestly interested in what her answer will be.

"I hadn't really thought about it. I mean I was just sitting there one day and this idea popped into my head. I started writing it down on paper and the words just started flowing."

"Like I said, I think you should go for it and see what you can do with it. There's got to be someone out there that can help you out."

"Are you sure? You don't think it's a silly dream and a waste of time?" she asks me, looking down and away from me.

"Kitten, I think what I've read so far is excellent and you have a real talent. Please, let me get things you need to do this for real and we'll see what happens. At the very least, you'll be tryin' somethin' that you obviously want to do."

"Okay. I'll give it a shot then," she says, taking the papers from my hand and heading back in the bedroom with them.

"Now, I'm goin' to go out for a little while. I'll be back and I think Melody said somethin' about you goin' over there to help her out."

"Yeah. She wants to basically just have company while she does her housework. Anthony is over with Jameson and Glock is doing something for the club."

"I'll see you in a little bit then."

Making my way out to my truck, I place a call to Irish. I need him to go with me since he knows way more about computers and that shit than I do. After explaining what I want to do for Keira, Irish is more than happy to go with me so I can make my girl's dream a reality. Honestly, I wasn't lying when I told her I thought what I read so far was amazing. I can't wait for her to get it finished and see what she can really do. We'll do whatever we have to in order to let her publish a story, or however many she can write.

Irish and I have been gone most of the day and I think I bought out the entire store. But, hopefully I got everything that my girl will need in order to write her books. If not, we'll go out and get what she does need. Money isn't an object for me and I have no problem spending it on her. Besides, who knows how much she'll be able to make by doing something she obviously loves.

We make our way into the house after placing a call to Melody and making sure that Keira was at her house already. I want this to be a complete surprise and she can't see anything until we have everything set up.

There's already a room in the house that we haven't set up yet. Now, we have something to put in there. I'm going to make Keira her own office so she has a place all her own to do what she has to do. I even bought extra baby monitors so she can write while Kenyon and Cory are napping. As an added bonus, she can make a living and stay home with the kids. I could tell when we've talked about it that she really wasn't looking forward to leaving them to find a job. Now she doesn't have to worry about it.

"You really went all out," Irish comments as we carry the last of the stuff in. "You sure it's worth it?"

"Absolutely. You didn't read what I did. Keira has the beginnin' of a really good story here and I can't wait to see where she takes it. Just so happens that it's an MC. And she hasn't even asked a single question about our club for her book. Somethin' tells me that she knows more than she lets on."

"What do you mean?" Irish asks.

"She doesn't bitch and whine when I have to leave on club business. When it comes to wantin' to know what's goin' on, she doesn't ask any questions. Just takes what I tell her and knows it's not everythin' there is to tell. I'm thinkin' she's been around a club before or she's done her research."

"You think she's attached to another club?" Irish asks me, the wheels starting to turn.

"If she has ties to another club, she hasn't had anythin' to do with them in a very long time," I tell him, not necessarily liking where his thoughts may be going.

"Blade, I didn't mean anythin' by it. I swear. I'm just curious."

"I may bring it up to her, but I don't need you runnin' your mouth to anyone until I know what's goin' on. If she doesn't have any ties to a club then I don't want to start trouble where none needs to be."

"I hear ya. Now, let's get this shit set up. I need to go check on the girl."

There's definitely something going on with Caydence and Irish. We've hardly seen anything from him unless it's mandatory club business. Even then, he's there the amount of time he has to be and then he's right back with Caydence and the baby. Ever since they adopted that little girl, things have changed with them and everyone has noticed it. We just can't do anything to help if they don't open up and let someone know what's going on.

It's been three hours and Irish and I are finally putting the finishing touches on everything that we've been putting together. Irish even went and put a few programs that she might need on her brand-new laptop and desk top computer. I wasn't sure what she would prefer and I couldn't ruin the surprise by asking her, so I just got both. Now, it's time for him to head back to his woman so I can get mine over her and show her.

"Kitten, I need you to come home now," I tell her, when she answers her phone.

"Is everything okay?" she asks, the concern evident in her voice.

"Yeah. I'll be there in a second to help you bring the kids home."

"Okay. I'll get them ready."

Hanging up, I make my way next door to help get my family home. Melody and Keira are just strapping the kids into the stroller as I walk up to the back door. Holding it open, I wait until Keira is through the door before pulling her in for a kiss.

"What's going on?" she asks me.

"Nothin'. I got a surprise for you and I'm excited for you to see it."

"Okay. Well, then let's get home so you can show me."

Walking into our home, I help Keira get the twins settled in so I can show her the surprise. As I lead her back downstairs, I can feel the tension mounting. Keira obviously has never had anyone do anything nice for her just because they wanted to. That's going to fucking change.

"Alright kitten, you ready?" I ask, putting my hand on the doorknob.

"As ready as I'll ever be," she tells me.

I open the door and let her go in before me. She stops as soon as she enters the room and just stares. In front of the wall is a desk so she can look outside while she's writing. I got her a filing cabinet, a printer and paper, notebooks, pens, a bookshelf, and a ton more things she may need.

"Why did you do this?" she asks, finally turning towards me with tears running down her face.

"So you can follow your dream. Kitten, if writin' and makin' books is what you want to do, then I'm goin' to make sure you can do it. Anythin' you need, I have no problem gettin' or payin' for," I tell her, wiping her tears away.

"I've never had anyone do this, babe. Never."

"I can tell. But, you need to get used to me bein' there to support you no matter what. I do have a question for you and I need an honest answer."

"What's your question?"

"I noticed you were writin' an MC book. How do you know so much about clubs?" I ask her, making her look me in the eyes when she answers.

"Well, you know the shitty upbringing I had. My dad wasn't necessarily a part of a club, but he did associate with one. I paid attention to what I saw because I wanted to stay as far away from them as I possibly could. They scared the hell out of me. Especially one of the guys. The looks he gave me were not the ones a man of his age should've been giving a young girl. We even went to the clubhouse a few times. You know, when my dad actually took me somewhere with him."

"That's why you don't ask me questions about what I'm doin' or want to know more than I tell you. Now, do you by chance remember the name of the club your dad had ties to?"

"I think it was the Soulless something or other."

"The Soulless Bastards?" I ask her.

"Yeah, I think that was their name."

"Well, you don't ever have to worry about them kitten. That club doesn't exist anymore. We made sure of that," I tell her, wanting her to know that she doesn't have anything to worry about.

"Are you sure? Because they were pretty big when I was younger. I mean there were a ton of members."

"I'm sure. We made sure that they don't exist and can never hurt anyone else again. Ever," I tell her, needing her to know that she won't ever have to think about them again. "Now, I'm goin' to leave you here so you can get started doin' your thing. I know that Irish put some office program on your computers so you can type out what you've already hand-written."

Keira just nods at me and heads over towards the desk. I did manage to get her a flash drive so she could save all of her work to transfer it from one computer to another. I close her in her new office and head upstairs to finish going through the boxes in the closet.

Keira

I can't believe that Blade went out and bought me what he thought I would need in order to write. I've always wanted to be an author, I've just never had the courage to follow through with that dream. There are a ton of stories that I've started and thrown away. The one that Blade found is an idea that I've been toying with for an MC story. Just recently I found the indie community where authors publish their own books and do a majority of the work themselves. Most of these books I've read have been MC. Now, I may not know much, but maybe this is some type of therapy for me letting out parts of my story of the small amount of dealings I had with the MC when I was younger.

Blade already has my handwritten story sitting on my desk, so I turn on my desk top and let it boot up. I get everything set up where I want it and turn on music once the computer is ready to go. I open the writing program and just go to town. Within an hour, I have every word I've hand-written typed out. And I had written close to fifty pages. From there the words just continue to flow. Before I know it, I've typed out almost forty pages in a matter of hours.

I've had no interruptions from Blade or the twins waking up. Blade has been true to his word and let me do my thing. But, I can't sit in here anymore and continue to sit in front of the computer. I need to get something to eat and check on my family. Even though I'm following my dream, I'm not going to cast my family to the side and ignore them. They are, and always will be, my number one priority.

Walking into the kitchen I see Blade starting to make dinner. He's taken a shower and is standing there in nothing but a pair of sweatpants. They're riding low on his hips and my mouth starts watering. It's been so long since I've been able to be with him. Hell, we couldn't even do anything on our wedding night. As long as the twins are still sleeping, I think it's about time to change that fact.

Before I can make any moves, he turns around and catches me staring at him. I can see the smirk that takes over his face because he knows where my head's at. His eyes darken and I know he's following the same thoughts that I'm having right now. I'm not going to make it easy though. So, I turn on my heel and make my way upstairs to our bedroom.

As I walk upstairs, I start removing one piece of clothing at a time. I leave a path upstairs and I'm hoping that Blade will be following me. Finally naked, I climb on our bed and lay back against the pillows waiting for my man to make an appearance. He doesn't disappoint. Within a few seconds I can hear him running up the stairs. A smile spreads across my face as I am finally going to get what I want.

Blade opted to also take his clothes off on his way upstairs. So, when he enters the bedroom, I get to see him in all of his naked glory. My man is hot as fuck and I love seeing him naked. Since I first met him though, he has added a ton of muscle to his body. I'm guessing it's from all the workouts he's been doing with Tank.

"Are you sure you're ready for this kitten?" he asks, standing at the end of the bed.

"I'm more than ready babe. It feels like it's been so long," I tell him, the need I'm feeling making me sound desperate.

No more words are said as Blade climbs on the bed and starts kissing his way up my body. My hands make their way to his shoulders as he stops at my thighs. As he stops and stares up at me, I can see every emotion running through his eyes. Breaking eye contact, Blade focuses on my pussy and I hold my breath as he lowers his head and swipes his tongue from my opening to my clit for the first time. The more that he runs his tongue up and down, sucking on my clit, the tighter my grasp becomes in the sheets. I can already feel my orgasm building and I know that it's going to be intense and quick.

"Blade…." I moan out.

"It's Michael now kitten. Only Michael when we're in bed."

"Mi-michael," I moan, my body starting to shake as the coil winds tighter and tighter. "More. Please!"

Blade inserts a finger in me as he zeros in on my clit with his mouth. He bites and sucks as he pushes and pulls two fingers in me. Because it's been a while I can feel him trying to stretch me a little bit, getting me ready for him.

"So. Close," I moan, starting to squirm on the mattress.

Blade wraps his arms around my thighs, holding me in place. I tell him he's torturing me when he does this, but he says he's giving me nothing but pleasure. It only takes one more nip on my clit and I feel myself explode around his fingers.

Before I can completely come down, Blade has his cock at my entrance and is kissing me like his life depends on it. Entering me slowly, I arch my back at the fullness I'm already feeling. Finally, he's completely buried in me and he stops moving. I don't want to wait though. So, I start to move my hips, letting him know that I'm fine without having to say anything to him. Taking the hint, Blade starts a slow pace, pulling almost all the way out before pushing back in. I meet him thrust for thrust and it's not long before his pace quickens. Knowing that he's going to wait until I cum at least once or twice more before he lets himself find his release, I move my hand down between our sweat-slickened bodies. Finding my clit, I start to rub circles around it before moving my hand lower to feel him as he's pulling out of me.

"Keep that up and I'm not goin' to last long kitten," Blade grits out.

I want to see him lose control though. I want the roughness that he used to give me, so I keep my hand where it is. After a few more pumps, Blade does what I want and I feel his control starting to slip away. He's not going to give up control that easily though. Pulling all the way out, he tells me to get on all fours, knowing I love this position.

Without waiting, I feel him slam back into me as soon as I'm in the position he wants me in. The pace is quick as he reaches an arm around me to rub on my clit. Leaning farther over me, Blade starts kissing down my back. As he's kissing his way back up, I turn my head to the side knowing that he's going to want my mouth next. Just as our lips touch, he brings his other hand to my hip and I can feel his fingers dig in. This is my first cue that he's getting close and trying to hold his release off.

"Give it to me," He grits out.

One hard pinch on my clit is all I need to send me flying over the edge again. I yell out his name and throw my head back. My entire body is shaking and I know that he's about to follow me over the edge. So, I squeeze my muscles around him and feel him still behind me. Blade growls out my name as his release overtakes him. Still slowly moving in and out, I can feel his body shake against mine before he lowers us to the bed. He turns us so we're laying on our side as he holds me from behind, not losing our connection.

"So. Good," I mutter, feeling my eyelids getting heavy.

Blade rubs my stomach as we both come down and try to slow our breathing down. I wrap my arm over his to get him to stop and just lay with me. When I was in Benton Falls, this is what I missed the most about being with Blade. Him just holding me while we gather ourselves. Before I can get too comfortable though, I feel him pulling away from me. I know he's only going to get cleaned up real quick before he brings a washcloth in to clean me up. It's the same every single time. As soon as he's done, he makes sure the baby monitor is on and lays back down behind me. We wrap ourselves around one another and I fall asleep before I can say anything to him.

Chapter Ten

Keira

IT'S BEEN AN INTERESTING few weeks. I've been working on writing this book and Blade has done everything in his power to help me. If I need the housework done, dinner needs to be cooked, the twins need to be watched, or anything else, he is all over it. I've enjoyed the time I've had to write and get this book closer and closer to completion. If anything, I'm writing for me and no one may ever see it. Other than Blade because he's already said that he will be reading this book.

I'm sitting in the office when Melody comes bursting through the door with Glen on her heels. She's panicked and telling me that Anthony is sick as fuck and needs medicine. She doesn't want to take him anywhere and she doesn't want me to stay with him because of the twins. So, she wants me to run to the store for her to get what he needs. Anthony doesn't get sick often, but when he does, it's bad. Saving my work, I grab my purse and keys before heading out the door.

Just before I make it to the pharmacy, I spot a beat-up, rusted-out truck following me. I've never seen it before and I'm not sure what to do. Blade had to go out of town for the day so I don't want to call him. The prospect that's been at the house, I can't remember his name, is supposed to be following me, but he's not. I wonder where the fuck he is.

I get to the part of the road that's got a slight curve to it when the truck makes its move. As I go to go around the curve, whoever is driving the truck speeds up and rams me in the ass end of my car. Because I'm going around a curve, the car starts to fishtail before going into a spin. I have no clue what to do other than not to touch the brakes. So, I just wing it and I think I end up making it worse. What the fuck am I going to do now? is the last thought that I have before everything goes black.

As I start to wake up, I can feel pain radiating through my body. The worst of it is coming from my wrist though. And it's even worse because my hands are tied behind my back wrapped around a pole. The angle is awkward and I know that before I get found, my wrist is going to be broken for sure.

Looking down, I see that my clothes are torn and I'm desperately trying to figure out what happened to me. Hell, right now I don't even know how long I've been gone. I don't know if anyone is looking for me, or if Blade's even back yet. But, the main thought running through my head is what Kenyon and Cory are doing right now.

Because there's hardly any light in here, I try to figure out where the hell I am. Based on the smell and the fact that there isn't any light, I'm guessing that I'm in a basement or some other dark ass, musty room. If I had one guess, I'm going to say that I'm at the house I was sharing with Jason. I really didn't venture down in the basement, but I know he had to be behind me being taken. There's nowhere else he'd take me. Only because he probably assumes that they wouldn't think to look somewhere so obvious.

Before I can try to figure anything else out, I hear a door open and someone walking down a flight of stairs. There's no point in pretending that I'm still knocked out so I stare in the direction I hear the movement coming from.

"I see your fat ass is finally awake," Jason says, turning on a light. "Thought you were going to die and then I'd be out the money I'm thinking I'm going to get out of you."

"You aren't getting shit from me, or from selling me," I spit out, letting my rage shine through. "My husband and his brothers will find me before you can do anything to me."

"What the fuck are you talking about?" Jason asks, getting even closer to me.

"I mean, Blade is my husband and there's nothing you can do to make that go away."

"You watch and see what the fuck I'll do bitch!" he screams, punching me dead in my face before landing a kick to my side.

I try my hardest not to scream out in pain or to flinch away from him. I swear it only turns him on to see the pain he's inflicting. So, I tighten my body up and wait for the next blow to land. Surprisingly, there's no other hit to hide from.

"I'll be back and you're gonna do exactly what I fucking tell you to do," Jason yells in my face, covering me with spit before leaving the room.

I have no clue what Jason is talking about. The only thing that I know is that I'm not going to do a fucking thing that he wants me to do. He can beat the shit out of me, hurl all of the insults he wants to, and whatever else he plans to do. There isn't anything in this world that could make me do anything that Jason wants me to do willingly. Well, if he decides to go after my family, I will have no choice but to do what he wants. I'm not risking them for anything in this world.

Apparently, I'm going to have nothing but time to think and plan on my hands. So, I try to figure out how I'm going to first get my hands undone so I can try to protect my wrist and hand. I can't take care of my family or write if I've got a busted-up hand.

I've all but lost track of time. Every time I get knocked out by one of Jason's goons, I don't know if it's been minutes, hours, or days. The only thing keeping me sane is the thought of my children, my husband, and my sister from another mister. I will do what I have to in order to get back to the people that own my heart.

"Ready for another round?" Jason asks, coming down the stairs.

"I'll go down fighting you nasty ass prick," I spit out.

"Today's the day that we take care of the pesky fact that you're married," Jason tells me, as I see the papers he's carrying out of the slit in my swollen eyes.

"What the fuck are you talking about?"

"I'm going to untie one of your hands and you're going to sign these annulment papers. That way my investors and buyers don't have to worry about a jealous husband trying to come after you."

"You think that me signing a piece of paper is going to make Blade and the rest of the clubs not come looking for me? You are so stupid if you think they won't come looking for me. And then I'll just marry the love of my life again," I tell Jason, getting ready to have the use of my hand to claw and fight my way free.

Jason walks slowly towards me and I can the see evil glint in his eye. "I know they won't come looking for you. I already have plans in place."

As soon as he gets close to me, Jason flips his phone around to show me pictures of my twins. In some they're with Melody and the rest of the girls, others they're with Blade doing various things. I can see the pain etched on Blade's face and I know these pictures are recent. I look up to Jason and see the hatred etched out on his features and wonder why I didn't see this shit coming from a mile away.

"You see, I can get to your little family any second I choose to," he tells me.

"You can go to fucking hell!" I spit in his face. "My family will never let you get close to them."

"I already am and your little club has no clue. You don't think I already have someone in place in that club? Then you guys are the ones that are stupid as fuck."

Jason unties my arm and I see that I have a small opportunity to make my move. Seeing Jason getting ready to turn his face back to me, I slam my hand up into his nose. I can hear the sickening crunch of his bones and for a second I'm stunned that it actually worked. Jason is stunned enough that I get my other hand free and I try to stand so I can make my way out of the dark, dingy basement.

My entire body hurts and it's crying out for me to stop and sit back down. I have to keep moving though, I have to do everything in my power to get away from here and back to my family. They are the only thing I'm concerned about right now. My health and wellbeing is at the back of my mind, it's not important to me.

I quickly make my way up the stairs and see that Jason left the door unlocked. Just as I go to open the door, he reaches out and grabs my ankle. Since my fight or flight instinct has kicked in, I kick my other foot out and land it square in his chest. He falls backwards and I don't stay to find out what happens to him.

The other men that work with, or for, Jason are only here at night. And Jason never comes down to see me when they're here. See, Jason has a small problem in that he doesn't know when to shut his mouth. He likes to brag and talk about every little thing going on. I guess it makes him feel like a big man to manhandle women and try to intimidate them. Since learning his game, it only makes me sick now.

Even though I'm sure that no one else is in the house, I still tread lightly, but quickly. We are in his house and that means that I know the layout and can figure out the quickest way to get out of here. Especially considering I hear Jason yelling and screaming from the basement. Going out the patio doors off the kitchen, I run to the side of the yard and the hole in the fence that never did get fixed. That's Jason's other problem. He's too arrogant to think that anyone can get one over on him.

I'm small enough to squeeze through the narrow opening and I know that once I'm through it, I'm home free. The neighbor is always up and I make my way to their back door. I pound and pound on it until Sue opens the door. She's in her mid-fifties and parties like she's in her twenties. Nothing illegal, she just likes to drink. A lot.

"I need your help," I tell her, the tears streaming down my face.

"What's going on dear?" she asks, ushering me inside and locking the door.

"I need you to call Slim. Please hurry before Jason figures out where I went," I plead with her.

Sue already has her phone in her hand and is putting it up to her ear. I can hear her talking and I know that she's talking to someone from the club. Before she can hang up there's a pounding on her front door and I start shaking so bad that I can't hardly stand. Jason can't possibly be here already. Seeing the panic overtake me, Sue pulls a chair out and sits me down while moving towards the front door.

"Are you sure it's one of your guys out there?" she asks Slim.

I can't hear his reply, but I hear Sue yell to the door. She's asking questions that only those close to me would know. And I'm guessing the person on the other side of the door is answering correctly. Soon, she's opening the door and I peer over to see that Killer and Wood are standing there. Wood rushes for me when he sees me sitting in one of her kitchen chairs and starts to check me over.

"Sweetheart, we have to get you to the hospital. Blade is on his way here and I know that he's goin' to want you there now," Wood tells me.

"I'm not going anywhere until I see my children and my husband," I tell him stubbornly, my tone letting him know that I'm not lying. I will sit right here until Blade, Kenyon, and Cory are here.

Blade

It's been days since my wife was taken from us. Melody is almost inconsolable, blaming herself. We've all tried to tell her that it wasn't her fault. Keira would have done the same thing for any one of the old ladies that asked her to run and get medicine for their child. Or anything else they asked her to do to help them.

When I'm not out looking for my girl, I'm with our children. Kenyon and Cory can both sense that something isn't right. They've been miserable and it takes shifts of everyone that's around the clubhouse to try to keep them from crying and getting at least a little bit of sleep. Hell, we're lucky if we can get them to eat most of the time. But, we keep trying until we can get something into their little bellies.

Tank has also stepped up the workouts again. I know he's trying to help me, but all I feel he's doing is taking me away from my kids and being out there looking for Keira. He keeps reminding me that he knows what I'm going through from when Maddie was kidnapped, but I can't hear it. Today is no exception. He's waiting on me right now to go over and get a workout in.

Just as I go to take Kenyon and Cory over to Skylar and Bailey, my phone rings. I look and see Slim calling me so I don't hesitate to answer it. This could be the call we've been waiting for.

"Tell me you got somethin'?" I ask.

"We might. I've had Killer and Wood sittin' on that fucker's house. There's been a lot of movement. Especially at night. It's all been guys, but they show up for a few hours and then leave," Slim tells me.

"What's that gotta do with anythin'?" I ask, confused.

"Why else would a bunch of guys show up to a house and then leave. I could see maybe once a week for a poker game or somethin'. But, not every night. I'm thinkin' he's got your girl there and they're helpin' dish out some punishment."

"Not one hair on her fuckin' head better be touched!" I scream into the phone. "I'm gonna head down there after makin' sure the girls will keep the kids."

"We don't know if she's there, Brother. You sure you wanna come down now?"

"No question about it."

I hang up the phone and make my way over to the clubhouse with the kids. Skylar and Bailey are waiting for me already. Without stopping to talk to anyone else, I make my way over to them. This makes the guys that are in the main room perk up. They can tell that something is about to go down and they're all getting ready to have my back.

"Can you guys keep the kids for a few days?" I ask, my tone is pleading. "Slim might have a lead and I need to be there for my girl."

"Of course we can. You do what you have to do and keep us updated," Bailey tells me.

As I go to turn around, I see most of my brothers have closed in around me. Grim, Joker, and Cage are the three closest to me.

"What's up Blade?" Grim asks me.

"Slim's had Wood and Killer on that douche canoe's house. There's been movement. If there's a chance that my wife is in there, I'm goin' to be there when she gets found," I tell my President. "I'm sorry Grim, but I have to be there for her."

"Go. Cage, Pops, Tank, and Rage are goin' with you. I'll take Kasey so you can go. She was talkin' about comin' over to play with Zander anyway," Grim tells Rage and I.

I don't even wait for anyone to finish talking or to see if they're getting ready. Making my way back to our home, I quickly pack a bag and make sure that my knives are packed. They don't call me Blade for no reason. I have special talents and can prolong someone's torture when it comes to playing with my knives. I've always had a fascination with them and I turned that into a talent when I got older.

Just as I go to leave our bedroom, I see the shirt that Keira stole from me. She doesn't wear anything to bed typically, but does like to have something on when she has to go to the nursery. My shirt was the first thing she grabbed one night and she hasn't given it back yet. I pick it up and it smells just like my kitten. Her touch is all around me in this house and I won't rest until she's back home where she belongs.

My bike was already parked at the clubhouse, so I head in that direction and see that I'm the last one there. Cage and Tank are already on their bikes while Rage is hugging his daughter goodbye. Before Kasey runs back into the clubhouse she runs over to me. Kasey hugs me and tells me to bring her auntie home. I look up at Rage and I know he can see the emotion on my face. Keira has felt like she didn't belong here, that no one noticed if she was around or not. Kasey telling me to bring her home just goes to prove that more people paid attention to her than she thinks. And I'm going to make sure she knows that when I bring her home.

"Let's roll!" Cage hollers after we all start our bikes.

I've ridden behind Cage and Tank on the way to Benton Falls. They knew if I were to take lead, I'd be breaking every rule of the road and almost kill myself in my attempt to get to my wife. They've been going faster than normal, but not fast enough for me. Nothing will be fast enough for me until I have my eyes on my girl and her in my arms.

We pull over to fill up. Since we weren't planning on making the trip, our bikes weren't filled up beforehand. In a way, I'm glad we did stop because I see that Slim called me about twenty minutes ago. I quickly call him back to see what update he has for me. I'm hoping that he's going to tell me that they know for a fact she's in Jason's house.

"Just stopped for a minute, Slim. What do you have for me?" I ask, getting surrounded again so I put my phone on speaker.

"Your wife got herself out. I'm not sure how she did it. All I know is that right before the neighbor called, Wood and Killer heard a ton of commotion coming from behind the house. They were on their way out back to check it out when I called them to tell them where Keira was. Killer went over to get Jason and he was already gone. We're keepin' her secure right now. Blade, she needs to get to the hospital and she refuses to go until you get here. Please tell me you're close," Slim tells me.

Cage looks at me and sees the torment on my face at hearing she needs to go to the hospital.

And that she got herself free. Don't get me wrong, I'm proud as fuck my girl saved herself. I just wish I were there for her. Instead I feel as if I let her down, like I wasn't there for her when I truly needed to be.

"We'll be there in about fifteen minutes," Cage tells Slim. "We're just outside town and I'm gonna let Blade take the lead. Where we goin'?"

"Blade, you know where her house was?" Slim asks.

"Yeah."

"Go past it and take your first right. You're goin' to go through four stop signs. I'll have Killer outside waitin' for you. It's on the right."

I hang up and head back to my bike. The rest of the guys are hot on my heels knowing that I'm not waiting for anyone. My girl needs to get to the hospital and she's being stubborn as usual. If she's going to wait for me, then I'm not going to make her wait any longer than she needs to. Fuck, I want to go as fast as possible but I'm not going to risk getting pulled over or laying my bike down and delaying her getting the help she needs.

Gunning my engine, I roar out of the gas station parking lot and make my way to the little house my wife used to call home. I'm not going to take fifteen minutes to get to her, it's not going to take that long. The rest of the guys are staying close and keeping up with me, though I'm not surprised.

They don't want me to do anything stupid and they want to make sure that I'm careful.

Finally, we pull up to the house I see Killer standing in front of it. Though with all the bikes sitting here, it's hard to miss where we're going. He's pacing back and forth and I can see the agitation on his face. Keira has made an impact on the men and women of the three clubs. Well, the ones that she's come in contact with and she has no clue. Killer is not so patiently waiting for us to park. Honestly, if it wasn't my only mode of transportation right this second, I would just lay it down in my haste to get to my girl.

"Come on Blade, she's not good and she still refuses to go. Even though Slim told her you were almost here. I've just put the call in for an ambulance and they'll be here any second now," Killer tells me as I quicken my pace.

"Killer hang back a second and fill us in on what you know," Cage tells him.

I don't pay any attention. The front door is already open and I burst through the members of Slim's club as if they're not even standing there. Nothing is preventing me from getting to Keira. Slim, Wood, and a lady I don't know are surrounding my girl on three sides, shielding her from anyone else getting too close to her. As soon as Slim sees me though, he moves the three of them back so I can get to her without anyone in the way.

Taking my first good look at my wife, I fill with dread. She's hunched over and her arms are close to her sides indicating that her ribs are fucked up. Her face is covered in bruises and cuts. Some are deeper than others and some are longer than others. I'm not sure what they used to cut her, but I know it wasn't any kind of knife. Keira is holding her one wrist in her other hand and I can see that it's got an odd angle to it. These motherfuckers touched my girl and they think they're going to get away with it. They've got another thing coming if I have anything to say about it.

Before she realizes that I'm here, I see that her clothes are now in tatters and I'm dreading finding out that they touched her more than just putting the beatings on her. I can't see her lap because she's got a blanket draped over her upper legs. The rage is just continuing to build and build within me. I'm trying my hardest not to let her see it though.

"Kitten, I'm here and we need to get you looked at. You should've gone as soon as you got here and knew Wood and Killer were here."

"No!" she screams, her face contorting with pain and tears running down through the narrow slits in her eyes. "I needed to see you needed to know you were okay. Where are our babies?"

Keira is frantic and I don't know why. My helpless eyes seek out Slim and Cage. I have no clue what to do here. So, I kneel down in front of her and gently lay my hands on her thighs. I don't know where she has any other injuries. I tip my head at an angle until I have her eyes on me so I can talk to her with her full attention. Not that it's easy considering they are so swollen.

"Kitten, the kids are home with Bailey and Skylar. Other than the few men I brought with me, all the guys are there to protect Kenyon and Cory."

"No!" Keira shrieks. "He's got pictures of them."

"What do you mean kitten? Who has pictures? Who are in the pictures?" I ask.

"Jason has pictures of Kenyon and Cory. Some of them are with you, some are with Melody. Jason has someone in the club he said."

Looking up, I see that Cage, Pops, and Slim are all on their phones. Tank is clearing people away as I hear sirens getting louder. Rage is staying close to Keira and I, shielding us from everyone and making sure someone is in range to pull me back if necessary. I go to move to Keira's side and she starts to flip out again. Telling her that the EMTs are here and I'm going no further than the side of her, I slowly move.

Thankfully, there's a woman EMT. At this point in time, I'm not sure how my girl would react to an all-male crew working on her. Not after what she's been through and I don't even know what that is. Part of me honestly doesn't want to know the hell that she went through. The other part of me knows that I have to find out what she went through so I can make sure the motherfuckers that put their hands on her pay for what they've done.

"Sir, you'll have to move out of the way," one of the paramedics tells me.

"I'm her husband and I'm not goin' anywhere. I tried to move here as you were comin' in and she flipped out. I'm not havin' my wife upset like that because you don't want me near her," I tell the guy that's trying to act tough.

"Bill, these guys are protective of their women. He'll stay out of the way so we can do our job because he doesn't want anything to happen to his wife. If you can't accept that, wait outside," the female tells him. "Hey Slim, nice to see you again."

"You too, Sam. Thanks for settin' him straight. My man here is hangin' on by a thread right now."

Sam nods her head in acknowledgement as she continues to get Keira ready to load on a stretcher. The man that tried to get me to move shrinks back among all of the bikers standing around the room before heading back outside. As they go to put a brace to support her wrist on, Keira cries out in pain. It's taking everything in me not to start throwing punches. And it takes Tank and Rage both placing a hand on each one of my shoulders to keep me in place.

We've been waiting at the hospital for hours now. I went back with Keira when we first got here, but they've taken her in to surgery now. Her wrist and thumb were broken to the point that her thumb needs a pin in it temporarily and her wrist is going to need to be fixed. Other than that, she's bruised on most of her body and there's cuts from various objects all over her body. On top of that, she's running a fever and is dehydrated. They're not sure if the infection she has is from all the cuts or something else at this point.

Sitting in the waiting room, I'm thinking about everything that could be going wrong right now. Once Grim was told that there's a mole in the club, he decided to send Joker, Glock, Melody, Skylar, Bailey, Ma, Maddie, and my kids down here. The rest of the kids are also coming down just to get the women and kids out of the clubhouse. Grim is staying behind so that he can try to figure out who is feeding Jason information and getting close enough to get the pictures of my children that he has. Keira is tortured by the thought that something is going to happen to them at Jason's hands and I'm not going to have her go through that.

"Mr. Branch?" I finally hear.

Standing up, I make my way over to the doctor that performed the surgery on my wife. I can't read his expression enough to know if the surgery went good or not. Tank and Cage follow me over and I know that they're staying close as a matter of protection for the doctor. If anything happened to my wife, there will be hell to pay.

"The surgery went well. She's in recovery now before we move her to a room. At this point she's going to be in here for about a week or so. It all depends on whether or not her body rejects the pin holding her thumb in place right now and what the infection does. Once she's in her room, we're only going to allow you in for tonight. Your wife has been through something seriously traumatic and we don't want to add any more stress to her."

"I understand," I tell him, shaking his outstretched hand. "When can I see her?"

"Give them a few minutes to get her settled in recovery and then someone will take you back. Tomorrow the rest of your friends and family can visit with her."

As soon as the doctor leaves, I'm surrounded by our family. Everyone is hugging me and telling me that they'll be back tomorrow. For now, the guys from my club, along with Wood and Killer, are going to be staying at the hospital. Because the hospital is used to the club and how many members show up, there's a room that the men can crash in while I sleep in Keira's room.

"I can't thank you all enough for bein' here, showin' my girl your support," I tell everyone before they start heading out.

"We're not just here for her," Slim tells me. "We're here for you too. It's time you learn that son. No matter what you need, you are family too."

I don't even know what to say to that. I knew it was like that with my club, but not Slim's. Keira is closer to them than I am. She's the one that spent time with them, they helped her when she left, she worked for them, and they were the ones that rescued her. To have Slim tell me that they're here to support me too means the world to me. It's honestly kind of humbling.

"Well, I'm going to see if I can get them to rush me into my girl," I tell everyone, making my excuses to leave.

Walking up to the nurse's station, I get their attention and tell them that I want to be taken back to recovery now. It's probably been more than enough time for Keira to be settled in. Honestly, I can't wait any longer to lay on eyes on her again. It's been too long since I've seen her and I need to make sure that she's okay. Well, as okay as she's going to be until she heals. It's going to be a long road and I'm going to be there to make it as easy as possible on her.

After a few minutes, a nurse tells me that she can take me back now. The entire time I can feel her undressing me with her eyes. More than likely, it's just the patch she's after. It's what they always want. I don't care though. Keira is my world and I'm not going to be like some men I know and have her at home while I use the club girls and anyone else that wants me.

"I can see you eye fuckin' me. I'm tellin' you now that I'm on my way to see my wife. I'm not interested in some quick lay because you want a patch. Lay the fuck off or I'll make sure you won't be workin' until my girl goes home. That understood?"

"Y-yes," she stammers and looks straight forward as we continue down the hallway. "She's right in here."

I don't wait to see what she's doing, my focus is solely on my wife and being with her. Our twins are in good hands. Hell, they're probably almost here now. The guys coming down with them were told to take them directly to the clubhouse and stay there until visiting hours tomorrow. I'm glad that I got the rest of the night alone with Keira. Even if she doesn't wake up to know I'm here.

As soon as I pull the curtain hiding Keira, I almost wish I could disappear. She looks so tiny laying in the hospital bed. She's got an IV going in her good arm while her other arm is covered in a soft cast for now. I'm sure it's so they can remove the pin in her thumb when it's time. One of her legs is elevated and an air cast is on it. I didn't even know that she had a sprained ankle or foot. They have the blankets up around her and the only thing you can really see is her battered and bruised face.

If I could take away the pain and recovery time my girl is going to have to go through, I would in a heartbeat. It's going to be hard on her and I'm going to be by her side the entire time. Although, I'm going to say now that the hardest part is going to be what she can't do with Kenyon and Cory. I know she still wanted to breast feed them and she's not going to do that. Not only has she been gone for almost a week and a half, now she's going to be on pain medicine and she won't be able to hold them to do it. She's going to get frustrated at how little she can do with the twins for the time being.

As I sit here by my wife's head and hold her one good hand, I think about everything that could've happened to her. In a way, I'm grateful that more didn't happen. But, I'm filled with a murderous rage at what was done to her. I'll have to think about that later though. I know that Slim has guys out looking for anyone that can be of assistance in finding anyone involved in what just happened. I'm just waiting to hear what's going on and if they managed to find anyone.

Wood and Killer took down some license plate numbers and Fox is running them through all of his programs. We got an update just before Keira came out of surgery and he had managed to get the names and addresses of at least two or three of the guys. Since most of the guys were here, they were going to send a few out later on to see if they could capture the men and bring them in for questioning.

Honestly, I'm torn as to what to do. On one hand, I want to be there and get my hands on the men that helped torture my wife. On the other hand, I need to stay with my girl and make sure she's okay. Not just physically but mentally too. Especially once the twins get here. If I know my wife, and I do, she's going to want them here with us. It's not that she doesn't trust anyone else with them, she'll just want to make sure that no one can get their hands on them. Jason is even closer now and she'll be worried and panicked more than ever.

Pulling my phone out, I see that I have a text message from Slim. It's short and to the point. Playboy, Fox, and Boy Scout managed to get their hands on two of the men and have them in holding at the clubhouse. This just makes my confusion even worse. Knowing that they are captured and waiting for us to get our hands on them has me itching to get to them now.

Me: I don't know what to do. Be there to get my hands on them. Or stay where I'm needed with my wife.

Slim: You let me know what you want to do. We can always start the questioning with Tank here and then make sure we leave some for you.

Me: Let me see what Keira is like when she finally wakes up.

Slim doesn't respond. He knows that I'm torn and it's going to depend on where she's at mentally and emotionally before I make my decision. Maybe with the twins and her girls here, I can get away for a few hours to do what I have to do.

Melody

The last week and a half has been absolute torture. I can't help but blame myself for my best friend being captured by her psychotic ex-boyfriend and having God knows what done to her. The absolute worst possible thoughts keep running through my head on a loop and I'm hoping anything that happens to her is not as bad as I'm imagining them to be.

Glock has tried consoling me and it hasn't worked. Anthony has tried to keep my mind occupied and I can't focus on anything at all. Hell, the house looks like shit because I can't even focus long enough to clean it up. My boys have tried to do the housework for me, but nothing measures up to my standards.

As much as I can, I'm with Kenyon and Cory. They are my remaining link to my best friend and sister. Blade is going out of his mind and I would rather take care of the twins so that he can concentrate on bringing Keira home. If he'd let them out of his sight when he's not out searching for his wife or working out with Tank, I'd bring them to our house. Knowing he won't let me, I haven't even brought the idea up to him.

Today is the day that we get to go down to Benton Falls. I'm so excited that I get to see Keira, but I don't want to see all of the damage done to her. It's only going to make my guilt reach higher and higher. I don't know how much higher it can go but it's about to happen as soon as tomorrow morning comes.

Tonight we've been told that we're going to the Phantom Bastards clubhouse and that's where we are to stay. It will be nice to get all the kids settled in after the long drive even if I want nothing more than to get to the hospital and see Keira. However, Kenyon and Cory are still having a hard time and it's important that I be there for them.

Skylar and Bailey have let me have them most of the time knowing how close I am to Keira and how guilty I feel. If only I had gone to get the medicine for Anthony myself, Keira would still be with her family. Glock has helped me as much as I let him. It's not much, but in a way I feel how Keira felt when she took on the role of Anthony's caregiver. She wasn't at fault when I was kidnapped, but I am for her being taken.

"Angel, you with me?" Glock asks as we pull into the clubhouse parking lot.

"Yeah."

"Still blamin' yourself and tryin' to keep Kenyon and Cory to yourself to make up for it?" he asks me.

"It is my fault babe. If I had just sucked it up and put Anthony in the car to go myself, she'd still be with her children. It's not like he had to go in the pharmacy with me for the two seconds it would've taken me to get what I needed."

"You couldn't have known what was goin' to happen. If I know your girl like I think I do, she's not goin' to be blamin' you either. I have no problem keepin' the twins, but you need to let the rest of us help you with them. You're runnin' yourself ragged and it's not good for you or the baby."

Knowing my husband is right causes the tears to come. I've been doing so good at not showing how deeply this is affecting me. The only time I cry is when I'm alone or with the twins. It's not like Kenyon and Cory will know that I'm the one to blame for this until they're older.

We get everyone in the clubhouse and Slim, who pulled in as we were pulling in, asks one of the prospects which rooms were gotten ready for us. The prospect leads our group down the hallway and starts pointing to doors. Since Glock has been here before I let him figure out what room the five of us will share. There's no way in hell that I'm letting anyone other than Blade and my girl take the twins. Not now when that asswipe Jason is so close to us.

"Angel, you know that there are plenty of other people here that can help with Kenyon and Cory. Why are you takin' this on yourself?" Glock asks me, setting the bags on the end of the bed and going to set the playpen up.

"It's my fault!" I wail, letting the dam break again.

"It's not your fault. We've all been tellin' you that. How were you honestly to know what was goin' to happen when Keira went to town?"

"I shouldn't have sent her to begin with. She could've kept an eye on Anthony. One of the prospects could have watched him while I was gone for fifteen minutes. Hell, one of the other old ladies could've done it too. I never should've let her go out knowing that a sick stalker is trying to get her to sell my best friend to the highest bidder."

"How were we supposed to know that Jason was already here?" he asks me. "Not a single one of us knew that Jason had left Benton Falls. And we've got three clubs watchin' him. He's a sneaky bastard and we will be more diligent from now on. Keira will not be left alone until he's dealt with."

"That's going to be a while," I wail, crying uncontrollably. "Who knows how long she's going to be kept in the hospital. We don't even know where the infection she has is coming from. What the fuck did she go through?"

"She went through some fucked-up shit, I'm sure." Glock states matter-of-factly. "But, like you, she's a survivor and she will get through this. Blade, you, me, and three different clubs will all be there to help her with whatever she needs. This is what we do. And you should remember this from when you got rescued."

"Do you think Karen will help her?" I ask, thinking of the help that she was for me and the rest of the old ladies that have gone through some shit.

"She'll be more than happy to help your sister. It's what she loves to do."

Finally, I have everything set up and I can get the kids in bed. As soon as I have the twins changed and back to sleep, I change for bed and climb in our temporary bed. Glock follows behind me instead of going out to see what the rest of the guys are doing. I'm hoping that sleep will claim me, but if it's like every other night, I'll spend it with my eyes wide open and thinking of everything that Keira has gone through.

As I predicted, last night was a sleepless night for me. Glock and the kids fell right to sleep and pretty much stayed asleep all night. The twins did get up a few times, but they went right back down. I don't know if it's the same shit that's kept me awake since Keira has been taken or if it's because I know that today is the day that we get to go see her and spend some time with her. Either way it was another sleepless night for me and I don't know when I'm ever going to get sleep again. Maybe I need to go see Karen again.

"Angel, you up already?" Glock asks, his voice full of sleep still.

"Never went to sleep," I respond, getting out of bed so that I can get ready to go see my girl.

"This has to stop Mel. You are goin' to make yourself fuckin' sick if you don't get some sleep. Then you try to be fuckin' superwoman and do everythin' yourself. Take the help that's offered and go to bed."

"I can't today. We get to go see my sister today babe. I promise that as soon as I know how she is, see her with my own eyes, I'll try to get some sleep."

"That's the best I'm goin' to get, isn't it?"

"Yes, it is. Now, let's get going so we can get to the hospital. I want eyes on Keira as soon as possible. And I don't want to keep Kenyon and Cory from her another second."

Glock gets out of bed and wakes Anthony up so he can help him get ready to go. As soon as they're done in the shower, I'll jump in so that I can get ready. Kenyon and Cory will be the last to get ready because they're the easiest. They had a bath in the middle of the night because they both wet through so I don't need to do that. All I need to worry about is feeding them and then getting them dressed in their new outfits.

I'm just getting done feeding Cory when Glock and Anthony emerge from the bathroom. Ever since he started hanging out with Jameson, our son now has to wear his hair just like Joker. It's so cute that instead of wanting to be like his dad, Anthony is choosing to have a faux hawk. The only thing we won't allow him to do is add color to it yet. As soon as summer's here, we'll let him do the temporary hair color, but that's it.

I scoop up everything I need for the shower and tell Glock that I'll change and dress the babies as soon as I'm done. Knowing that I can take all the time I want and that Glock will watch over the kids is a comfort, but not one I indulge in. I quickly hop in and wash as quick as possible before getting out. Dressing is easy considering I chose a summer dress for today with the unseasonably hot weather we've been having. My hair gets brushed and thrown up in a messy bun and I don't worry about make-up. My girl has seen me at my absolute worst and doesn't give a shit what I look like.

Practically running back into the bedroom, I stop dead in my tracks when I see it empty. Where are the twins and my son? Where did Glock go? Frantically searching for them, I leave the room and head towards where I hear the most noise coming from. Sitting at a table in the middle of the room is everyone I've been looking for. My heart beats out of my chest and I'm finding it difficult to breathe. There was no way in hell I would've been able to go to the hospital and tell Blade and Keira that something happened to their children after causing Keira to be kidnapped and abused.

"Angel!" I distantly hear Glock yell. "Angel, come back to us! Everyone is okay and we're all waitin' on you. The kids were gettin' fussy so we just walked them around a bit. I'm sorry I didn't let you know before we left."

"How could you?" I scream, my breathing becoming semi-normal again. "You know it's my fault their mom isn't with them right now. How could you make me imagine that I'd have to go there and tell them that something happened to Kenyon and Cory too?"

"Melody, we've got you covered," Bailey says, coming over to me and placing a hand on my shoulder. "We would never let anything happen to any of you. What happened to Keira is not your fault. If you keep blaming yourself, then you're going to harm that baby you're carrying right now."

I stare at Bailey, stunned into silence. We haven't told anyone other than Keira and Blade that I was pregnant. How the fuck does Bailey know? I look at her, the confusion clearly written on my face. I'm not going to ask any questions right now though because Keira is more important.

"It is my fault though."

"You made Jason decide to become possessive over someone that wasn't his? You made him decide to sell her to the highest bidder? And you made him decide to plant someone in Grim's club before kidnappin' her?" Slim asks me. "No, you didn't. Whether you sent her to the pharmacy for you or not, Jason was goin' to get his hands on Keira. He's psychotic enough not to give a fuck if he's alone or surrounded by three clubs. You are not to blame and I don't want to hear that fuckin' shit anymore!"

I do get where everyone is coming from, but I'll always feel responsible. They're all right though in the fact that I need to calm down and stop because of the life I'm carrying now. If something were to happen to our baby, I wouldn't be able to go on. I know it.

"Fine. Let's get going. I want to see my girl and I'm not going to do that by standing here having a panic attack and worrying about everything. I'm sorry, I just didn't know where you guys went," I say, apologizing to everyone that just witnessed my outburst.

We all make our way out to the vans and SUVs that are waiting in the parking lot of the clubhouse. It's going to be easier to keep as many of us together as possible so Slim is using one of the large vans they have along with one SUV. We'll be in the middle of a group of bikes as we make the ten-minute drive to see Keira. The children will mainly be in the large van, but Kenyon and Cory will be in the SUV. It's bullet proof and the windows are tinted so no one passing by can see who's in there. Glock, Slim, Playboy, Ma, and myself will be riding there. Anthony wanted to go with Jameson, so I'm allowing that.

As we pile in the vehicles, I notice a car sitting just outside the gate. I motion to Glock and pull him in acting like I'm kissing him. Instead, I'm telling him about the car. Once I'm done telling him, he kisses my neck and I know that he's looking to see what I'm talking about. We pull apart and get in like nothing is out of the ordinary.

"Car at the gate, Slim," Glock says after all the doors are closed. "Angel noticed it and I don't like it just sittin' there.

All the men turn and look at the car since the windows are all tinted and no one can tell. Slim's already on his phone talking to one of the guys riding on his bike. They're changing plans and the way that we're leaving. Apparently, there's more than one entrance and no one but Slim and a select few know about them. Just as we're pulling off, I see about ten bikes go out through the gate and surround the car. I'd be worried it was Jason, but I know he's not dumb enough to sit outside the clubhouse. No, he's got someone else watching and waiting to see what our movements are.

"Good eye Melody," Playboy tells me. "I was scannin' the area and didn't even catch it."

Pride warms my body as I realize that he's not lying to make me feel better. These men are trained to catch that kind of stuff and he didn't. No one did except for me. It kind of helps ease the guilt I feel a little bit, but nothing will ever take it completely away.

The rest of the ride is uneventful. Even when the bikers that surrounded the car join us, it's done seamlessly. Kenyon and Cory sleep the short ride and I know they're going to stir as soon as we come to a stop. Any change for them these days wakes them up. Hopefully being able to see their mom today will help calm them down though. These poor babies have been through hell since she's been gone. We all have.

Glock and Slim help get the carseats out before we all make our way up to Keira's room. I don't try to take either one of the babies back. It's time that I let someone else help me. I don't know what made me realize that, but it's a fact I have to deal with. More than likely they'll be staying here with their mom and dad anyway.

Slim leads us all up to a private room that's larger than most. Blade and a few guys are currently sitting with Keira. I'm the first one in the room and seeing her banged up; battered and covered in casts and other medical equipment has my breath freezing in my lungs. Glock almost runs into the back of me because I can't make my feet move me any closer to her.

"Bitch, you better get the fuck over here and give me some lovin'," Keira's voice says over everyone else talking.

My focus is solely on her as I make my way closer. I'm moving at a snail's pace and I can see her becoming impatient with me. I don't care though, this is what she must have thought when she first saw me and I was mainly healed by then. There's no words to describe the pain I feel for my best friend right now.

"It's about fucking time," she murmurs in my ear as I hug her gently. "This is not on you. I know where your head's at and I'm telling you to stop it now."

Tears shimmer in my eyes as I hold her and nod my head in response. "I love you sister from another mister."

"Love you too. Now, where did you hide Kenyon and Cory. I'm not done with you, but I need eyes on my babies."

Glock and Slim step forward and Blade takes Cory. He lifts his daughter out of the carseat and hands her over to her mother. Cory instantly cuddles down into Keira as much as she can and I know everything is going to be alright. As Glock hands Kenyon over to her, he does the same thing as his sister. The twins know they have their mama back and aren't going to want to move anytime soon.

"I know that in a minute or two all you men are going to be leaving and it's just going to be us girls. So, leave now and go do your manly protective things," Keira says, trying to lighten everyone's mood.

Blade saunters back over to her and whispers in her ear. I can see her eyes grow round and I know he's telling her what's about to happen. None of us are dumb, we all know they're going to dish out punishment to someone. They just want to spare us the details and make it so none of us know anything that happened in case the cops get involved.

"We'll be back as soon as we can, kitten," Blade tells her, kissing her like it's going to be the last time.

"I know you will be. Now, leave a man or two and get out of here. I need some time with females without you men around. And Blade, take a shower before you come back here please."

Even with everyone around her laughing, Keira doesn't hear a single thing. Her sole focus is the two babies snuggled on her chest and side. There's going to be a long period where she doesn't let them out of her sight. I know because I was the same way with Anthony when I first came home.

As the last guy leaves and closes the door behind him. Keira starts to bombard us with questions about her children. She feels like she's missed so much time with them instead of a week and a half. We all answer her questions and try to keep the conversation steered away from anything too serious or about what happened to her. We all know that she'll tell us if, and when, she's ready to. Not a single person in this room will push her, but we'll all let her know that we're here when she needs us.

After an hour or so I can tell the pain is getting to Keira and I motion to Bailey to clue her in as well. She takes one look at her and understands what I'm saying. "Ladies, let's let mama have some time with her babies. We can go get the kids fed and hang out for a while before we come back. Slim left enough men here that we'll all still be protected."

Everyone but me leaves the room. I'm not going to be letting her out of my sight for a while. I sit next to her bed where Blade was sitting and watch her. She pushes a button and a nurse comes over an intercom asking her what she needs. Once she relays that she needs some pain medicine, the nurse tells her someone will be here in just a second.

"Mel, can you take the twins and put them in their seats please?"

"Of course," I respond getting up and doing as she asked.

"We're goin' to talk about the guilt you're feeling. It's not going to be today, but we will be discussing it. I'm going to be seeing Karen and I think one or two appointments should include you. Mel, I don't blame you for what happened. If it didn't happen that day, it would've been the next time I left the clubhouse. I'm just thankful that I didn't have Kenyon and Cory with me. I knew they'd be taken care of by all of you. So, please stop. My little niece or nephew can't handle it."

"I'll never forgive myself. Now, I'm going to drop it so that we can have a good rest of the day," I tell her, sitting back so that we can all talk and try to forget everything that happened.

Blade

I really didn't want to leave the hospital. But, these cocksuckers need to be dealt with and I'm going to have a hand in dealing out their punishment. We left three prospects right by Keira's door and there's more guys throughout the hospital. No one should be able to get to her or the rest of the old ladies.

"You here with us?" Tank asks me. He always knows when I go in my head.

"Yeah. Tryin' to forget that I left my girl and kids by themselves."

"They're not alone," Grim pipes up. "We've got guys on them and he's not goin' to get them."

"I know. I really need to be here. I need to have a hand in takin' these guys out."

"Slim's guys have already been questionin' them. They've gotten some good intel, but it's not enough."

Grim quickly tells us what they've learned so far. Jason was the one behind kidnapping my girl. They were just hired hands. He's also got a bigger backing than what we originally thought he did, though we're still not sure exactly who Jason is working with. If I had to guess, I couldn't even begin to tell you any groups. He's just so unknown and we're having a hard time finding any information on him. Fox has been at his computers almost nonstop and he still can't hardly find out any information on the motherfucker.

Pulling into the clubhouse parking lot, Grim pulls the SUV we're all riding in around the back. Since a few of us didn't bring our bikes, we figured this was easier than any of us having to ride bitch or splitting up. Keira is someone they're definitely after, but we don't know if they're going to try to take any of us out in their quest to get my wife.

"You ready Blade?" Grim asks, pulling to a stop in front of one of the out buildings.

"Yeah. Did someone get my toys ready for me?"

"Trojan did. Killer may have used one or two, but he's almost as pissed off as you are. Wood and him have gotten close to your girl."

"I know they have and I appreciate them for protectin' her as much as they could."

The five of us make our way into the building and see the two men hanging from one of the rafters. They're beaten and bloody and I don't know if there's going to be much for me to do. Both men look like they're about ready to just give up and let themselves die. Not before I get a go at them though. The rage flowing through me needs an outlet and I need to do something to them.

"So, these are the men that put their hands on my wife?" I ask menacingly.

"They are. I'm not sure what part they did, but they did touch her," Killer tells me, taking a position against the wall so he can watch.

"Do you know what I do when someone hurts someone that belongs to me?" I ask them, picking up one of my favorite knives. "No? Let me tell you. I make sure that all the pain my girl felt at your hands is felt by you. You will know the suffering she felt. But, you'll feel it worse."

I walk up to the guy closest to me and rip what remains of his shirt away from his body. My girl has cuts all along her body and I'm guessing part of them are just from the rings these fuckers are wearing. The patterns fit. Taking the blade of my knife, I run it across the guy's lower stomach. I push in hard enough that a trail of blood starts dripping down his exposed flesh. It's not enough to kill him by a long shot, but he's definitely feeling the sting.

Asshole number two is hanging there watching me. It's not going to make it any easier when I get to him. If he wants to watch and see what's about to happen to him, I'm not going to stop him.

"How many men in total touched my girl?"

"There were ten of us," the second asshole tells me. There's no way they're not going to talk after the rest of the guys have already had their fun.

"What was Jason's plan?" I ask, moving on to the side of the guy I've been carving up.

"He was going to get her to sign the annulment papers so you wouldn't come looking for her. She gave him hell and told him that wouldn't stop you and that you'd just get married again."

The guys from the club still didn't know that we got married. They probably figured it was going to happen and that's why I was already calling her my wife. Killer steps forward and asks if he's telling the truth. I tell him we did get married the day she came home from the hospital and that only a few people knew about it.

"Who was he goin' to sell her to?"

"I don't know. We were just brought in for this job. We don't know the guy other than when he hired us to help him with her."

"Did you see anyone else he was talking to?"

"No. We heard him on the phone a few times, but he always went in another room when he got a call. Or made one."

The guy that I've been carving up finally passes out and I know it's just a matter of time before he dies. So, I move on to the next guy. Now, he's starting to squirm knowing that he's going to be carved up. Only, he's going to get it a hundred time worse because I didn't get to do too much to the first guy.

"You know, I just got thinkin'," I start. "You got a family? A wife and kids maybe? I know my wife just had twins. Did anyone look in his wallet?"

I look at the guys that have been here and they all shake their heads no. We wouldn't dream of touching a woman or child, but this asshat doesn't need to know that. Reaching around, I find the guy's wallet and pull it out of his torn pocket. I make a show of flipping it open to see the pictures that he carries with him.

"Would you look at that? You got a pretty little wife and what, four kids at home. I wonder what your wife will look like when she's all carved to shreds. You want us to go get her now so she knows this is all because of you?"

"No!" the guy screams. "Please don't hurt her. She doesn't know anything about this. I'll do anything."

"You've already done enough. You touched my wife. Were you all supposed to rape her too? Because I know that's about the only thing that didn't happen to her."

"No. We were just supposed to teach her a lesson and get her to sign the papers so that Jason could sell her. The guy didn't want someone that was married."

"Did Jason try to rape her?"

"No. He just hit her."

The guy says this like hitting a woman is no big deal. Fuck that! He's going to learn that hitting women is a big deal. One that we don't accept and that we stop from having happen whenever we see it. That's why we are turning the house into one for victims of domestic violence. Not only are the women behind helping these victims, we all are too. Even Slim's club is going to be looking into starting to buy houses for this use.

Taking a different blade, I carve the words 'Woman Beater' in his lower stomach. Killing this one is going to be too easy. I think we need to let him live and let other people know that he thinks it's not only okay, but funny, to beat women.

"Hey guys, this one thinks it's okay to beat women. Let's let him live and a few of our buddies know that he thinks it's okay. Killin' him wouldn't serve any purpose except tryin' to fulfill our rage. This way he gets the proper treatment more than just at our hands."

The men in the room take a minute to think this over and one by one all start nodding their heads. This doesn't mean that I'm still not going to have my fun with him. It just means that I'm going to make sure that he lives and can get to the hospital to get patched up.

I take a knife and start making small little cuts all over his upper body. This one is trying not to squeal and scream like a little bitch, but it's not working. He's screaming and yelling to stop and knock it off. I'm not going to though. I can just imagine that Keira screamed and tried to hold in her pain but these fuckers didn't care. They just kept right on torturing my wife.

After having some fun for a half hour or so, I put my blade down and step away. He's had enough and he's ready to pass out. I don't want that to happen before he can get to the hospital. So, I nod to the one prospect, Boy Scout, that was allowed in the room and he gets moving to let the guy down. He'll place him in one of Slim's vans for the club and drop him off outside the hospital.

Someone will eventually find him and make sure he gets the help that he needs. When he gets out of the hospital, there are some people that will make sure he's reminded of the fact that women do not deserve any man to put their hands on them. These men won't kill him or put him in so much pain that he dies, but they will make sure he feels the aftereffects for a long time to come. Until they've decided that he's had enough and won't put his hands on another female again.

I've cleaned up and we're all making our way back to the hospital. I need to get back and make sure that my girl and kids are okay. Yeah, I've talked to the prospects that are right outside her door, but it's not the same as keeping my eyes on her.

Walking in the room, I see all the old ladies surrounding my girl on her bed. They're laughing and talking about things we probably don't want to know about. Especially considering they all immediately stop and try to look innocent when they realize we're in the room. I really don't want to know what's going on now.

"Girls, I need time with my wife. You can all come back later," I tell them, moving closer to the bed and giving her a kiss.

"Wait a minute," Skylar starts. "What do you mean that you need time with your 'wife'?"

"We got married the day I came home from the hospital with the twins," Keira tells them. "We just wanted something quiet and simple."

The women all stare openmouthed. Well, all of them except for Melody since she was there. I can see the expressions on their faces and know that not only are we going to get hell from them for getting married without telling anyone, but that at least two of them are already planning the party to celebrate.

"How could you not tell any of us?" Bailey asks. "We would've helped you plan it and get you ready. Wait, that's why we took the twins for a while that night."

"It is," I answer, putting my arm above Keira's head.

"Now, this is bullshit that you didn't tell us," Maddie says. "Why couldn't you at least tell us?"

"I didn't want a lot of fanfare," Keira answers. "We just wanted simple and small. We were planning on telling you all soon. Then all this shit happened. And no, Melody, I don't blame you for any of it."

"Hold up," Ma says. "Why aren't you surprised by this news, Melody?"

"I may have been there," She says, looking away.

The girls stop talking amongst themselves and instead they stare at her and can't believe that she kept the secret from them. Melody finally looks up at everyone and goes to say something before stopping.

"Listen, they wanted it kept a secret and I had to keep my word. If she said I could tell anyone, I would've told you."

"Okay. Well, moving on, we're going to be planning a party for you guys then. We didn't even get to have a house warming party. You two really don't like to draw attention to yourselves. Do you?" Skylar asks us.

Instead of answering, we both just shake our heads. For various reasons, I don't like calling attention to myself. With Keira I know it has to do with wanting to stay under Jason's radar and the fact that she's never had anyone care about her enough to do this kind of stuff. For her, it's about trying to make friends with these women and not about what they can do for her, or us.

Finally, all the old ladies and men leave the room and it's just the four of us. I sit here and look at Keira, Kenyon, and Cory for a few minutes without saying a word. Not only did Keira manage to break through any walls I had put up against falling in love but, Kenyon and Cory also have me wrapped around their little fingers already. I couldn't imagine my world without any of them. Now, we just need to get Keira home so that our family can get back on track and living our life.

Chapter Eleven

Keira

I'VE BEEN HOME FROM the hospital for about a month now. Blade and I have been finding a balance between work, the twins, and time for one another. Kenyon and Cory are growing like weeds and they're learning something new every day it seems. This is why I'm glad I get the chance to stay home and write instead of having to send them to a babysitter or daycare. I get to see every new thing they discover without having to be told about it. Blade even stays home as much as he can. He hates missing out on things, but he's got a job and things he needs to do for the club. Thankfully, he hasn't been away on runs or anything since we returned home. I think he told Grim that he didn't want to be too far away from me with the threat of Jason still out there.

The book that I started writing is almost finished. I'm hoping that by the end of the week I'll be typing 'The End'. Since deciding to become an author, I've made some amazing friends and connections online through the miracle of social media. I just don't get into my personal life and the fact that I am actually an old lady and married to a biker. I just read all the comments about how much these women want bikers and can't wait to meet one. They all just go based on characters in the stories they read and see on *Sons of Anarchy*. It's much different in real life.

"Kitten, where are you?" Blade asks, coming downstairs.

"In the laundry room," I answer, throwing another load in the washer. It seems I spend more time doing laundry than anything else.

Blade comes in carrying Cory. He's smiling down at his daughter and I know all thoughts of him not being a good dad have vanished. When it comes to our children, Blade is so attentive and hands on. We won't even go into how protective he is. There are days I'm glad they're only babies and don't understand the crazy man their dad is right yet. They'll have years of dealing with that. Especially Cory.

"What's going on?" I ask, as he just stands there.

"I have to go on a run tomorrow. Grim can't go because he needs to be here for a meetin'. I've tried to get out of it, but there's no way I can."

"Blade, I never asked you to get out of going on these runs when you have to. You need to do what you have to do."

"I know you didn't ask me not to go. I just don't like the idea of leavin' the three of you without me bein' close by. So, can you please do me a favor?"

"It depends on what that favor is."

"Will you please stay at the clubhouse? Just while I'm gone."

"I don't really want to stay there. There are things I need to do here and I can't do that if I'm over there," I tell him, pouring the soap in and starting the washer.

"The stuff you have to do will still be here when I get back. I'm only goin' to be gone a day, two at the most. I don't want you here alone," Blade tells me, and I can see that he's not going to give up on this. "You can take the laptop with you and still write when the kids are nappin' or whatever. Plus, you won't have to worry about things here so that just gives you more time to write. I really need you to do this for me."

"Fine, Blade. When are we going over there?"

"Not until tomorrow mornin'. It will be early though, like six."

"Wouldn't it make sense to just go there tonight then? That way I don't have to wake Kenyon and Cory up if they're still sleeping," I answer, heading upstairs to start packing a bag for us.

"Yeah, it would. I just didn't want to get you even more pissed at me. I'm not sleepin' on the couch or in another room again," Blade tell me, and I can't hide the laughter that bubbles up.

Blade and I had taken the kids to the store one day. Everything was going fine until a man got a little too close to me. I thought that Blade was going to beat the man's ass right in the middle of the store. After finally settling him down and getting the other guy to stop running his mouth and leave us alone, I didn't talk to Blade for a day and a half. I get that he's scared I'm going to be taken again, but his reaction was ridiculous. There was no reason for him to be such a drama queen and almost get us kicked out of my favorite store. So, he slept on the couch and has been on his best behavior ever since.

Blade starts packing his bag as I'm packing up a few things for myself. Thankfully he still has his room in the clubhouse so I already have some stuff over there. I just need a change of clothes and my toothbrush really. The kids are a different story though. We haven't taken anything for them there because we have our home and haven't had to go on lockdown. Something the girls explained to me in great detail so I would know what to do if it ever happens.

"What do we need to pack up for them?" Blade asks, following me into the nursery.

"Everything. Clothes, diapers and wipes that we can just leave over there, toys, bath stuff, the playpen. The list goes on and on. I think the only thing we don't need is baby food and cereal. Melody took some over there the other day."

We work together in silence until we have everything ready to go. Blade loads it all in the bed of his new truck and I get the kids ready to go over there. They may only be a few months old, but they've been on cereal and baby food since we came home. Kenyon was constantly hungry, so we decided to start with the cereal in his bottle. It helped so we started doing the same thing with Cory. Now, they both get a little cereal mixed with some fruit a few times a day. Cory is really starting to gain a little weight and Kenyon is just a chunky monkey.

Once I have them strapped in their carseats, Blade helps me carry them out. Melody is on her way over and I quickly explain what's going on. She tells me that Anthony and she are going over there too. At least I'll have company when I'm not writing and the kids are asleep. I'm pretty sure that most of the women are going to be over there then. I'm more than a little nervous about that because Blade and whoever helped him buy the stuff for my office are the only ones that know I write. I don't have the courage to tell anyone else.

"Kitten, you get your computer?" Blade asks, heading back in the house.

"No, can you grab that and the flash drive for me babe?"

"Yep," Is his muffled reply.

"Why are you taking a computer with you?" Melody asks me.

"You're my ride or die, my sister from another mister? I can trust you to keep this to yourself?" I ask warily.

"Of course, you can. I didn't tell anyone about the wedding."

"I don't even want Glock to know," I tell her seriously.

"I won't even tell him then."

"I've been working on writing a book. Blade went out and bought me everything he thought I'd need for it and it's actually almost done. There are some other authors online that are going to help me get it published."

"Are you serious right now?" she asks, shocked.

"I am."

"How are you going to get it published? Why didn't you tell me sooner? When can I read it?" Melody asks in rapid succession.

"I don't know if I want you to read it. I'm not sure it's any good. That's the next step in the process, sending it out to a few people to see what they think and letting me know if I have to change anything up."

"Then let me be one of them for you. You know I'll give it to you straight and won't bullshit you," Melody says, trying to convince me to let her read my story.

"How about we'll see when I finish it. I can't promise anything right now."

"Okay," she answers, pouting.

Blade comes back out and loads the last bag into the cab of the truck. I'm ready to get over there and unpack everything. That way he can help set the kid's stuff up and then I can help make dinner or something. I have no problem helping do whatever I have to in the clubhouse while we're there. I just hope they leave more than just Grim with us. Jason is not someone to trust or take lightly. If he sees most of the men leaving, he will make a move.

As soon as we pull in, Glen is there grabbing bags out of the bed of the truck. He takes them inside and I follow him to the room that I used to share with Blade. It hasn't changed other than the fact that most everything is not here now. All of our stuff is in the house and that's the way it's going to stay. Well, other than his posters of half-naked women. He can keep those here.

"Kitten, where do you want the playpen set up?" Blade asks, setting the carseats down next to the bed.

"Why don't we put it on this side of the bed so it's not between the bed and the bathroom door?" I tell him, moving the bags that Glen already set down.

"Okay. I'll set that up so we can get the kids out of their seats. When we're done, you want to go get some lunch or find somethin' here?"

"Let's just stay here. I don't want to wake the kids up and it's just going to take time away from being with you before you leave," I tell him, wrapping my arms around his waist and laying my head on his chest.

It doesn't take that long to unpack everything we brought over with us. As soon as we have it done, we head out to the kitchen to make lunch so we can go back and relax. I'm sure that Blade has other things he could be doing, but he's going to spend his time with us before he leaves. It kind of makes me think that whatever he's about to go do is dangerous and he's worried about coming back to us. I don't know what I'd do if he didn't make it back home.

"Kitten, what's got you thinkin' so hard over there?" he asks, pulling me in his lap to straddle him.

"Wonder if you're worried about makin' it back to us or not. If what you're about to do is dangerous. I don't know what I'd do without you babe."

"You don't have to worry about losin' me kitten. I'm not goin' anywhere. This run is just to gather information. Nothin' more," he tells me.

I lean my head against his shoulder and press a kiss to his neck. He tilts his head away so I have better access and I can feel him starting to grow hard beneath me. Just before anything can really get going though, Kenyon wakes up and starts crying. Blade groans and drops his head.

"Cockblocked by my own son," he says chuckling. "You better be ready to finish this later."

"I'll finish it. But it depends on you." I tell him, not knowing when he's going to be leaving for sure.

The day has been spent mainly lounging around in the room with the twins. We've watched movies, cuddled, and spent some time talking about the future. Blade wants more kids and I'm kind of on the fence about whether or not I want any more right now. Eventually, I'd like to have one or two more, but the twins are only a few months old. He wants them close in age though so that they can be close and he knows that they'll watch out for one another as they grow older and away from us.

Night is coming on and everyone decided that we were going to have a small party to send the guys that are leaving off. I've never been to a party here before other than when the kids are included. Tonight they will definitely not be going. Ma and Pops are going to watch over all the kids with the help of the older ones. So, the rest of the girls are all getting ready together. I think this is so that they can let me know what to expect when I get out there. Blade sure as hell hasn't said anything to me about them.

"Are you almost ready?" Bailey asks, coming in our room where we all are.

"Yeah," we all say in unison.

We're all dressed similar but different. Similar in that our clothing is tight, but not tight enough that a little isn't left to the imagination. Skylar is the only one wearing pants while the rest of us are wearing skirts of varying lengths. I'm wearing a short black skirt that comes to the middle of my thighs with a spaghetti strap tank top. Both are black and I added a splash of color with red high heels. It's been so long since I've gotten to dress up for anything. Melody is doing my hair while Maddie is doing my make-up. Bailey looks like she's ready to go and Skylar is just putting the finishing touches on herself.

"You are going to be seeing a lot of shocking things tonight," Bailey tells me, breaking out a bottle of Jack Daniels and pouring us all shots. "People will be having sex right out in the open and no one will bat an eye about it. Hell, some of the guys will be having conversations while they're balls deep in some club girl or getting a blow job."

"Okay," is my only comment.

"It's actually kind of hot to see everyone let loose and trust one another enough to know that it's a safe environment to fuck wherever you want to," Maddie pipes in.

"You guys actually watch them having sex?" I ask.

"I have. It gave me ideas about what I wanted to try with Cage and Joker since I had never been with two guys at once before. We all look, it's just a matter of how comfortable you are," Skylar tells me, a faint blush creeping up her face.

Just as we're about to leave the room, Ma knocks on our door. She's carrying a crying Cory with her. Cory isn't just crying though, she's full on screaming and crying to the point that she's having a hard time breathing.

"I'm not quite sure what's wrong with her. We were sitting there watching a movie and she started throwing up. I got her all cleaned up and then she started crying so hard I got her right here to you. I didn't even get a chance to give her anything for her fever," Ma says, handing Cory over to me.

"Thank you so much!" I tell her, cuddling Cory close to me. She feels warm and I know that I won't be attending the party tonight. "You guys go ahead. I'm going to stay in here with Cory. Tell Blade to have fun and I'll see him when he comes in."

The girls all leave and I lay down on the bed, keeping Cory close to me. Once she settles down, I give her some infant medicine to help try to break her fever. I don't want to try cool cloths or anything like that just yet. For now, I'll keep an eye on her and see what happens.

Closing my eyes, I try to rest while keeping my daughter close to me. Just as I'm starting to doze off since Cory is finally resting, the door opens and Blade walks in carrying Kenyon. I'm not sure what he's doing, but I didn't expect him to come back to the room. There's no reason for him to be here.

"What are you doing babe?" I ask.

"If you're in here with our daughter because she's sick, then I'm goin' to be in here with you. You are not in this alone kitten," Blade tells me, laying Kenyon down in the playpen. "I don't need to be out there when my family is in here. If she stays asleep, we'll have Ma come in for a few minutes so you can go get a drink. How does that sound?"

"Okay I guess. I'm not sure that I want to leave her when I don't know if her fever is going to break or if she's going to be sick again."

"I know kitten. But, if we do go out, it will only be long enough for you to say hi and have one or two drinks. Not all night."

"I'll think about it."

Blade lays down on the other side of Cory and starts gently rubbing her back. It's something he's done since she was born and she snuggles closer to his hand. Even in sleep she knows her daddy and wants to get closer to him. It's the cutest thing I've ever witnessed. Other than when she falls asleep on his chest before he falls asleep. I've got more than one picture of that.

It's been a little bit and Cory is still sound asleep. Blade is looking at me and I know he wants to go out to the main room for the party. I quietly tell him to go and that I'm fine in with the kids. He quickly kisses me and tells me that he'll be back in a little bit. I truly don't need him in here when the kids are sleeping and it does feel like Cory's fever has broken. I'm not sure what made her sick, but she seems to be over it already. Just as I go to get up and go in the bathroom, I hear a light tapping on the door. Ma sticks her head in and asks how Cory is doing. I tell her that she's doing fine and Ma comes in the door.

"Blade wants you to go have a drink with him. I got the kids in here. You need to get out for a little bit and have some fun dear," Ma tells me, settling in on the bed in the spot I just vacated.

Since she's already here, I guess I don't really have a choice but to go see Blade and join the party. First I go to the bathroom and then touch up my hair. Then I check on Cory again before leaving the room. They are right and I do need to get out and have some fun, but my mind is on our daughter and whether or not she's going to get sick again.

As I come to the end of the hallway, I stop and take in the scene before me. There are a few couples having sex in random places, one or two club girls dancing almost naked on tables, and the men are just eating it up. Well the men that are single are eating it up. I notice that all the other men are with their women and they're off to another side of the room. All except Blade. He's sitting at the bar and I watch as some little fucking skank walks up to him and starts rubbing on his back before moving to his chest. Blade is trying to get her hands off of him, but she's not having it. Guess it's time for me to step in and let a bitch know he's very taken.

"You mind getting your fucking hands off my husband?" I ask, walking up to them.

Blade turns his head to look at me and I can see it register on his face how pissed off I truly am. There's no going back though since the bitch looks at me, laughs, and then steps closer to my husband. I know she's not going to try to get in his pants right now, right in front of me. Who the fuck does this bitch think she is?

"Honey, if you think you can make me get away from your man, go ahead and try," she snarls back, stepping even closer and letting her hand stray down towards his cock.

I don't say a single word as I grab her hair and slam her head off the bar. Pulling her back, I land a punch directly to her nose and I know instantly it's broken. She's crying and trying to get Blade to make me stop, but he's just enjoying the show I'm putting on right now.

Taking her hand, I twist her arm behind her back and get right up in her face. "Do you see this ring on his finger? It means that he's taken and doesn't need any loose fucking pussy like the one you have. There are plenty of single men here that wouldn't mind giving you a ride. So, I suggest you don't even look in my husband's direction again. Do you understand me?"

"You're going to pay for this bitch!" the club girl screams. "I know more about you than what you think. I know that you won't be here soon and I'll have your man all to myself."

I stop and instantly look at Blade. He heard the same thing I did and I know we just found out who Jason has in the club. There's no other way she would know that someone is trying to get to me, unless one of the other guys told her that. And, I highly doubt anyone would share any information like that with her. She's nothing more than a hole to these guys.

Blade

I'm sitting at the bar waiting for Keira to come join me. I knew she would try to argue if I told her I was getting Ma to come sit with the kids, so I just didn't say a word about it. Keira should be out here any second, even if it's just to yell at me for sending Ma in. Instead I see the club girl that I told to leave me the fuck alone the day I was going to Benton Falls heading directly towards me.

She starts rubbing on me and I can't believe that she is back here after the last time I had her thrown out. I'm trying to pull her hands off of me, but it's not workin'. Not even when my wife starts getting in her face does the girl leave me alone. It's like she takes it as a challenge and wants to see how far she can push Keira. It's not going to be very far.

Before anyone can say anything, Keira starts beating the shit out of her. I just sit back and watch my girl take care of the trash. Well, until she says that Keira won't be around for much longer. Grim never did find out who the mole was and I think we just found out why. I'm sure he looked at the club girls, but I haven't seen this one around very much. And every time I do, she's always trying to get me to fuck her. Keira is more important than any loose pussy so I've stayed away from all the club girls.

I look over towards Grim and the rest of the men and see that they also heard the bitch's comment about Keira not being here. Slowly they all start making their way over to us and surround the bitch. She's not going to be getting out of this one any time soon.

"Take this girl to the holding cell downstairs," Grim tells Glen. "Glock, go down and don't let anyone in the room with the bitch. Make sure Glen ties her up nice and tight so she can't go anywhere. We'll be down in a minute."

I grab Keira by the waist and pull her into me. Nuzzling her neck, I can't believe the way she put that bitch in her place. It makes me realize that Keira was the right choice to make as my old lady and at the party that the girls are planning for next week, I'm giving her the rag that I ordered a while ago. There just didn't seem to be a good enough time to give it to her until now.

"I'll be back in a little bit. Make sure the kids are in the playpen. That was hot as fuck kitten," I tell her, kissing her until we're both breathless.

"What if I'm sleeping?" she asks, coyly.

"I'll wake you up. You know what you do to me and I already told you that you better be ready for tonight."

I get up and make my way down with the rest of the men. There's no way I'm going to miss finding out exactly what this bitch knows and what the plan is for my wife. Obviously, there is one if she's saying she won't be here much longer.

Grim walks in the room first and we see that Glen tied her to a chair in the middle of the room. Now, we're not going to put our hands on this woman at all, but she doesn't have to know that. So, as I take my spot along the wall, I make a big show of pulling out the longest blade I carry on me. I start playing with it and the entire time her eyes are getting bigger and bigger. She thinks that I'm going to be using this on her. If she were a man, she'd be one hundred percent right. But, we'll end up sending her away like we did the last one and hope she doesn't talk to Jason.

"What are you talkin' about with Keira?" Grim asks her, getting close to her face.

"I don't know what you mean!" she answers, trying to lie her way out of the situation she now finds herself in.

"Yes, you do. I suggest you tell us before I let my boy loose over there. Yeah, the one you're watchin' play with his favorite blade."

"All I know is that Jason paid me to come in here and try to fuck Blade. He wanted proof to show that girl as soon as I did it. Blade hasn't wanted a thing to do with me though and I can see that he loves his wife."

"You thought you could help that fuckin' psycho take one of our women and we wouldn't do anythin' to you?" Joker asks, stepping up.

"I didn't think you'd ever find out," she whines.

"How did you figure we wouldn't find out?" Grim asks. "If you've spent any time here at all, you know we value any woman associated with us. Our old ladies have the utmost respect of everyone around here. We've already been lookin' into who the mole was, you just didn't pay enough attention to know that," Grim tells her, taking a step closer as she tries to shrink back.

"Listen, I thought I'd fuck him, or at least make it look like we fucked, and then be gone," she cries out.

"How do you know Jason?" I finally ask.

"I've been fucking him for years. He helps me supply my habit and then he holds it over my head. Telling me how I'm never getting my son back because he'll make sure of it if I don't do everything he says."

We all look at one another and I know we're going to end up helping this bitch. She needs to get help if she truly wants her son back. But, it won't be here. Maybe one of the other clubs would be willing to take her in and help her get clean and then keep an eye on her to make sure she stays clean.

"Listen," Grim says. "Do you want to get help, get off the drugs you're on?"

"Yes! Jason's the one that got me hooked to begin with. I may not be the most upstanding person, I've done what I've had to do to raise my son. Jason took it to a whole new level so he could control me though. I want my son back and I want as far away from Jason as I can get."

"If we help you, are you goin' to turn your back on us and go back to Jason and continue helpin' him?" Joker asks.

"No. I told you, I want as far away from him as possible. The only reason I haven't tried to leave him before is because he has someone keeping an eye on my son. I get pictures every week to show that someone's always there watching him. Kind of like he had me to do your wife with the twins. I'm so sorry!"

Grim tells Glen to untie her as he pulls his phone out. I know he's calling one of the other clubs, I'm just not sure which one yet. Though, if I had to guess, I'd probably say Gage's. Slim's club is a little bit harder than ours and we're not going to send her to a club whose members do drugs. I'm trying really hard not to fall for this chick's words, in case she's playing us, but something tells me she's not. She truly wants to get away from Jason and get her life back on track so she can get her son back.

"One more question," I suddenly ask. "Who is Jason workin' with?"

"What do you mean?" she asks, confusion clearly written on her face.

"He's not smart enough to get you hooked on drugs to control you, kidnap my wife, and everythin' else that he's done. We know he's in bed with someone else."

"I've heard mention of a cartel. But, I'm not sure which one and I don't know how true it is," she answers. "If I asked too many questions, I'd get hit so I learned real quick not to ask him anything."

"Okay," Grim says, hanging up his phone and turning to us. "What's your name?"

"Sally."

"Sally, one of our other chapters are goin' to take you in. They're goin' to get you clean and then they're goin' to help get you on your feet so you can get your son back. You fuck us over and we'll make sure you never see your son again. Is that understood?"

Sally nods her head furiously. She knows that this is her one opportunity to get clean and away from the lifestyle that Jason got her into. Now, it's up to her as to what she does with this second chance she's being given.

We head back upstairs and I see all the old ladies standing around in a circle. They're protecting my wife and I couldn't be more proud than I am right now. She's got more friends and family now then she knows what to do with. I can see her looking at me until her eyes land on Sally. Suddenly her face takes on a whole new demeanor and I see her claws coming back out.

"What's going on?" she asks.

"Sally here is leavin' the clubhouse and goin' out of town. For good," Grim tells her.

"I'm so sorry that I made it seem like I was making a play for your man. I really wasn't," Sally tells Keira.

Keira takes in the scene before her and starts heading our way. I'm not sure what's going through her head right now, but I'm bracing for anything to happen. Before she gets too close, my girl comes to a stop and really looks at Sally.

"He got to you too. Didn't he?" she asks.

Sally nods her head and I look over at her. Now that everything has calmed down, you can see that she's got so much make-up on it's caked on her face. Usually, this isn't out of the normal when it comes to club girls. Looking closer though, you can see the bruises that she's trying to hide. She's not caking on the make-up to try to impress anyone, she's doing it to cover the evidence that she's been hit.

Joker and Irish make their way to the door with Sally in between them. They're going to be taking her to the half-way point between here and

Dander Falls. Once they get there, they'll hand her over to a few guys from Gage's chapter. He'll figure out the best way to get her clean and protect her. She's not safe here now that she's turned on Jason. Especially if he's working with a cartel. This whole situation just got a lot fucking bigger than what we originally thought it was. We need to be prepared for anything now.

"Listen up!" Grim hollers out. "As soon as Joker and Irish get back, we're havin' church. We need to figure out what our next move is after what we just found out. Get some rest while they're gone and see if you can come up with any game plans. Blade, it's up to you how much you tell Keira. This involves her otherwise I wouldn't be tellin' you to say anythin' to her."

Everyone breaks up and I lead Keira to our room. Ma is sitting on the bed next to a still sleeping Cory. She's clearly concerned about my little princess and I wonder if she got sick again. Seeing the worry on my face, Ma quickly tells me that she's fine and has been asleep the whole time. She leaves the room and heads back to where all the kids are so she can bunker down with Pops and try to get some sleep.

"Can you tell me what's going on?" Keira asks, moving Cory to the playpen.

"I will. Only because I need you to be extremely cautious for now and I don't want you out alone. At all. There is to be at least a few brothers on you at all times. Even when I'm here with you," I tell her. I'm not trying to scare her, but she needs to know the severity of the situation.

Sitting her down on the bed, I relay everything that Sally told us. Keira has tears in her eyes and I know they're for Sally and the son that she can't see right now. When I get to the part about Jason being involved with some cartel, Keira's eyes about pop out of her head in shock. This definitely gets her attention.

"So, now I'm not just being sold, I'm being sold by a member of a cartel?" she asks, her voice shaking.

"We don't know what part Jason plays in the cartel, kitten. Sally just said that she's heard talk of him being involved in one. It makes sense, but it doesn't necessarily make it true," I tell her, pulling her down in my lap.

After taking a few minutes to take in the fact that a cartel is now more than likely after her, Keira sits up and stares at me. I feel her grind down on my hardening length and she moves in to kiss me. I meet her halfway and just before our lips touch, she tells me to make her forget about it. There's nothing I wouldn't do for my wife. So, if she wants to forget for a little while, then I'm going to help her do that.

Taking her mouth with mine, I lay back until I'm the one laying against the pillows. Keira might want to forget, but she's going to be the one to take lead tonight. I'm giving her complete and total control over what happens and what doesn't happen.

Sitting up, Keira pulls my shirt over my head and I feel her running her hands up my stomach and to my chest. As she moves her hands lower, I feel her scoot back so that she can get to my jeans and undo them. Once she has them undone, she pulls my pants off and makes her way back up my body. Before I can stop her, she takes me in her mouth and my head falls back to the pillows. My eyes automatically close at the sensations she's creating by licking, sucking, and reaching down to massage my balls. I don't want to cum in her mouth though.

I pull her hair just hard enough for her to release me. Pulling her up my body, I bring her mouth to mine and kiss her deep as hell. By the time I pull away from her we're both breathless. Keira doesn't need any further direction about what I want from her. She needs me as much as I need her right now. Keira lines herself up with me and pushes herself down. She goes slow as fuck and it's absolute torture. But it's torture of the best kind.

"Kitten, are you goin' to move faster at any point or are you just goin' to torture us both?" I ask her, gritting my teeth.

Instead of answering, Keira starts moving a little bit faster and twirling her hips as she's moving. I drop my head back again and my eyes close on their own. For Keira taking top, she sure as fuck knows what she's doing. She throws her head back and her long hair brushes against my thighs adding to the sensations she's already creating. I reach up and start playing with her tits, knowing that she loves this. Hell, I love playing with them. It's not enough for me though. Sitting up I take one nipple in my mouth and start nibbling and sucking on it.

Keira doesn't miss a beat with the change in our position. The only thing she does is throw her head back even farther and let out a moan. From this position, I can thrust up as she's coming down and hit every spot to make her reach her release. With one hand, I grab one of hers and bring our hands between us. I lay mine on top of hers and rub circles on her clit. She takes it a step further and moves her fingers down enough to slide on each side of my cock while I'm sliding in and out of her.

"Give it to me kitten," I grit out, feeling myself getting closer and closer.

I bite down on her nipple again as I pinch her clit, just hard enough to give her the slightest amount of pain. Keira may not know it yet, but she loves a little bit of pain with her pleasure. From what I get out of conversations we had in the past, no one ever took the time to see what she liked and didn't like. No one experimented with her or let her try new things.

"Michael!" she screams out as I feel her muscles clenching around me. It's too much and I moan out her name as my release finds me.

I lay back against the pillows and pull Keira on top of me. Rubbing her back, I help her come down as I try to get my breathing back under control. I can feel her hands running up and down my sides in a soothing manner. Well, it's soothing until she hits the one spot that has me jumping because it's tickling me. Keira starts to apologize and I put my finger over her mouth. There's nothing for her to apologize for. She didn't know and it's not like she meant to do it. Sometimes it tickles and sometimes it doesn't.

"Kitten, I need you to be extremely careful when I go out of town on this run in the mornin'. I don't want you goin' outside for any reason." I tell her, letting her know once again the severity of the situation.

"I'll stay inside baby. I don't need you focusing on me and what may or may not be happening while you're away. What I need is for you to be safe and come back home to us."

"Always," I answer, knowing I'll do everything in my power to come back to the three people that mean everything in this world to me.

Chapter Twelve

Keira

IT'S BEEN ALMOST A month and a half since Sally told us all about the possibility of Jason being involved with a cartel. The guys have decided that it would be best if I stay in the clubhouse for now since it's easier to get in our home than it would be here. If I go out anywhere, I need to take an army of men with me and I can only ride in the vehicles that have been made bulletproof. It's not one hundred percent safe if anything else were to happen, but Blade and I feel a little bit better if I have to go anywhere.

For the most part, I don't go anywhere. I've changed any appointments I had and have only taken the kids to a doctor appointment for their monthly check-up. Other than that, prospects take care of everything else I need to do. Blade has stopped going on runs and has been sticking close to me. Some days it grates on my nerves to know that he's taking this whole protective thing above and beyond what it needs to be. Other days, I can't help but love how protective he is.

Ma and the rest of the old ladies have also been sticking to the clubhouse. Mainly to keep me company, but I think the guys want them all here for their protection too. If Jason is involved with the cartel then they won't hesitate to grab anyone they can to get to me. I've learned a lot about the rest of the old ladies and they've been telling me about everything they've been doing to try to help victims of domestic violence. That's definitely something I can get behind, so I tell them I'll do whatever they need me to do.

By the time I leave the room with the twins, most of the old ladies are in the kitchen getting things ready for the party today to celebrate our wedding. Blade has been acting nervous and strange so I have no clue as to what's really going on with him. It's not like we're getting married today, so I have no clue why he's acting the way he is. Bailey, Maddie, and Melody all look up and smile when they see me. Skylar isn't here right this second, which is surprising because she is usually the one in charge of any food being prepared.

"Hey!" Skylar says, walking in behind me. "Now, I don't know what you think you're doing in here. There's nothing for you to do."

"I can help do something, guys."

"Nope. Your party, you're not helping. Darcy should be here soon to give you the full treatment. So, I'd be thinking about what you want done to your hair and stuff," Skylar tells me, continuing over to the stove.

"Well, before I leave, I need to get the kids fed. And I might need to get something too."

Skylar tells me that I'm allowed to do that but nothing else. As I'm preparing lunch for the twins, I'm thinking about what I want to do to my hair. Blade told me before that he doesn't ever want to see me cut my hair. Maybe a trim and then I'll have her do something different to it. Put it up in a way I haven't worn it before.

As soon as I have our lunch, I take the twins back to the room with the help of Ma. She helps me get them fed really quick before going back out to help the rest of the women and club girls get everything ready for the party. I sit down to finally eat just as there's a knock on the door.

"Come in!" I call out.

"You ready to get pampered?" Darcy asks, peeking her head around the door.

"I am. We'll just have to stay in here so I can keep an eye on the twins," I tell her, standing up to jump in the shower. "You mind sitting with them for a few minutes?"

"Not at all."

Darcy has been working on me for hours now. I've been massaged, had a manicure and pedicure, and now she's doing my hair. I told her I just wanted a trim and maybe some layers put into it. Crash and Trojan are camped outside the bedroom door and I know part of it is so Wood and Darcy can't have any more incidents like the last one I was a witness to.

"Almost done sweetheart. Am I putting it up?" she asks, not once stopping what she's doing.

"I want you to put it up. Do something I haven't done before. That's not hard though considering I usually just throw it up in a messy bun or a pony tail."

"Alright. I think I know what I want to do to it. I'll put it half up with curls flowing down your back. How does that sound?"

"I trust you. You do what you think will look best."

Blade comes in the room and grabs a change of clothes before heading in the bathroom to shower. I don't know what he's been doing, but he's been gone all day long. There's no reason for me not to trust him and I don't need to know every little thing he's out doing. If I need to know or he tells me, then he does. If not, then it's because it's club business and he'll only tell me what I do need to know.

Darcy is just putting the finishing touches on my hair when Blade emerges from the bedroom. He gives me a kiss and leans down to pick Kenyon up. They're just starting to wake up so Blade feeds Kenyon and changes him before moving on to Cory. Darcy stops what she's doing and watches Blade for a minute. I guess she's never seen a guy so hands-on with his children before. At least without his woman asking them for help.

"I'll see you out there, kitten. You gonna be much longer?"

"I'm almost done with her," Darcy answers.

"As soon as Darcy's done, I just have to change and then I'll be out," I answer.

"Okay. Some of the other clubs are startin' to show up, so I need to show my face."

Before leaving, Blade gives me another quick kiss and makes his exit. The twins are sitting in their bouncy seats and Darcy is gabbing away about things I don't understand. I think it's a nervous habit she has and doesn't even realize she's doing it.

"Darcy, can I ask you a question?" I ask, during a pause.

"Yeah."

"What's going on with you and the two men stationed at the door?"

"Oh. Um…..nothing really. They just want what they can't have."

"I don't think so. From what I've seen and heard, they've been chasing you for a long time. If it were really all about the chase, they would've given up by now."

"No. When they get something in their mind, they won't stop until they get between her legs. As soon as they do, it's over and they're moving on to the next one. I'm not dumb."

"What makes you so sure?"

"Those are two fine as fuck men. I'm a curvy, boring hairdresser. It's all about getting in my pants so they can say they did and then moving on."

"We'll see. I think you're gonna be surprised and they will end up getting what they want. Besides, even if it is just a little bit of fun, why not take it while you can?"

"Is that what Blade and you started out as?"

"It is. Even before he found out I was pregnant he said he was already getting ready to find me and bring me back here with him."

"I don't know if I can handle the lifestyle though."

"I think you can. You're already in it if you think about it. You spend time with us, I know they keep eyes on you, and you'll have more protection if you're with them."

"I don't know. Right now, there's things going on that no one knows about and I don't want to open up about them. To anyone."

"They're going to find out and then you'll have no choice but to take what they're offering. I've been watching the three of you and I see the way they look at you. The way their eyes follow your every movement. You just don't see it because you don't want to see it. You want to keep believing that they only want a piece of ass and nothing more."

Darcy doesn't say anything in response. She finishes up my hair and make-up so I can get dressed. Blade was still acting funny and I don't know what to make of it. Before I go in the bathroom, Darcy tells me that she's going to go make sure none of the other girls need help getting ready. I ask her if she sees Blade if she can send him in to help me.

As I walk out of the bathroom, Blade is sitting on the end of the bed holding Cory. I pause and watch father and daughter for a minute. Blade is staring at his daughter, a look of pure love shining down. Kenyon is still in his bouncy seat at Blade's feet.

"Babe, what's going on?" I ask, sitting next to him.

"What do you mean?"

"You've been acting weird. It's like you're changing your mind and I don't know what I can do to fix whatever changed for you," I tell him.

"Nothin' changed, kitten. I'm actin' weird because I'm nervous as fuck."

"What are you nervous about?"

"We're already married. Married couples get divorced all the time. I have somethin' for you, but it's different than bein' married. It's for life and I don't know if you're goin' to change your mind about bein' with me."

"What do you mean? You're not making sense to me, Blade."

"I want you as my old lady. I know the other old ladies already consider you mine, but today I am goin' to make it official," Blade says, standing up and going over to the closet. "I was goin' to do this at the party, but maybe we need to do this in private. Especially with the other two clubs comin' in."

Blade hands me the box and I sit there with it in my lap for a minute. He's just watching me, a nervous expression on his face. I can't make him wait any longer, so I pull the ribbon from the box and lift the lid. There's tissue paper inside and I lift it up to reveal a rag just like Blade's. I take it out and hold it up. The back is facing me so I open it all the way up and read what it says; *Property of Blade*. Their patch is in the middle and the words are surrounding the words like Blade's.

Looking up to Blade, I see the hesitation on his face and I know he's waiting for me to say something. I'm just so stunned that I don't know what to say.

"If you don't want, or like it, you don't have to wear it," Blade tells me.

"It's not that babe. I'd be proud to wear it. I just wasn't expecting this and I don't know what to say."

"Are you sure?"

"Baby, did I marry you? Am I staying with you when everything in me is telling me to leave and never return before you get the chance to move on? I want everyone to know that you're my man and I want to wear this rag."

I see Blade visibly relax as I put it on. The hesitation leaves his face and the smile he saves just for me shines through. Blade sets Cory back in her seat and wraps his arms around me, pulling me as close as I can possibly get to him. I wind my arms up around his neck and pull his face to mine, kissing him like my life depends on it. I can't believe that he was so unsure of himself because of this. He should've known better.

"We better get to the party since it's for us," he tells me, breaking the kiss. "If we don't go now, we're not leavin' this room for a very long time."

"I wish we didn't have to leave the room. That I could show you how much I love you and how honored I am to wear your rag."

Blade

We've been at the party for a few hours. I can't believe I was so nervous about what Keira would say when I gave her my rag. She's sitting at a table with the twins and I constantly have her in my line of sight. My girl is talking and laughing with everyone. Not just the other old ladies that she knows, but old ladies from other chapters, brothers from other chapters, and the guys from Slim's club.

Keira is in her element and if she's nervous about being around everyone she's not letting it show.

"You made a good choice," Pops tells me, coming to stand next to me.

"She's the best woman I know. I didn't stand a chance against her and she didn't do anythin' special to try to get me."

"The best ones don't have to do anythin' special. They're themselves and they don't pretend to be someone they're not. That girl loves you more than anythin' other than your babies. Keep her close and don't ever let her go."

"I don't plan on it. Those three are my world and I don't know where I'd be if anythin' were to happen to any of them."

"Blade, I think you might want to go get your girl," Bailey tells me.

"Why is that?" I ask, setting my beer down on the closest table.

"You're goin' to dance with her. We're celebrating your wedding and what's a wedding without a bride and groom dance? Hurry up, Grim's getting ready to announce it."

I walk over to Keira as Pops and Ma make their way over to her. Apparently, they already knew this was coming. They take the twins and I hear Grim calling for everyone's attention.

"Everyone is here to celebrate the marriage between Blade and Keira. They didn't want anyone to cause a scene or make a big deal of it, but we all know our old ladies aren't like that. Now, for the first time, I'm goin' to introduce Mr. and Mrs. Branch as they enjoy their first dance."

Everyone starts clapping and whistling as I lead Keira to the make-shift dance floor. Keira is blushing and I know this is hard for her. She hates calling attention to herself. We no sooner get to the middle and I wrap my arms around her when *Tangled Up In You* by Aaron Lewis comes on. Keira smiles up at me before laying her head against my chest.

We sway to the music as everyone surrounds the dance floor. I look at Cage and make a motion with my head for him to bring Skylar out to dance with us. Keira has her eyes closed so she doesn't have to look at everyone watching us and I know this will make it easier for her. It's still our song, our dance, we're just going to be joined by our family.

Slowly other couples make their way to dance with us. The members from my club are the ones that surround us though. Even Irish manages to get Caydence on the dance floor with us. She finally made an appearance a few minutes ago. Keira opens her eyes and sees everyone surrounding us.

"Thank you," she tells me.

"I got you. I've always got your back kitten," I tell her, leaning down for a kiss.

After our dance, I see Pops making his way over to us. I'm not sure what's going on now, but I hope it's something good and not one of the twins. He waits until he has Keira's attention before he holds out his hand to her.

"Everyone deserves a father-daughter dance." He says. "I don't know your situation, but I walked you down the aisle and I'd be honored if you would let me share that dance with you."

Keira has tears in her eyes as she looks over to Bailey. Bailey just smiles and nods her head. She knows how Pops is and that this is something that he would do for anyone. Seeing that it's okay with Bailey, Keira takes his hand and lets him dance with her. I don't know who chose the song, but my girl has tears cascading down her face as *I Loved Her First* by Heartland plays.

Even though the song doesn't fit the relationship between my girl and Pops, the girls are trying to give her a traditional reception. If that means dancing to this song with Pops, then that's what they're going to do for her. Since they've all moved to stand together, I look over at the old ladies and smile. They're all crying and watching as Keira finally realizes that she's a part of our family.

We've eaten, danced, talked, and just relaxed throughout the day. The guys are starting to light the bonfires around the party area and we're getting ready to send the kids in with a few of the old ladies. Not many, but a few of the club girls are going to be showing up for the brothers that are single, but this is still a party for Keira and I. Only certain club girls are going to be allowed here. Summer was given the job to choose the best ones, ones that won't cause any drama or problems.

"You want to take the kids inside, or stay out here?" I ask Keira, pulling her in my lap.

"I'll take them in. I love you so much," she tells me.

"I love you too. Will until after I take my last breath."

I stand up with her and help her get the kids inside. She packed a bag so that everything they would need was already together and we didn't have go looking for anything. Ma, Pops, and Summer are in with the kids tonight. Ever since we lost Storm, Summer hasn't been big on the parties like she used to be. Honestly, I don't even know when the last time I saw her with a brother was.

Keira hugs and kisses our kids before handing them over to Ma and Summer. We turn around and make our way through the back door of the clubhouse. Just as we go to sit with Grim, Slim, Wood, Killer, and Tank, all hell breaks loose.

We hear one explosion from out front of the clubhouse and all of the brothers begin to run that way. Before I can get too far, there's another explosion at the very back of the property. One by one there's explosions starting to come from every direction. I grab Keira and pull her with me to get to the clubhouse. People are screaming and yelling, trying to rush to wherever they think it's going to be safe for them to wait out the explosions and fires that are starting to burn rapidly.

Before we can get inside the clubhouse, there's an explosion at the front side of the building. Keira screams louder than I've heard anyone else. All of the kids are inside along with Ma, Pops, Summer, and Glen. I know the thoughts running through my wife's head because they're running through mine right now.

Grim doesn't let anyone get near the building though. He's directing everyone to find cover and stay together as much as possible. Meanwhile, he's running around trying to find people that are too scared to move or do anything. Bailey is screaming for him to take cover and before anyone can do much it seems like there's multiple explosions at one time. They're in no certain places, just all over the place. I can see that one of the explosions catches Caydence who actually came out for the first time in months. This is not going to end well for anyone.

After covering Keira for what seems like an eternity, the explosions stop. There's dead silence surrounding us with no one daring to move in case more start going off. Grim is standing in the middle of the yard and he's looking around cautiously. Looking up, I see that at least two walls of the clubhouse are completely caved in, letting me see right up to the front gate. There's nothing left to the garage we store our bikes in and most of the bikes and other vehicles in the parking lot are completely destroyed.

Panic is starting to set in after seeing the walls caved in. The kids, Ma and Pops, and Summer are in there. I can't even tell you if anyone else had made their way in there. Keira looks up at me and I can see the tears in her eyes knowing that our kids are in that building right along with the rest of the kids. Jumping up, I run as fast as my legs can carry me towards the clubhouse. Cage, Joker, Tank, and Glock are also running that way. Grim is the closest one there so he makes it to what used to be the doorway first.

"We need to tread carefully. Where did Ma and Pops have the kids?" Grim asks.

"They were in the back room closest to the door," I answer. "I don't think they would've moved them once the explosions started. Unless they took them to the panic room that just got finished."

Not that long ago, we all decided that we would turn the back section into a panic room. Grim hired a contractor from out of state to ensure our privacy and paid them extra to keep their mouth shut about it. If there was any way they could get there, I know Pops would have made sure that's where they were.

Once we enter what used to be the back door, we see that there is no hallway left. It's completely caved in and there's no doors or anything left standing. My heart is in my throat as we start moving debris trying to make our way to the area of the panic room. We can see that it's still standing, but we have no clue who's in there or if any of them made it there.

After what seems like forever, we move the last piece of wall that's blocking the door. Grim punches in the code and after a minute the door unlocks. As soon as he pushes it open he's greeted by Pops pointing a gun right in his face. Pops slowly lowers the gun as he realizes that it's us and not some threat. Shock is evident on his face and I glance around the room to see all of the kids in one piece. They're crying and in shock but they're all whole. Summer is holding Kenyon and Cory in the corner and I feel like I can take my first real breath since this all started. Upon further inspection though, I don't see Ma. She's nowhere in the room and I don't know where the hell she would be. Unless.

One by one, the rest of the men come to the same conclusion that I do. Ma is either trapped somewhere or she didn't survive one of the explosions. Losing her is going to cripple this club. She's been the backbone behind every member for as long as anyone can remember. Any time one of us had a problem, she was the one we went to. If someone in town needed anything at all, including the shirt off her back, she was there with no questions and not wanting anything in return. Pops will not survive losing the love of his life either. I honestly don't know what he'll do.

"Pops?" Grim asks. "Pops? Where's Ma?"

"In the game room. I tried, I tried with everythin' in me. She told me to go and make sure the babies were okay and safe. Grim, she wouldn't let me bring her. Told me to lock the door and not come back for her," Pops tells us, finally breaking down and not caring who is there as a witness.

I make my way back out to find Keira and see who else we lost. All around me there's crying, screaming, shock, and everything else you can imagine. Some of the men are moving all the women to an area of the backyard that will be the safest for them to be in right now. There's coverage, but nothing will fall on them.

As soon as I step out the back of what used to be the clubhouse, I can already count at least fifteen bodies lying on the ground. Some are just injured but others didn't make it. The first guy I see is one of the nomads. His body is at an odd angle and I know without a doubt he did not survive. Glen, the new prospect, is not too far away from him and I know that we've lost him too. Before I can make it another twenty feet away, Caydence is lying face down and Irish is at her side. He's bent over her and I can see the tears streaming down his face. As soon as I saw her in the one explosion I knew she was not going to survive the damage done to her body.

Keira is in the middle of the women and I can guarantee that they're trying to make sure she doesn't leave and go in search of our children herself. Anyone that knows my kitten knows that she'll fight tooth and nail to protect those she loves and there's no greater love than what a mother has for her children. Well, from the good moms that is. She finally meets my eyes and I nod my head to let her know that Kenyon and Cory are safe. Her entire body sags in relief. Until she starts looking around at all of the destruction surrounding us.

Keira

The day that was supposed to be one of joy and celebration has turned into one of the worst days anyone in the Wild Kings MC has experienced. I know without a doubt that this is my fault and I don't know how I'm going to look anyone in the eye after this catastrophe. Jason is behind this attack and he's cost multiple people their lives just to try to get at me.

The women have surrounded me because they know I'm about to go find my children and not care what happens to me. I can't relax and I'm trying to figure out how to break away when I see Blade make his way outside again. After taking a glance around to see the casualties and damage, our eyes meet and he lets me know the kids are safe. I can't help the relief that spreads through my body.

We're all standing here waiting to hear some news about what's going on when I know we're all thinking about who made it through this and who we've lost. I can already see that we've lost Caydence. Even though I didn't know her, the rest of these women I consider my friends and family did. Her man is draping himself over her body and I can see the sobs wracking through his body. The rest of the men are taking stock of who's just injured and who has not made it. Those that are injured and can be moved are being brought closer to us. Unfortunately, there's a lot of bodies that are not being moved which doesn't bode well for anyone.

I can hear the sirens in the distance coming closer. And I know that they're going to have to call in more than just the few fire trucks and ambulances that this small town has. Instead of standing here waiting, I want to be helping do something. Anything to get my mind off of what's going on and what's going to happen next.

"I need to go see what I can do to help," Bailey says, as if she's reading my mind.

"We were told to stay put so that they could concentrate on what they had to do instead of worrying about us," Skylar says, trying to get Bailey see reason.

"I know. But as someone that's grown up with this club, I need to do something. My mind is racing and I can't shut it off," She tells us, the tears and her control finally slipping.

"I feel the same way Bailey," I tell her, letting her know that she's not alone. "For right now, let's stay put. The emergency help is almost here and we're going to need to stay out of their way so people can get the help they need."

No one says anything to that, we all just think whatever thoughts we have and one by one sit on the ground. Melody pulls me to her and we take comfort from one another while the rest of the women do the same thing. I can see the doubt, questions, guilt, and a host of other emotions on the faces surrounding me. Guilt is probably the main one on my face right now.

"This is all my fault," I say to no one in particular.

"It's not," Bailey says, adamantly.

"If I had just stayed with Jason, none of this would've happened. It's retaliation for me leaving and not letting him sell me."

"You would've been found one way or another. Jason and his cronies took it upon themselves to rain terror down on our club and family today. The hell that is about to rain down on them is going to be like nothing they've ever seen before." Bailey says, making sure I'm looking directly at her. "You can't blame yourself for wanting to survive, wanting to come home to your man and amazing children."

The rest of the women surrounding us all nod their heads in agreement. They may not know the situation, but they're agreeing to what Bailey is trying to make me understand. I just don't see it though. How can I when I know that Jason is the cocksucker behind this?

It's been hours and we're all finally being released from the clubhouse. About the only thing that wasn't destroyed were the homes that were built across the field from the clubhouse. So, we're all splitting up who's left and bringing them home with us. The space is going to be cramped, but I wouldn't have it any other way. We all need to be here for one another with the list of names we have already that haven't survived and for the ones that have been rushed to different hospitals surrounding the area. Bailey has been inconsolable at the news that her mother didn't survive. Grim left with her as soon as they possibly could and Skylar took their son and daughter. Pops left with them and I know that he's just as distraught as his daughter is. He's just trying to be strong for the rest of his family right now. He'll break eventually and we'll all be there to support him.

We've taken in a few nomads, a few of the guys from the Dander Falls chapter, and Darcy. So, yes, Crash and Trojan are at our house with her. Wood just so happens to be here too. He didn't want to leave my side knowing that Blade was going to be busy doing what has to be done now. Wood has become a close friend and someone that feels the need to protect me. With the somber mood though, I can guarantee that there's not going to be any shenanigans between the foursome that seem to make a habit of becoming the entertainment for everyone.

I'm sitting upstairs in the nursery with Darcy and we're each holding one of the twins. We're not saying much and I'm personally in my own head and not finding a way to get back out of it. I haven't been this bad since being with Jason and I don't think that Blade or Karen are going to be able to help me this time. The guilt I feel is just becoming all consuming.

Before too long, the three men in our lives make an appearance. For a minute, I can feel them just standing in the doorway watching us, waiting for us to break. I can't afford to break though when I have the twins to think about, a houseful of people, and things that need to be done concerning funerals, hospital visits, and just being there for the individuals and families that have lost their loved ones. These are the things I need to focus on right now.

"Kitten, Cory's sleepin' why don't you let me put her in the crib?" Blade asks me.

I look down and see that he's right. "Yeah, I didn't realize she passed out already."

"It's okay kitten. You've got a lot on your mind right now. We all do."

Hearing those words, I break and start crying uncontrollably. Blade pulls me into his arms and tries to comfort me the best that he can as I watch Trojan take Kenyon from Darcy and put him in his crib. The three of them surround us to be there for support even though there are other people downstairs that need support too.

"What's goin' on kitten?" Blade asks, the concern evident in his voice.

"I've been saying it since it happened. This is all my fault. Jason did this because of me. You all lost family and friends because of me."

"Jason did do this, I guarantee it. It's not your fault though. Would it still be your fault if Slim's club were the ones to get you free and this still happened? No. They chose to do this instead of acceptin' that you weren't theirs to sell or do anythin' else with," Crash says.

Everyone is saying this isn't my fault, but it's barely breaking through the fog in my brain. It's like I need to take on everything that happened so there's someone to blame for it. Jason is to blame, but I'm the one that led him here. Blade isn't going to stand for this though, I already know he's going to do everything in his power to prove that I'm not at fault. Including bringing in Karen, Grim, Slim, Gage, and whoever else he has to.

Chapter Thirteen

Grim

IT'S BEEN ABOUT TWO WEEKS since the bombing at the clubhouse during Blade and Keira's reception. Keira has been blaming herself and we've all been trying to tell her that we don't blame her at all. Jason is the one to blame along with whoever else helped him do this to us.

If the information we have is correct, then he's working with the cartel and they were already going to be gunning for us. They're pissed we released all the girls when Maddie was taken. It was honestly only a matter of time before they got their retaliation and we all know this. Keira may not because she wasn't here during that time. So, today is the day I educate her.

Knocking on Blade's door, I wait for someone to let me in. I don't want to be away from my wife for too long because she's not handling the loss of Ma, and everyone else, at all. I don't think she's even gotten out of bed since it happened unless I make her take a shower. And I know for a fact she hasn't been eating. So, Karen is on her way over now to spend some time with her.

"Grim, what are you doing here?" Keira asks, opening the door. "How's Bailey?"

"She's not takin' it too well. But, I'm here to see you. We need to have a chat before this gets any further out of control for you. I know you've been wearin' yourself thin tryin' to be there for everyone and the guilt that you're feelin' right now."

"Oh. Well, I'm not doing anything that anyone else is doing. I go where I'm needed to do what I can."

"Let's go out back and talk," I tell her, waiting for her to close the door behind her.

We make our way out back to the patio and take a seat at the table they set up for cookouts. Keira takes a seat across from me and waits for me to begin talking. She doesn't look at me and I know she thinks that I'm going to be yelling at her. I'm not though.

"I know you think this is on you. It's not," I begin. "But, we've been dealin' with the people Jason's workin' with since long before you made an appearance. We've honestly been waitin' for retaliation and they're just now makin' their move."

"They wouldn't have done it to this extreme though if I wasn't there," she tells me, honestly believing what she's saying.

"Yes, they would have. I'm goin' to tell you somethin' no one outside of the members know. Jason is workin' with a cartel. So, yes, they would've done the same thing they did regardless of you bein' here or not. Now, I'm trustin' that you're not goin' to say anythin' about this to anyone."

Keira sits there in stunned silence for a minute as I watch to make sure she's going to be okay. Finally, she looks up at me and I can see that I'm getting through to her with the knowledge that this is not her fault.

"You have to believe that I didn't know that's who he was working with. I would've told Blade or someone if I had any idea that he was working with a cartel."

"We know. He kept you in the dark the same way we keep our old ladies in the dark. His reasons weren't the same, but he did it none the less. So, go back inside and let the guilt leave you," I tell her, knowing that she can breathe a little easier now.

Standing up, I make sure Keira is inside before making my way back over to my house. We all took members into our homes, and I'm glad that I have the extra help right now with the kids since I've been trying to be there for Bailey. She's needed me more than ever and Pops has too. He's trying to be strong, but we've had a few talks and I know this is eating him alive. Ma was his whole reason to live and get through the day. I don't know how he's going to handle this. Especially come tomorrow when we go to bury everyone.

After having church a few days after the bombing, we all decided that we'd bury everyone from here on the same day. Afterwards, we'll have a memorial service for everyone that lost their lives that day. We managed to lose four people, Gage's club lost two, Slim's club lost three, and one nomad didn't make it. There are two guys that were about to become prospects for our club in the hospital and it doesn't look good for them. We'll make sure they're either taken care of or their family is taken care of depending on what happens to them.

When I walk in the door, Pops tells me that Karen is in with Bailey so I go see Zander who's sitting outside by himself. He looks up at me and I can see the unshed tears threatening to spill over. Zander quickly looks away and I know he's trying to be strong and not cry in front of me. Time for a talk with him. Zander may be young, but he's smart as hell and knows more than he should.

"Son, what are you doin' out here?" I ask, taking a seat and pulling him into my lap.

"Just wanted to be alone daddy," he says, snuggling in.

"You know it's okay to cry, right buddy?" I ask. "I've cried, Pops has cried, and a lot of the other men have cried to. We've had somethin' real bad happen."

"I know. But, I'm trying to be strong daddy. You need me."

My heart breaks at hearing my young son telling me that I need him to be strong for me. I pull him in and give him a hug, holding him close for far longer than he probably wants me to. But, maybe I need this now and he's letting me without argument or complaint.

"Daddy doesn't need you to be strong little man. I need you to cry if you want to cry. You need to lean on us as much as we're all leanin' on one another. Can you do that for me?"

Zander nods his head and I know that he's going to break down. So, I continue to hold him close and give him the comfort and strength that he needs right now. It breaks me to know that I've been so busy trying to help everyone and figure everything out that I forgot to be there for my son. One of the main people that I should always be there for no matter what.

Pops

Tomorrow is the day that I bury the love of my life. I've been with Ma so long that I don't know how I'm going to go on. I can't believe that Ma wouldn't let me go back for her and try to save her after making sure that Summer and the children were in the safe room. I tried to leave there, but the kids were not going to let me walk away from them. It was honestly one of the hardest decisions that I've ever made in my life. Ma would've wanted me to stay with the kids though, that's just who she was. I just can't help thinking that it should've been me that was about to get buried and not the greatest woman that I've ever had the pleasure of being around.

Every day, Ma is the only thing I can think about. The only time I've even left Grim and Bailey's house is when Grim called church and we all had to make an appearance. I dream about her smiling face and the memories that we've made over the decades we were together. When I'm awake, I go to tell her something only to remember that I'll never be able to tell her anything again. If it weren't for our grandchildren and the promise she made me make when Joker and Bailey first started having kids, I would've laid down and died right alongside Ma. However, she made me promise that I would live the rest of my life if anything ever happened to her and help guide the next generation to be the kind, loving, respectful people that they need to be. So, I'm going to honor the love of my life and do this for her.

Tomorrow is going to be hard for everyone and I need to pull my act together and start being there for everyone else. Not just mourning my loss when other people lost loved ones too. Irish lost Caydence and I have no clue how he's doing at all. He's now all alone with a small daughter to care for and he lost the only woman he's ever been with. Even though something was going on with them the last few months or so, Irish loved that woman with every fiber of his being. Maybe I should walk over to Skylar's and see him before tomorrow

Bailey

I've been in bed for weeks now and I can't seem to pull my act together. I know that the other members of the club need me and there's things I need to do being the President's old lady and wife. Unfortunately, my grief is so strong for the loss of my mother that I can't even lift my head to see my own children. Ma was loved by everyone and I know I counted on her more times than not. No matter what happened to me, what kind of trouble I got into, or anything else, I could always pick the phone up and my mom would be right there. She picked up the pieces of my broken heart countless times before Grim and I finally got our shit together. And when I lost Ryan, my mom was the rock that I leaned on when I finally started letting others in to help me.

Karen just left me after sitting here for an hour and I didn't say one word to her. We just sat in silence and she let me know that she's going to be there to help all of us through this. Hell, I can't even begin to imagine what my dad is going through, but I can't seem to care enough to get out of bed and see him. I know he's been in here sitting with me for hours and hours, but I didn't even acknowledge him.

Grim is being the rock that I've been leaning on lately and I know that he's going to be there to get my head out of my ass. He's made me get up and take showers, washing my hair and body, made me eat and drink when I don't want anything to do with food, and he's making sure our children are looked after. On top of that, he's doing everything he needs to as President of the Wild Kings.

"Hey crazy girl," he says, walking into our bedroom. "Karen will be back tomorrow after the funeral services and before the memorial service. She's goin' to be here every day until you're ready to start talkin' this shit out."

"What's there to talk about? My mother lost her life because of whatever is going on," I tell him, finally getting out of my head for a second. "Is this only about Keira?"

"No, it's not. These guys are probably the same cartel from when we rescued Maddie. We knew it was a matter of time before they came at us. You did too. Just didn't think they'd take it to this level."

I don't respond to Grim, I just pull the blanket back up over my head and try to digest that information. We did all know that we were dealing with a cartel when it came to getting Maddie back. It looks like they go big when they're pissed and want to let you know it. I just don't understand how they can go after women and innocent children. Our MC would never do that no matter what kind of problem we had with anyone.

But, I know that I can't lay in this bed anymore. I need to get up and continue living my life. I need to be there for my children and the rest of the members, old ladies, friends, and family of the MC. Before I can move though, I hear someone else come in the room and start whispering with Grim.

"Baby," my dad starts. "I get that you are so lost right now that you can't see an end in sight. Fuck, I feel the same way. But, do you honestly think this is how your mom would want us to be? So lost in our own grief and misery that we forget about everyone else around us? We forget about our children?"

"No, I know she would want us to live life to the fullest and get through every day the best we can. It's just so hard daddy," I mumble, taking the blanket off my head.

"I know it is. But, you have a son and daughter that need their mama. There's a ton of extra people here that need support and love, and we have to get ready to say our final goodbye to those around us that lost their life. So, I need you to get out of bed, get ready for the day, and start livin' again. Honor your mother by takin' her role over and fillin' her shoes by bein' there for everyone the way she would be. When you need to break down, you'll know when the time is. Grim will be there to catch you and be the strong that you need."

I nod my head and start getting out of bed. It may not be what I want to do, but it's what I have to do. We will get through this and every day it will start to get a little easier to handle. I just need to remember that there are a ton of people here for me to lean on when the day gets too hard to make it through. Grim being the biggest one there is. I know this is killing him, so it's time that I step up and take some of that pressure and stress off of him. Let him start dealing with his own grief.

Irish

I honestly can't believe that Caydence is gone. She's been the love of my life for so long now that it's hard to imagine never seeing her again. Never seeing her smiling face, watching the crazy things she wanted to do, seeing her face light up with joy when she got an idea she knew would get us all in trouble, and seeing the devastation when she found out we'd never have children of our own. We've been through so much together and I know without a doubt that I would've been able to get things back to the way they were before Cassidy Rose came into our lives.

We were having issues for the last few months. As soon as little Cassidy became ours, Caydence changed. All of a sudden, she didn't want to leave the room, no one was allowed near our daughter, and she was so terrified that someone was going to try to take her from us. I was trying to get her the help she needed to work through this and we had an appointment to go see Karen for tomorrow. It's taken that long for me to convince her that she needed to talk to someone. Now, I'll never know if I would've gotten my girl back.

When I saw the explosions start, I tried to get to Caydence. It's the first time she's been out of our room in months for more than a few minutes. She wanted to go celebrate with Blade and Keira though so I thought we were already starting to make some progress. Now, it's like she knew something was going to happen and wanted to be there for what happened to happen to her. I can't explain it. As the explosions started hitting around the back yard, instead of running for cover, Caydence just stood there. Her eyes locked on mine as I started moving towards her and a smile lit up her face. For the first time in months I saw her relax and relief fill her body. It was like the old Caydence was back. Then I realized that she was going to use the bombing as her way out. She didn't think she could get out of her own head long enough to start getting better so she chose the easy way out.

Am I pissed as fuck that she chose the easy way out? Yeah, I am. Instead of getting help and making sure she was there for Cassidy, I'm now a single father. I wouldn't trade my daughter for anything in this world, I just wish Caydence had been stronger and would be here to help me raise this little girl. Because we all know she's going to get the short end of the stick with me as a dad. I don't know the first thing about raising a little girl, other than the fact that she's not dating until I'm buried in the ground. No one will ever be good enough for my little princess.

As I sit here, holding Cass, I know that life is about to get hard. We're going to be seeking vengeance for what Jason and his assholes did to us and I'm going to have to navigate the role of being a dad. It's time that I get back to the land of the living though and join in things that I've put on the backburner while I was trying to help my girl.

Keira

Today is the day that we say our final goodbye to Ma and everyone else that lost their life. The guys decided that they needed to wait for a bit for the guys that were in the hospital to get out and for the ones that are fighting a battle to see if they were going to get better or not.

Blade and I are helping get everyone gathered in what used to be the parking lot of the clubhouse when I see Bailey, Grim, Skylar, Cage, Joker, and Pops making their way over to us. Grim pulls Blade aside and I'm not sure what he's talking to him about, but I see Blade continually nodding his head yes. As I go to turn around, movement on the other side of the fence catches my eye. Looking closer, I see Jason standing there, a smug smile on his face. Today is really not the day that he's going to want to be pulling some shit. But, I'm not scared of him anymore.

"Joker, make it look like we're having a normal conversation," I say, leaning in just a little bit more.

"What's goin' on Keira?" he asks, confusion clearly on his face.

"Jason is right over there. He's standing on the other side of the fence watching us. Now may be your only chance to get him. But, you have to play it smart."

"Okay. How about we make it look like a few of the guys are goin' back to the houses and sneak through the yard at my house. We can sneak up behind him."

"It would probably work, but I know a guaranteed way to keep him right where he is. You just need to make sure that Blade is one of the guys that leaves the area."

"What are you goin' to do?" he asks me.

"Don't worry about it. Just make sure Blade is one of the guys goin' over to capture him."

Joker makes his way over to Grim and Blade taking Cage with him. After they all talk for a minute, I can see Blade catch my eye and nod his head in my direction. Without a word to anyone, about four men start heading over to our homes. Blade is one of them. As soon as he's far enough away, I start making my way over to the gate and I see Jason moving in closer to me. This is going to be easier than I thought if he really thinks that none of these guys are going to be going after him with all the chaos and destruction he just caused.

Before I make it thirty feet, the men have him surrounded and are tying him up to take him somewhere. I don't want to know any more information than that right there. Grim and Bailey walk over to me and he tells me that I did good, letting one of the guys know I saw him and telling him how to get him. I can tell he's not happy that I was heading that way myself, but he's not going to say anything about it right now.

By the time Blade and the rest of the guys make it back, we're ready to head to the cemetery. Grim, Gage, and Slim have lined everyone up and told the old ladies who is riding where. I'm riding with Bailey and Melody with our kids. We're the first car in line behind some of the bikes. Bailey is a mess, but she's trying to hold it together. I don't know how she's going to get through today, but she's trying. I'll be there to help her in any way I can. We all will be.

The ceremony is over and we're getting ready to head back to the houses. Since the clubhouse is no more, we're going to have the memorial service at Skylar, Cage, and Joker's house. They have that huge yard and the pond. As soon as we get back, I'm going to make sure the twins are good and then I'm going to be helping get everything ready.

Bailey won't be doing much except for going back to her house. She tried to give a eulogy and broke down. Before Grim or anyone else could make their way to her, I stood by her and finished reading what she wrote. It was beautiful and while it was mainly about her mom, it included everyone that lost their lives that day.

"Kitten, need you a minute," Blade calls before heading over to his bike.

"What's going on babe?"

"I'm gonna head out for a bit. I'll be back as soon as I can. You stay close to the other old ladies and don't take your rag off for any reason."

"Okay. You make sure that motherfucker pays for what he's done," I tell him, making sure he can hear the pain and anger in my voice.

"Kitten, don't think we won't be talkin' about you walkin' his way later on either. I saw that shit and I'm not happy. But, I got a few plans in mind for him. He'll pay kitten, for everythin'."

"I know he will. I'll see you when I see you. Love you."

"Love you too, kitten."

Blade takes off with a few of the guys, leaving the rest to take us back to Skylar's. The car ride back is silent and I know that Bailey is in her own head again. I wish I could take the pain away from her, bring her mom back to her. Bring everyone back and have Jason never get the chance to do anything like this.

We've been at the memorial service for a few hours now. Drinks are flowing, food is disappearing as soon as we set it down, and people are sharing memories of their loved ones. Bailey has been here the entire time, right on Grim's arm. She's laughed, cried, and tried to be there for everyone as much as she can right now. I'm sitting here, people watching while holding Kenyon and Cory. Since I don't know too many people and I really didn't know those that passed away, I don't feel right mixing with everyone. I'll just wait until Blade gets back before I mingle. Besides, I'll be of more help letting Skylar, Bailey, and the rest of the girls mingle and do what they do while I make sure everything is set out for everyone. Darcy has been helping me too. I think she feels the same way.

"So, have you made a decision about what you're going to do with those two men that follow you around like little lost puppies?" I ask her.

"Yeah. I think I'm going to give them a shot. But, I'm not letting them know and I'm not going to make it easy on them by any means," she says, trying to laugh.

"I hope that you get what you want Darcy. I think they'll be good to you and treat you the way you deserve to be treated. Right now, they're mingling and doing their part, but they don't take their eyes off of you for too long. And they don't move that far away from you. Trust me honey, they want more than just a few nights of fun with you. They want it all."

"How did you know Blade was it for you?" she asks me.

"At first I didn't. We both just wanted some fun with no strings. When I found out I was pregnant, I knew I had to leave. Blade made it clear he didn't want kids and I knew I wasn't giving my baby up. As soon as I made the decision to leave, my heart started to break and I knew that my life was going to be empty without him in it."

"How long before you took him back?"

"He had to work for it. You go from just wanting some fun and nothing more to telling me you want me as your old lady, I was skeptical. I didn't want to get hurt by him and I wasn't going to give him a chance. But, he wormed his way back in my heart and I knew that I would never love anyone the way that I love him. So, here we are."

Darcy and I spend a little more time talking and making sure everything is kept filled. Just as dark is settling in and the guys are starting to light bonfires, I see the guys pull back up. Instead of coming over here, they all head to their respective homes. Must be they need to clean up and get ready before heading over here. I know I can relax now since that lowlife piece of shit is no longer walking around here. So, I settle in and wait for Blade to make his way over to me.

Chapter Fourteen

Blade

JUST BEFORE WE GOT ready to head to the cemetery, Keira saw that douchebag Jason. We got him before he had any clue what was going down. Keira could have something to do with that because she started walking towards the gate where he was. I got so angry when I saw her heading that way and I know she was trying to distract him so we could get him, but fuck.

We took him around the back of Joker's yard and through a hole in the fence. One of the outbuildings that was saved during the bombing is where our guest is currently waiting for us. I can't wait to have fun and get my hands on the sick fuck that has taken so much from us. The rest of the guys are feeling the same way and I know he's not going to last long once we get in the building with him.

"Blade, you want first or last?" Grim asks me.

"I'm gettin' my hands on him first. But, I get to deliver the kill shot. That's all mine," I tell the guys surrounding me.

"I know I'm gettin' my hands on him for sure. You didn't see what the fuck he did and said to her when they were in the middle of Vixen," Killer says. "You can bet that I'm goin' to get out what I couldn't when we were watchin' your wife."

I nod my head, thankful that Killer was one of the guys assigned to my old lady. Wood is another one I'll never be able to repay. He'll be getting to dish out his own justice as well. Right now, he's making sure everything gets set up in the yard with no problems. I know he's just making sure that my girl and twins are settled in before he leaves to join us.

We all walk in the building and Grim turns on the lone light hanging high above Jason's head. The smell of piss and shit hits us and I can't help gagging at the stench filling the small room. He's only been in here a few hours and he's already being a little fucking pussy. Keira held out longer than that. My girl's a badass though. She'll hold her own against anyone and come out on the other side.

"Look here boys, the shithead can't make it a few hours without makin' a mess of himself. Bet the women that he beats on and takes without their consent last longer than him," Killer says, and we all start laughing at him.

"Pl-pl-please let me go," he stammers out. "I'll do anything you want me to."

Stepping up, Jason instantly recognizes me. "Did my wife beg you for mercy? Did she scream out in pain when you and your buddies beat the living shit out of her? Or was she strong as fuck like I know she is?"

Jason doesn't say a single word. He just shakes his head back and forth, trying to get the image of me looming over him out of his head. Too bad I'm going to be the last motherfucker he ever sees before going to hell. And I'll make sure his last moments on Earth are as painful as they can possibly be.

"Killer, you want to help me carve this fucker up?" I ask, bringing my knives out.

"Absolutely," he says, unfolding the roll of knives I have laid out on the stand with the rest of the tools.

I grab my go-to when I want to inflict damage but not kill the person yet. Killer goes over each and every blade I have, making a big show of picking one out. It's strictly for Jason's benefit, to scare him more than what he already is. We all know this and I can't help the smirk that overtakes my face. The rest of the guys are wearing the same smirk because we know that Killer is putting on a massive show just to get in Jason's head. It's working.

Finally, Killer grabs a blade and we make our way over to where Jason is strung up. Killer rips open his shirt, not going anywhere near his pants and the mess they are. Both of us begin to make small slices all over Jason's body. Deep enough to make him feel it but not deep enough to kill him. We spend probably a half hour marking him up all over his back, chest, stomach, arms, sides, anywhere we can get our blades to.

Joker brings over some salt and hands it off to me. I know what he wants us to do and I'm all over it. Putting my hand on Killer to stop him, I begin to dump the salt over the wounds that we've made on him. Killer holds his hand out so I can dump some salt in his hand. As soon as there's a good amount there, he takes his hand and rubs it into the wounds on Jason's chest. Jason screams out finally, he just can't keep his mouth shut.

"Did my wife scream to you to stop? Scream out in pain?" I ask, my voice full of contempt and malice.

"Yes!" he screams out. "It was my favorite part."

That was the biggest mistake Jason could've made. He just pushed my buttons to the point that I'm not going to care about keeping him alive or not. Every other man in the small building can see the look on my face and knows that shit is about to get real. He's about to be in so much pain that I don't know how I'm going to keep him awake and feeling the maximum amount of pain we can dish out.

"I got somethin' for this fucker," Killer says, going over to the bench and reaching behind the table.

He walks back over and I see a bottle in his hand. It's a spray bottle and I can see the closer he gets to me that it's a glass bottle, not one of those plastic spray bottles. That can only mean one thing; he's got a bottle full of acid. Killer is not playing around when it comes to this fucker.

"You want the honors or do you want someone else to have a shot with it?" he asks me.

Wood picks that moment to walk in the building. So, I motion my head over towards him and Killer hands the bottle off to him. There's no pausing or asking questions of any sort. He just starts spraying the acid over the cuts on Jason. Meanwhile, Pops gets another one of my blades and tells one of the prospects to strip his pants, shoes, and socks off. The only thing he wants left on are his underwear. Irish also gets in on the fun with his own blade. He starts with Jason's fingers slicing them off slowly and methodically, one by one.

Jason is screaming uncontrollably and you can see that he's about to pass out from the pain and the acid eating away at him. His head is hanging forward and the screams die in his throat as Pops and Irish are cutting off his fingers and toes. The rest of the guys step forward and get their hits in before Jason dies. They leave just enough for me to get the last shot in and take the life from the dumb fuck that thought he could mess with us.

I take another blade from my collection and walk up to him. Using one hand, I pull his hair to make sure his head is up and that he's looking directly at me when I take the last breath from his body. With my other hand, I bring my blade up and agonizingly slowly drag it from one side of his throat to the other. Killer is now dumping the acid all over Jason's body to make him feel the maximum amount of pain before the life leaves him.

Grim tells the prospects that came with us to clean up the mess, get rid of the body, and then make their way over to the service at Joker and Cage's house. The rest of us make our way over to the houses to get cleaned up so we can make an appearance and spend the rest of the day with our brothers, old ladies, and the rest of the people here for our fallen brothers and old ladies. Personally, I want to get to Keira, Kenyon, and Cory. I don't want this shit to cloud my time with everyone before they all start heading out and making their way back to their own clubs and families.

The party is starting to get a little rowdy and I want to get Keira and the kids home. It's been a good day full of memories being shared, spending time with brothers from other chapters we don't usually get to see, and enjoying the time we need to as one family.

"You ready to go kitten?" I ask, picking Cory up from her bouncy seat.

"Yeah. You stay and visit with everyone. I got this. Darcy is going to help me get them settled in and then I'm just going to crash. Stay and be with everyone."

"I don't want to kitten. I want to be with our family."

"This is your family. I'm not going anywhere and most of the people here are leaving soon. Be with them before they leave and I'll see you when you get home. Wake me up."

"You don't have anythin' to worry about anymore," I tell her, hoping she'll understand what I'm telling her.

"I know I don't. That's the only reason I'm going home with Darcy and her only. We don't need any protection or someone with us. Please stay. I love you with everything in me Blade. Please give me this," Keira practically begs.

"I love you too kitten. I'll be home shortly."

I hesitate and Keira can sense it. So, she leans up on her toes and kisses me before taking Cory from my arms. Yeah, I'd love to stay and continue catching up with everyone here, but I want to be there for my girl too. Apparently, she's telling me that she doesn't want me to be with her right now. Maybe Darcy and her need some time to decompress too. Get away from the people that they don't know but they've spent the day with regardless because they knew it was needed by them.

I nod to Crash and Trojan to let them know the girls are heading over to the house. The three of us follow behind, making sure that we stay covered so they don't know. Jason might be gone now, but that doesn't mean that we're going to let them out of our sight, walking alone. So, we'll make sure they get home and then rejoin the party. And it is a party. We're celebrating the life of the men and women that died being a part of something that we all believe in. Family, loyalty, respect, and watching out for one another.

Epilogue

Irish

IT'S BEEN SIX MONTHS since I lost Caydence.
I'm learning how to be a single dad while balancing
work and things I have to do for the club. This is
one of the hardest things that I've ever had to do,
but the old ladies of the club have been amazing.
When I need to leave, they practically fight over
who's going to take Cassidy for the day or however
long I'll be gone. If I can't get her to calm down or
stop crying, Skylar is the first one to come running
over to help me.

The old ladies have shown me more about
raising a child, especially a daughter, then I ever
thought I'd need to know. Changing diapers and
cleaning up when she gets sick is easy for me. It's a
matter of putting her in clothes that match, not
treating her like a little boy, the right things to eat
and drink for her age, and what medicine I can give
her to name a few things. I've taken her to the
doctor and the days she has shots are over for me. I
can't leave her with someone else when I know my
little girl is in pain. The women all check on us
throughout the day, but they leave us alone for the
most part.

When I'm not busy, my thoughts are always
filled with Caydence. I've been told I need to move
on and let myself fall in love with someone new,
but I just don't ever see that happening. Caydence
and I were together for so long that I never
imagined my life without her. Now it's not just

imagining what it would be like, I'm living it every single day. I try to keep her memories alive so that I'll be able to tell Cass about her mom as she gets older. I want her to know how much Caydence truly loved her and wanted the very best in life for her.

Today, we're getting ready to move someone into the house the club bought to help out domestic violence victims. Skylar apparently ran into this woman and her teenage daughter in town and knew she needed to help her. From what we were told in church, the woman was covered from head to toe in bruises and her daughter wasn't looking much better. I'm on my way to the grocery store to make sure that the kitchen is fully stocked for them. It's something I can do and take Cass with me, so I jumped when Grim was looking for volunteers. Plus, it ensures that I'm helping out, but that I don't have to be around anyone else right now.

I don't know what the future is going to hold for Cass and myself, but I know that I never thought it would be like this. I'm having Rage build a house for us that I always thought I'd share with Caydence. It's now just going to be for the two of us. I'm making it large so that my daughter will have some place to raise her own family one day. And if she chooses to leave the club, then my grandbabies will always have a place to call home. For now, I'm just going to take it a day at a time and concentrate on my daughter, my club, and my work. Everything else is meaningless.

The End

Blade's Awakening Playlist

Anywhere But Here – Aaron Lewis

Tangled Up In You – Aaron Lewis

Vicious Circles – Aaron Lewis

Over You – Ingrid Michaelson

Hello Goodbye – Tyler Farr

Hurt – Christina Aguilera

Just A Fool – Christina Aguilera

Closure – Hayley Warner

The One That Got Away – The Civil Wars

Right Here – Staind

See You Again – Wiz Khalifa

Say You Won't Let Go – James Arthur

Give Me A Sign – Gavin Mikhail

For Whom The Bell Tolls – Metallica

Nothing Else Matters – Metallica

Until It's Gone – Linkin Park

Weak And Powerless – A Perfect Circle

It's Been A While – Staind

Failure – Breaking Benjamin

Broken – Seether

I'll Be – Edwin McCain

I Loved Her First – Heartland

About the Author

Growing up, I was constantly reading anything I could get my hands on. Even if that meant I was reading my grandma's books that weren't so age appropriate. I started out reading Judy Blume, then graduated to romance, mainly historical romance, and last year I found an amazing group of Indie authors that wrote MC books. Instantly I fell in love with these books.

For a long time, I've wanted to write. I just never had the courage to go through with actually doing it. During a book release party, I mentioned that I wanted to write and I received encouragement from an amazing author. So, I took a leap and wrote my first book. Even though this amazing journey is just starting for me, I wouldn't have even started if it weren't for a wonderful group of authors and others that I've met along the way.

I am a wife and mother of five children. Only one girl in the bunch! My family and friends mean the world to me and I'd be lost without them. Including new friends that I've met along the way. I've lived in New York my whole life, either in Upstate or the Southern Tier. I love it during the summer, spring, and fall. But, not so much during the winter. I hate driving in snow with a passion!

When I'm not hanging out with my family/friends, reading, or writing, you can find me listening to music. I love almost all music! Or, I'm watching a NASCAR race.

I look forward to meeting new friends, even if I'm extremely shy!

Here are some links to connect with me:

Facebook:
https://www.facebook.com/ErinOsborneAuthor/
Twitter:
https://twitter.com/author_osborne
My website:
http://erinosborne1013.wix.com/authorerinosborne
Spotify:
https://open.spotify.com/user/emgriff07

Acknowledgements

First and foremost, I have to thank the amazing team that I work with. Vicky is my amazing PA and she is venturing out and trying new things to help us even more than she already does. We couldn't do this without you!! Love ya girl!! Darlene, you help calm me down when no one else can. Yes, there are times when our bossy PA can't do it. We bounce ideas off one another and are on the phone all hours of the night. Jenni, I can't wait to see what the year brings with you as the newest addition to our team as our assistant PA. I love ya all!!

I have a new team of beta readers and I can't wait to see how we learn and grow together. Here's to the first of many more books to come!!!

Finally, my family. Even with all of the ups and downs, you continue to support me in continuing my dream of writing. I love you all!!

Made in the USA
Middletown, DE
23 June 2019